Bad Press

Bad Press

by

Rob Hadley

RaveN
STONE

published by Ravenstone
an imprint of Turnstone Press
607–100 Arthur Street
Artspace Building
Winnipeg, Manitoba
Canada R3B 1H3
www.TurnstonePress.com

Turnstone Press gratefully acknowledges the assistance of the

The Canada Council | Le Conseil des Arts
for the Arts | du Canada

Canadä

Canada Council for the Arts, the Manitoba Arts Council and the
Government of Canada through the Book Publishing Industry
Development Program for our publishing activities.

Cover design: Manuela Dias
Interior design: Sharon Caseburg

This book was printed and bound in Canada
by Friesens for Turnstone Press.

Canadian Cataloguing in Publication Data

Hadley, Rob, 1963–

Bad press

ISBN 0-88801-250-0

PS8565.A27 B34 2000   C813'.6   C00-920185-8
PR9199.3.H24 B34 2000

This book is dedicated to everyone who made it possible.

To my wife, Therese,
who gave me a life.

To Kevin Carter,
who won a Pulitzer Prize, and then took his own life.

To Charlene Smith, Dave Sandison and Juhan Kuus,
who prove that above the cynicism of the media,
there is honour and sincerity to be found there too.

To Horst Faas and Jimmy Soullier,
who prove that there really are "gentlemen of the press."

To Rosie Livingstone, Marti Daniels and Lia Wolfe,
who worked so hard to keep me on track while writing this book.

And finally to Chris Collingridge
and all the other foot soldiers of the print media
who I've had the pleasure to work with.

Contents

Chapter 1

I WATCHED THE CRIMSON GROWTH spreading across the white carpet. Blood. And lots of it. Coming from the foot of the closet.

I reached for the handle and everything seemed to happen at once. Suddenly I was pushed back onto the bed. There was a person on top of me – naked. Worse – dead.

I kicked the body away and rolled off the bed to my feet, ready to bolt. Then I saw what was happening. The body on the bed was female. She was probably about seventeen, I guessed. Long hair, brunette, looking awful in red.

She was draining blood everywhere. I was covered with it and when I wiped my face, sure enough, I spread it further. I tried to think clearly – was there a phone in the apartment? The kitchen? I had to call the cops right away.

There were terrible marks on the girl's wrists – she'd been shackled, by the look of things. As I rushed back to the kitchen things suddenly got a whole lot worse. The front door opened. In the doorway stood a London bobby, his radio in his hand, and someone right behind him – another policeman. There's no one quite as helpful as a London bobby. He looked at me and said something into his radio.

"Quick," I said, "in the bedroom." I shouted at them to come in, panic welling up inside me.

"You just stand here, sir," said the first one firmly as he brushed past me. His partner came to my side and stood there, solid and menacing.

"I found her," I said weakly.

"Sir, at this point I should just keep quiet and wait while we see what's been going on here."

"Going on?" I said. I didn't really understand yet.

"Okay, Jack," the first cop said as he came out of the room, "I think we'd better take this young man down to the station."

The policeman named Jack gripped my arm. His hand was large and wrapped around my upper arm in a cast-iron grip. Meanwhile, my knees turned to jelly.

"But I was about to call you!" I glanced around for a way out.

"Yeah," said Jack, "and I'm the Queen of bloody England."

I SMOKED IN THOSE DAYS. Horrid habit. Dirty. I lit up almost immediately after I got to work each morning. There was something both repellent and satisfying about having that first smoke of the day, while looking onto Fleet Street.

From the office, when things were quiet, we could watch the people in the street buying our newspaper. An old man on the corner across the street had been selling the *News* for thirty years. He called out the day's headlines to passersby, a distinctive, stooping figure with his flushed, red face. He wore a West Ham Football Club scarf and woollen bobble hat every day, winter and summer. Never knew his name.

First time I'd got a picture in the *News* I bought a copy from him. "That's one of my pictures!" I said. He looked at me as though I was daft. I *was* daft. Daft with pride, I guess, the rush of making the paper for the first time.

Inevitably, no sooner had I tossed the match into the ashtray then I was handed a slip by Bonnie, the picture editor. It detailed where I was to go and what I had to bring back for the paper. Not so much an assignment as a work order. Often it was a court job: "Head and shoulders plus," the description would read. I could have been working on a shampoo advert. Sometimes the instruction would even specify the shape of the space the photograph would have to fill. I was doing more than my fair share of court work at the moment, but that was okay. I enjoyed court work. Most snappers hate court jobs. I suppose there's something sadistic about it. Maybe something dark and disturbing, but whatever it was, it worked for me.

Bonnie handed slips out to each snapper as s/he arrived for work. She had been in the office since about 7 a.m., assigning work for the day as it came down from the newsdesk. She was a good picture editor, and a fair one. She rotated the good jobs among the staff and the regular freelancers. If there was a trip to be had, or a band to be covered, she saw it was dealt with fairly.

When football game passes came in, she'd see that any photographer following the team got to cover the match. She was good for each photographer, and good for the paper. And when there was trouble, Bonnie would be there to cover for us.

This particular morning I left my camera bag at the office, grabbed a few rolls of film and slipped the Nikon into my overcoat pocket. It sometimes pays to travel light. Court jobs need more cunning than anything else, and I quite enjoyed the deception. I left the office feeling bouyant.

I stepped out of the *News* building and crossed a sunlit Fleet Street before disappearing into the London Underground. Maggie Thatcher had done her best to break the inner-city transport system, but somehow it remained, crumbling but still standing.

The tube carried me south of the river and almost directly to the court I was supposed to cover. I slipped inside, leaving a pair of photographers and a journo outside. I recognized one of the photographers; he might be after my guy, he might not. There is always a lot of activity around a court. Sometimes all the papers are there, working on totally unrelated cases. Other times, you all show up for the same case, and a real bun fight develops as photographers jostle for position to get a picture.

The snappers hang around just off the court property, usually, an overcoat concealing their gear or maybe a camera slung around the neck. You can recognize them by the stomping feet and Styrofoam cups of coffee, and an inevitable cigarette hanging from the lip, the badge of those of us who wait. Waiting is the largest part of the job, usually.

Inside the court was like any local government building. I hope they got a discount on the gray paint that adorned every inch of the place. There was so much of it someone must have thought it was a good idea, though I never met anyone who liked that color. On a notice board near the entrance was a roster of cases to be heard in the different courtrooms. I quickly found the one I was to shoot for the *News*. The man I was interested in was in courtroom number four. His was to be the second case of the morning. That could mean anything. Things didn't usually get going till 10 a.m., but the first session might be over quickly. I could be back in the office by lunch.

Mark Willsworth, the assistant to the clerk of the court, was pinning up a notice next to the rosters.

"Hey, Mark," I called. "This guy in number four, John Hanson ... you know what he looks like?"

"Sure," he said. "Bald as a coot. Tall guy, and heavy. He lands one on you and you won't be round for a week or two," he laughed. He'd seen me dodge a few, and he's seen me swallow one or two as well.

"Right," I said. "Thanks."

Mark was all right. Few of the court people cared much for the press. We were the enemy for most of them, an unnecessary evil. But Mark would sometimes tip us off, telling us which exits would be used. He risked plenty by doing so, even though he obviously liked his job. Usually only one photographer was assigned to cover the court and all its exits. Any help at all was welcomed. During the release of the Guildford Four, acquitted after their tragic wrongful imprisonment, there were seven of us assigned to cover the exits alone. But that was different. Today's entertainment only warranted one snapper. When the case was a child molester, or a rapist, something real bad, Willsworth would let us know where we might get him. And we usually did get him, somehow. Nasty job it might be, at times, but it took its own brand of skill and cunning.

I made my way upstairs to the cafeteria. It was probably the worst coffee in London, but it was hot and sweet. And there was a tall, bald guy across the room from me. He was big, too. There was only a handful of people in the cafeteria. The law in England says you can't shoot in the court, otherwise I'd be walking up to this great oaf, shoving my Nikon in his snout and blasting him, before legging it back to the tube.

Press photographers pay attention to a rule like that ever since some senile judge came out of court to find a photographer shooting just inside the car park. The old bigot called a constable, had the snapper hauled into court and hit him with a thousand-pound contempt of court fine. That kind of news travels real quick. Especially when a drug pusher gets off with a light fine and a slap on the wrist. Still, most of the judges appear certifiable to anyone with even a glimmer of sanity. In England a judge can't be fired. Consequently, they stay on the bench until they are way beyond senile. The pay is better than pension. Trial by a jury of one's peers is a great concept, but sentencing by a drooling Victorian relic seems a little harsh at times.

I maneuvered over to the bald guy. John Hanson was "known to the police." For this delightful British euphemism, read: the police have your number and they're just waiting to nail you. The file on Hanson was thick, and the journalist assigned to cover him had found it easy to get details. He was involved in marrying illegal immigrants off, to get them their British citizenship. Not exactly a master criminal, this one. It was a simple enough scam: you just find someone who wants to make some money, and organize a wedding with someone (preferably of the opposite sex) who wants to get into the country. The woman, or man for that matter, would get a sum for the trouble, and meanwhile the poor sap immigrant would be charged some other figure entirely. Hanson had got greedy, by the look of things. He had actually got his own name onto a marriage certificate and no doubt charged someone handsomely for the doubtful privilege. Trouble was, he already had a wife. Someone had made the connection at the City Hall, now that the records were freshly computerized, and turned the file over to the police. The charge itself was bigamy, and all he had to do today was enter a plea. Nothing serious yet, but this thing had all the earmarks of a story that would grow as the wheels of justice rotated – excruciatingly slowly. In the meantime, it was a tasty morsel for the paper.

He was about forty, fairly fit, and looked like a typical south London thug. You can see the type in the playground of any secondary school, bullying or strutting around. Twenty years later he ends up in the local court. As predictable as an adolescent's punch line.

"Excuse me," I said. "Er, can you tell me what time the court goes in session?"

He looked up from his coffee, surprised that someone would be talking to him.

"Dunno, mate," he said. "Maybe ten, that's what I heard, anyway."

"Oh," I mumbled. "Gotta be in court four, myself."

He looked up, curious.

I was feeling lucky, so I played it out. "Licensing. You'd think they'd let me serve customers in my bar till midnight. This is the third time this year they've had me up here."

"Oh, sorry," he mumbled into his coffee. "Which pub?"

"Nag's Head, just round the corner." I looked to my left as though I could see the place through the cold hard concrete of the building. Sure there was a pub there, and sure it was called the Nag's Head, not that I'd ever set foot in the place.

"Oh, I know. Been there," he said, loosening up a little.

"Well, I'm third up, in number four."

"You must be just after me." He didn't sound embarrassed in the least. Strange the way people like to talk, once you open the door. It never fails to amaze me.

"Well, I wish they'd get on with it."

On cue, Mark Willsworth came in and said in his best "assistant to the clerk of the court" voice, "Court number four is now in session."

I hovered as John Hanson got some things together and moved in the direction of the door. Mark glanced at me, and seeing I had something going, he didn't speak to me.

I tagged along with Hanson into the courtroom. I sat next to him in the public area of the courtroom – in spite of the dozens of empty seats. This was the most annoying of characters, one that latches onto people, and a surprisingly enjoyable role to play. If a courtroom isn't a theater,

I don't know what is. Half the cast are even in fancy dress. I love it. Hanson must have been too depressed to bother getting rid of me, which suited me just fine.

The first case was just a plea to be entered and took all of fifteen seconds. Hanson's lawyer had obviously thought he could manage to say "Not guilty" without any handholding. Maybe this was not his first time in the gray room.

I noticed a young girl in the press gallery, a row of seats ahead of the public area. There was something about her that made her stand out, perched there in the front row. A sort of visual loudness in the silence of courtroom number four. I never sat in the press gallery, of course. Blowing the element of surprise was the least intelligent thing a photographer could do. But the journos liked to, setting themselves apart. I didn't know who the young journo was. Young and quite pretty, but not from the *News*, as far as I knew. Funny having so many earrings in that ear, though. Uneven. There were more in the left ear than the right. You didn't see that so often. I wondered if it meant something. She was probably a trainee somewhere, or a college student on a journalism course.

Hanson did his bit and the judge named a date for the trial. Hanson was released with conditional bail. Nothing out of the ordinary. He came back to his seat and picked up his coat, which he'd left over the chair. He nodded to me and said good luck and then left.

I waited an awkward thirty seconds and walked out. I got lucky – Hanson was disappearing into the gents. I positioned myself just outside, by a window that looked out to the front of the building.

As he stepped out I said, "'Ere, look at this!"

He came over towards me and peered out the window. A few photographers were visible, ready for the kill.

"There's press boys out there!" I said. "I reckon there's three I can see, maybe more! Who's coming here today?"

"Dunno," he replied, more motivated this time. He was shifting around uncomfortably.

"Well, I ain't leaving the front way, that's for sure. Don't want my face in the paper. I think I'll take the side exit."

"What side exit?" He was looking at me intently now. When you fish for trout, you feel the mouth on the hook. This was like that feeling. It's evil and it's thrilling.

"There's a service entrance the staff use. It's open to the public – just no one uses it. One of my girls does some serving up here in the cafeteria. Look, I'll show you."

I moved down the corridor and led the way downstairs. He followed me obediently. When I reached the unmarked door and pushed it, it opened as nicely as I had hoped. The light outside was excellent. It was coming from the left. Perfect – when he looked back his face would be fully lit. "Let's go," I said, walking smartly outside, pulling up the collar of my coat.

He paused, then followed briskly, walking to the road that ran along the side of the building. And then he was beyond the bounds of the court. Here he was – mine, like a lamb to the slaughter.

"Damn, I left my umbrella," I said, turning back. He kept walking. This was good. A little distance, that's what

I needed. Just in case he took a swing. I could close it up tight on the zoom, if I had to. Just like so many times before.

I drew the Nikon out, a dagger for the sacrificial lamb, then called loudly, "Eh, Hanson!"

He was startled by my use of his name, and turned.

"Smile, my old son!" I called after him. Click, click, click.

First there was an incredulous pause. Then as it dawned on him he'd been had, he started coming at me. I kept on shooting. They always do this. The powerful motordrive on the Nikon dragged four frames a second through the gears and Hanson realised that whatever he did, he was there on film. He turned and pulled his raincoat up around his head in an effort to mask himself. Again, the usual reaction, too late by far. Next, he began running down the road in the hope of an escape. I could have let him go, but that shadowy part of me kicked in. I wanted to see him squirm. Had I just backed off then, perhaps what happened later would have fallen out differently. I suppose it's a karma thing.

Instead, I decided to have fun with this one, and watch the lamb twist in pain as I turned the blade of the sacrificial dagger in its wound. For a moment I thought, *This is a bad decision, don't do this.* But something inside demanded that secret sadistic pleasure. I ran after Hanson. It was all so easy. He turned and saw I was still with him, and, livid with rage now, started shouting something. He ran backwards, retreating down the road, his raincoat covering his face. I snapped a couple more frames. This was so simple, it was cruel.

I could see it happening, even though he couldn't. I

can relive that moment in my mind as though I were watching it in a silent movie, in slow motion. The road was quite busy, the noise of traffic drowning out a road crew at work. As Hanson backed towards them blindly, they actually stepped aside. He disappeared down the hole they'd been digging, just like a cartoon. I rushed to the edge of the hole and there he was. Flat on his back, six or seven feet down. Sore, stuck, but okay. That's where I shot the rest of the roll, the film churning through the spinning gears of the motordrive until none remained.

"There you go, you stupid bastard!" I shouted down to him as I lowered the camera and hit the rewind button.

He staggered around in the hole, but couldn't get out. That was about the time I chose to make a swift exit. Hanson was in the bag. Head and shoulders plus.

I GOT THE MESSAGE from the newsdesk about a month after Hanson fell in the hole. My picture had got some good play, piggybacking on a story about upcoming leg-islation changes affecting immigrants. That was a piece of good luck, giving the picture more play than it really deserved.

The newsdesk was asking for the archive copies of the pictures. Photographers routinely keep a handful of frames printed and accessible on stories that are not yet fully played out. Hanson would be making other court appearances, so I had some close at hand. The desk was pleased, and the fact was, they were "spoiler shots." Papers always want to be first with a picture, to show they're on the ball. One tactic is to make the subjects' first experience of being photographed so terrible that they always "cover up" at subsequent court appearances. This denies other photographers the opportunity to get a picture. The result is that the original pictures become the only ones – and therefore play again and again. It's a lousy thing to do, but it happens all the time. It's a dirty business sometimes.

I handed the 10x8 black and white prints to Marlene, the *News* editor, shortly after she'd called down for them. I had a great relationship with Marlene. She smoked cigarettes with a cigarette holder. Never knew anyone who did that before. She'd nearly fired me for a captioning problem once. I had shot Princess Anne and her horse in the winner's circle of a three-day event prize-giving. It was a nice tight headshot of Princess Anne and the head of the horse. At the foot of the caption sheet I had written "Princess Anne and four-year-old eventer Sunburst (horse left)." Unfortunately, someone had left the "(horse left)" on the caption when the picture was printed, and three editions ran with the error before anyone called the newsdesk.

Marlene tore me to pieces for my little joke, but subsequently defended me and let me keep my job. I didn't make jokes like that any more. I liked Marlene.

"You talked to Hanson?" she asked.

"Sure, but I don't think he'd talk to me again." I didn't want to go into specifics. We'd had a good laugh about the guy down in photographic, but the newsdesk didn't need to know the details.

"What d'you make of him?" Marlene squinted at me, studying my face as she listened.

"He's hard. Probably been in court before, might have a record. Maybe we should get someone to look into that. Why?"

"Well, we're digging around. His name came up in conversation on another story. Have a chat with Cass. She'll need anything you've got on him. I want you to work on this with her for a little. Just shake a few things and see what comes up."

"No problem," I said, hoping she wasn't expecting me to knock on his door and invite myself in for tea. Marlene never let anything go unless she had to. I had no idea what her special interest might be, but that's just the way she was. I was used to it. She was already immersed in the next problem of the day. I left her with her head buried in an early pre-press copy of the front page. Outside her office, in the newsroom, phones rang and keyboards rattled, just like any day in newspaper town.

I crossed the busy newsroom floor. Cass Collingridge had a desk in the corner of the open-plan floor. It was partially partitioned, giving her some tiny (but pre-ciously guarded) privacy. On the shoulder-height parti-tion was a poster of George Michael. It was autographed and the signature looked real.

"Hi," I said. "You're interested in Hanson?"

"Oh, yeah, you're the photographer, right?" She spoke without looking up from her work.

"Right." I wanted to add that I had a name, but let it go. I had never worked with Cass before. She was just one of probably sixty journos on the *News*, split between three shifts, seven days a week.

She was typing something, and I had a moment to look at her desk and the stories pasted on the partition.

They were her stories, some getting very good play, mostly left-wing, some environment and women's issues. I wondered if the south London hoods had upset the Greenpeace weenies, and she'd tripped over it.

She finished what she was doing and spun her revolving chair round to face me. She had a pretty face, delicate but intelligent. Just the right mix of hard and soft.

"What's he like?" she asked.

"A thug. Not a nice guy. Probably has a history." I added, "You'll like him."

She followed my gaze towards the cuttings. "I do other stuff, too." She sounded a little petulant. "You have some pics?"

I placed what I had on her desk.

She examined them closely, frowning. "Where is he in this?"

"Down a hole," I replied. "We burned the background out."

"Seems angry."

"Yes," I said. "Some people just naturally are." I wondered why Cass had drawn this job, and said, "This is hardly your thing, is it? I mean, you usually cover environment, don't you?"

"Sure," she replied indignantly. She reached for her black leather handbag and rose to her feet. "I didn't choose this story; it chose me."

"What d'you mean?" I followed her towards the elevator.

"Strathclyde dumped this one on me. I wouldn't normally go near this stuff. I guess he's trying me out on something new. He does that, you know. Just rattles us a bit, now and then. Says it keeps us on our toes."

"Great," I muttered under my breath. "Now I'm breaking in trainees."

"Smartass!" she replied. "Get your gear and meet me at the parking lot in five, okay?"

I felt I was getting off on the wrong foot with Cass. That's always ominous.

Half an hour later I was in Cass's car, heading south over Tower Bridge towards Purley. I hadn't wanted to go and scope his house, but when Cass mentioned that Hanson was currently in Jersey, I felt a little easier about it. He was apparently away for a week, with the full knowledge and consent of the police. His lawyer must have worked hard for that.

Cass drove a battered two-door Ford. It was better than walking, but in the heavy London traffic, the difference was marginal. We found the address easily enough, then circled the block a couple of times and parked across the street. The house was dark and there were no cars in the driveway. It had a neatly tended set of rose bushes close to some windows, which would provide a little cover for snooping. It looked good.

It was still light, and we'd be seen from the road if we just walked up to the windows. Instead, we slipped off down the road and ordered a curry at a nearby restaurant. We'd come back an hour or so after dark.

Cass didn't look the sort with the stomach for this work. It was a little risky, in a schoolboy prank sort of way. She was a tall brunette, intelligent looking, more like a literary critic than a street hack. Her car stereo was better than the car, and probably worth more. She had tapes stacked all over the place. Vivaldi, Bach, Rachmaninov. Heavy stuff like that. And George

Michael and something called Psychedelic Furs, which I'd never heard of. Personally, I felt if it wasn't Clapton or Floyd, it wasn't worth listening to.

The curry was all right, and Cass loosened up. It was dark by the time we arrived back at the house. We killed the lights and coasted to a halt outside the house. It was a still night and a waning moon slid behind the clouds. We left the car and walked purposefully up to the front door. It was obvious there was no one home, but she knocked anyway.

She tried the letterbox, but couldn't get her hand down to the letters lying there. Never mind. We slipped into the garden and looked into the living room. It was immaculate and boring. Pictures on the wall and a grandfather clock in the darkness radiated qualities designed for a magazine shoot. It was modern and affluent, but not a place that seemed lived in; it was more like a show home for a real estate company. There were no stains on the coffee table, and no books pushed down the sides of the chairs.

On the other side of the house we found a study. This was better. On the desk, which looked out over the rose bushes, was a computer, and we could see the winking red LED of an answering machine with messages on it. The window was secured but partially open. No one could get in through it, but I could hear the hum of the computer's cooling fan. I could get my hand in, but I couldn't reach the catch on the window. Silently Cass pushed me aside and slipped her hand through the window. She could reach further, but the answering machine was still far beyond her reach.

Cass opened her handbag and rummaged around for

a moment. She withdrew a six-inch aerial, which she extended. She twisted the end around into a hook shape, and then slid the aerial through the open window. I was quietly impressed by all this. Not what I had expected from her at all. She began dragging the answering machine towards the window. It took a couple of tries, but soon was within reach.

"Where did you pick that trick up?" I asked.

"I grew up in Kenya. They use fishing rods to steal stuff through the windows there. Socks, trousers, wallets. In fact, anything."

The answering machine was close enough now. She wrapped her hand in a handkerchief, reached in and pressed the release button. Then she removed the tape and pushed the answering machine back across the desk.

"Very clever," I laughed. "Now, let's get the heck out of here."

When we got back to the office I left Cass and took the tube home. There was still a little shaking we could do with Hanson. I had a few ideas, though now that I thought about it, there was still a very fundamental question unanswered.

Why the heck were people so interested in Hanson, anyway?

TRANSMITTING PICTURES is a relatively simple process. The negative is scanned and then sent down a phone line to a receiving unit. A special portable computer called a Leafax does this, and manages to retain the quality of the image very nicely. A skilled user can have an image on film, process the film and transmit in a period of about twenty minutes. That's really going for it, but it can be done. More often than not the skill in operating the Leaf is getting it connected to the phone system correctly. It's an intricate tool, and goes far beyond a PC. But things are changing now, and the digital cameras are already displacing much of this technology. Knowing how the equipment was set up, and the way we used to jerry-rig things, meant that most photographers were pretty familiar with computers and the various modem systems around.

As I walked over to Guy Mctavish's office in the Information Technology department, I wondered if he'd be able to help with an idea I had hatching. He had his head inside a PC casing when I arrived. He looked up and stopped what he was doing, removing a pair of glasses that looked like the severed bottoms of beer bottles fastened inside a frame. The word "geek" was not far from my mind. Guy looked after most of the network and IT wizardry on the editorial side of things. He'd become a one-man department accountable to no one but the editor. That was a long way from being the boy with the damaged spectacles held together with tape that he must have been at school. Sure to be the one the bullies picked on, somehow he'd excelled. He was a bit of a mystery, and I suppose that drew me to him in a strange way.

"Don't get many visitors in here," he said. His office seemed to be a broom cupboard, which had been equipped with industrial shelving for the purpose of stacking computer parts. "What can I do for you?" he asked.

"I wondered if you could help me with something?" I said, looking at the racks of equipment behind him.

"I'll try. You're in photographic, aren't you?"

"Yeah, Steve Sinclair. You trained me on the Leaf upgrade last year."

"Yes, I remember. Nice system, that one! Come on through." He disappeared behind a rack of monitors and disk drives.

"Well this isn't a photographic problem really . . . ," I said as I followed him. After skirting through a deceptive maze of racking, we emerged into a large, airy office, with a cathedral-like window. Part of one wall was taken up with larger computers and what looked like a complex system of switchgear. These were the company servers, the centre of the computer network. LEDs blinked and large boxes hummed. It all looked very impressive.

"Uh-huh? Not photographic, eh? Sounds better already." He settled into a comfortable chair behind a huge desk, empty except for a chessboard and a laptop. I wondered how Guy had swung such a great office, but then I looked around and began to understand. Guy was a scavenger. The desk was a little older than the current issue. The chair had a slight tear in the leather. The space was so nicely concealed behind the spare parts that I suspected no one was aware it was there. This, too, was probably scavenged somehow. I admired him already.

I picked up a piece of equipment on a nearby shelf and looked at it more closely, trying to figure out what it was.

"Just put that down, would you?" said Guy, a firm edge in his voice. "We're not really meant to have that: it's still illegal in this country," he added. A little pride showed through his words.

"What is it?" I asked.

"Never you mind. Now, how exactly can I help you?"

"I'm working on a story, and we're getting pretty much nowhere. We need a break soon, or it'll be dropped. Anyway, we're pretty desperate."

"Is it a hack?"

"No – unless you can hack into a stand-alone unit."

"Can't be done," he shrugged.

"No, but what about this? He leaves his machine on at night. It's near a window. I might be able to get a cable in there."

"That's very naughty," he said in a conspiratorial tone, "but very easy. As it happens, I think I have exactly what you need."

THAT NIGHT I FOUND MYSELF outside John Hanson's place once again. This time I was well equipped. When Guy heard what I was suggesting, he wanted to come along, he found it so funny, but apart from being illegal, this sort of thing upsets people enough to mean some risk of violence. It was best to work alone under the circumstances.

I crossed the front garden and went to the study window. I was dressed in black and practically invisible from more than twenty feet away. Knowing the house was empty was reassuring.

The window would open only a couple of inches, but it was enough for my needs. I reached in and disconnected the printer cable. Into the free printer port I slipped a cable provided by Guy, which ran back into my shoulder bag. Once I was connected I sat down and faced the road, partially shielded by the flowers growing in the nicely tended garden. From my shoulder bag I pulled the laptop Guy had loaned me. I turned it on and ran a connectivity utility. Guy had taught me some geek-speak, which I repeated in my head as I worked. If John Hanson's computer was running a Windows system, it probably came installed with the same product, and would detect the request for a connection.

I waited as the utility ran. If it failed, I would disconnect and skip out quick. Just as I was beginning to think I was doing something wrong, a flashing text box pulsed to let me know a connection was established with the remote unit. The laptop displayed a screen split down the center, with my directories on one side and Hanson's on the other. I was tempted to look in his files, but instead did as I had agreed with Cass to do. There was no time to waste, just transfer the lot and get the hell out of there. We'd have plenty of time to get into the files in the comfort of our office.

I began the transfer routine. Guy had given me a good unit – my hard drive was three times the size of the computer I was linked to and I could accommodate his entire hard drive comfortably. The progress indicator gradually grew as file names flashed across the screen, confirming their transfer was complete. In a couple of minutes I was looking at a twenty-five percent complete transfer.

That was when a passing car slowed and then swung into the drive. It was a cherry red Porsche, nicely appointed, too. The headlights swept past me as I crouched in the flower bed. I froze and watched a middle-aged woman climb from the car fifteen feet away and walk to the porch. She wasn't badly appointed, either. The light caught her blonde hair, and it reminded me of a record cover my mother had in her sixties collection. I like retro.

I heard keys rattle, and then the door open. Lights went on inside, and then I heard the sound of the study door opening. I considered running, but a quick look at the screen said I was over halfway done. Better sit tight and see what would happen.

I could hear her moving about in the study. I sneaked a look. She walked to the desk, paused, and then I heard something click off out of sight. Could be the monitor. Had she seen the file transfer in progress? Would she know what it was? Almost certainly not. As she approached the window, I slid down out of sight. She was moving towards the answering machine. I heard the sound of the tape compartment opening. Then a long pause. That was odd – I could almost hear the thoughts going around in her head. She was wondering where the missing tape was. Then she was on the move again.

A few moments later I saw an upstairs light go on. The file transfer had finished. The entire contents of Hanson's hard drive were now in my shoulder bag. I reached in through the window and disconnected the cable. All the lights were off downstairs, but then I heard the footsteps descending. Clutching the shoulder bag to my chest, I lay in the flower bed, willing myself to be invisible. The door opened and she came out, walked quickly to the car, and moments later was gone.

As soon as the coast was clear I slipped away down the road. Two hundred yards away, I climbed into Cass's car, and drove to the office. I could hardly believe what I'd just done. With luck, it would pay off.

THE NEXT MORNING at 8.30 a.m. we had the weekly news conference. The various departments filtered into the boardroom and gathered around the mahogany table, some taking seats, others leaning against the wall. The news conference was about the only time you'd ever see the whole team in one place. At the head of the table was Marlene – this was her show – and by her side was Strathclyde, the editor.

Strathclyde, also known as "Smiling Death," was a good editor. He had opinions. You couldn't always agree with them, but at least you generally knew where he stood. Having said that, he could be unpredictable and brutal. I'd heard him fire someone at the Christmas party the previous year. "Happy Christmas, how are the kids, and by the way, you're fired." Nice. That's how you get a name like Smiling Death. Still, it was better having Strathclyde than some of the limp editors who were on other papers. An editor has to be a character, he has to have a personality that shines through the pages, good or bad. Anything else is just plain bland.

There were a few journos sitting around, some junior reporters and some photographers, straggling in late. The sub-editors moved together in their little clique. "Who's the suit?" a voice next to me asked. Rory, the horse-racing correspondent, was offering me a smoke. That was still allowed at the time, though even Marlene was reluctant to light up in a news conference.

"No thanks," I said, declining the cigarette, and then looked in the direction Rory was indicating.

I checked out the man taking a seat next to Strathclyde. Young, well dressed, tailored even, but not hard enough around the face to be anyone in the advertising department. I'd not seen him before. The advertising people sometimes sent someone up to the news conference to scope out the possibility of a special ad sale on the strength of some news angle, or a sports event. Strathclyde sometimes invited people in to see the news conference so they'd have an idea how the business worked. We'd had journalism professors from his old college (though God knows what sort of deranged institution turned out people like Strathclyde), shareholders and government ministers sit in on news conferences in the past, though it was unusual.

"Don't know," I said. "Just some guy, I guess."

"I know that face," said Rory enigmatically. "And he ain't just 'some guy'."

"He could use a chin," I said under my breath as the room began to quieten down.

Cass was there, sandwiched between someone from the Arts pages and Tricia Williams, well-known female columnist and confidant of star-crossed lovers. Of course she wrote a lot of that mail herself.

For all her high-collared blouses and prim, almost Victorian graces, I knew Tricia before she was a virgin, when she was working on court jobs and doorsteps. To see her now you'd think butter wouldn't melt in that rosebud-like mouth, though in truth she was the greatest trollop that had ever worn out a mattress. It takes all sorts to make up a newsroom. She was deep in conversation with Bonnie.

Just as Marlene began speaking, the door opened and Mitch, the showbiz editor's own photographer sidled in. Even on the *News* there's a distinction between 'Arts' and 'Showbiz'. Mitch was sleazy, gutter press at its worst. He made you want to take a bath after just looking at him. Still, you had to respect his work. He always got his picture. A real craftsman, actually.

Marlene started the meeting. First she ran down a list of scheduled jobs, allocating them to various journalists. Then the columnists each said what they were working on, and a couple of journalists threw in a few news angles. The political desk was in a tizzy over the upsurge of pressure groups planning marches with the onset of summer. Marching season was about to get into full swing, and one of the young, white-faced research boys said something that lodged in my mind. These people do research ahead of time that primes the newsdesk, and is an invaluable resource, even if they never do actually get their hands dirty.

"We've been looking at the way these marches are scheduled with the police and the metropolitan district council. It seems there's an increase in race issues on the agenda this year. Normally, we expect numbers to be evenly split between international human rights issues, same-sex issues and local political issues, with race issues being a significantly lower factor than the other major issue types. We think this change in emphasis may be something to do with amendments to existing immigration legislation, which are due to go in front of the Cabinet in the next few months. There's a government think-tank called the Immigration and Nationality Review Board that's due to present its findings, and they're expected to suggest some sweeping changes.

"Interestingly," he droned on, "we're seeing public opinion shifting already." He consulted his notes as he spoke. "It's all over the place, actually. Race is the big issue this summer, according to the number of scheduled marches, with human rights and a few local political issues coming next, and same-sex issues bringing up the rear."

There was a ripple of laughter, and the young man looked up, unaware he'd said something amusing. I was looking at Strathclyde and he smiled a little before setting his face in a cold study of concentration. I don't think anyone noticed as the man next to him whispered something in his ear and took the opportunity of this diversion to move discreetly to the door and step outside.

No one else noticed the man leave. I looked round as Marmaduke Wellbelloved, the Arts editor and a well-known homosexual, commented on the appropriate positioning, and shared in the joke with great composure and charm. "That would appear to be a position mutually acceptable to all concerned," drawled Marmaduke, to the embarrassment of the young political researcher, who blushed into a crimson silence.

Marlene moved the meeting on, with the control of a woman who had seen it all before, and done it all before. She handed out a number of assignments to photographers and the meeting broke up shortly afterwards.

IT TURNED OUT TO BE a typical, slow news day. There was a Royal visit to cover at Great Ormond Street Children's Hospital, an arrival at the airport of some has-been pop star who was in trouble with the tax department, and a couple of court jobs.

I drew the court coverage and had what amounted to a wasted day, as the defendant in one case failed to appear, and another pleaded guilty and was led away to the cells. It went like that some days. I ended up standing around the Old Bailey and outside on the pavement, drinking bad coffee in Styrofoam cups and smoking with the boys for most of the morning.

When I got back to the office Cass told me she was getting away for a couple of hours, so I took the opportunity to slink off with her. She was heading to St. Johns Wood, which would give me a chance to pick up some negatives I had left at home. On a slow day like today I could spend my time more enjoyably working on some prints for my walls. Bonnie had my cellphone number, and would call me if anything came up.

Cass wanted to check on her parents' apartment. They'd been away for the last week, and would be for another six on a long cruising holiday. The idle rich, what a life! Leaving their poor daughter to look after their apartment, like Cinderella. Well, not quite.

We'd swing by my place to pick up my neg files. After a quick stop, shopping for a few bits and pieces Cass needed, we arrived at the apartment building near the old Abbey Road Studios. The nearby pedestrian crossing had been featured on the front of a Beatles album. I remembered the image. What kind of bastard would shoot John? We'll always love you, John.

"I'll be back in a minute, just let me drop this stuff off," she said, parking in a no-parking zone. The way this area was patrolled I would be amazed if we didn't get clamped in seconds. But we didn't. After ten minutes she was back.

"I'm gonna have to stay for a while, I haven't even watered half the damn plants yet!"

"Oh, I'm sorry," I said. "You want a hand?"

"No, better you stay with the car and make sure it doesn't get clamped. If you want to go to your place and get your stuff, go ahead. Just don't trash my car, okay? And if you get any tickets, you pay!"

"It's only ten minutes from here. Thanks, I won't be long."

It was early afternoon and the traffic was light. I made it to my apartment a few minutes later and parked across the road. Strictly speaking, this was a no-parking zone, but I'd never seen a police patrol down this dead-end street. It wasn't even on half the local maps.

I still wanted to talk to Cass about the answering machine tape we'd got from Hanson, and to arrange a time to go over the contents of the hard drive we'd copied. That was all going to happen, but it was happening in slow motion. Not that it mattered. We had plenty of time to inspect every item of information we'd collected. Then the fun would start.

To be quite honest, I was just enjoying time slacking off for a change.

Chapter 2

MOST HAMPSTEAD APARTMENTS are both expensive and exclusive. Mine was neither.

It was in one of five remaining houses that had once been a long terrace by the heath, until the Luftwaffe had dropped bombs and flattened most of the street. My apartment was part of what was left of the last house. It looked as if it would fall down at any moment, but in the meantime gave me an excellent address, relatively close to the centre of town, in one of London's nicest areas. It was almost on the heath, and retained something of an older time. Maybe it was the way the walls sagged or the fact that I could hear birdsong.

The place had character, and Gunner Sykes, the mad soldier landlord. He was very much alive, though he looked like a ghost. He had a sort of natural pallor that goes with the perpetually disappointed. His disappointment stemmed from returning to "a land fit for heroes," which never really was. Sykes still wore the uniform on Remembrance Day, and had gone to the Cenotaph every year since the end of the war. He had the kind of face that would be chosen without fail by the TV news crew as they panned over the crowd. They would zoom in on the somber time-worn lines, the heavy-lidded blue eyes. What memories and experiences lay behind that look, a television audience could only guess at.

Sykes was seventy-nine, had served in the Western Desert in the war, and probably saw me as an example of all that was bad in Britain today. "To think I fought in the desert so the likes of you could wreck the country!" was one of his favorite themes. I shouldn't mock. If it weren't for him and his friends, I'd be speaking German.

I climbed the stairs to the third floor.

I heard the commotion as I was walking up the stairs, and then saw Sykes slamming a freshly fitted bracket closed and fastening a heavy padlock to the front door. It clicked tight shut, and he turned towards me. "Ah, so you're back! Thought we'd seen the last of you! Thought you'd hopped it and not paid yer rent, like the last one."

"No, I'm still here." I looked at the lock. "You seem to be locking me out!"

"I seem to be, don't I!" Sykes was grumpier than usual. Locking me out of the apartment was a new departure, even for him. He stood, slightly hunched, in his faded tweed jacket with leather elbow patches.

I tried to appeal to his inner generosity, buried so deep I held out little hope of locating it. "Won't you open up, just so I can get a change of clothes?" I said.

"I won't open this until I gets your rent. Two months it is, now!"

"I get paid at the end of the week, I can give you something then," I offered weakly.

"Well, that's fine. Just don't be expecting to sleep here till the end of the week then."

"Oh, come on, Sykes, be reasonable, man!" I braced myself for his standard lecture on the shortcomings of today's youth.

"I'll be reasonable when I get my rent." That was his position and he wasn't moving from it.

"Look, I don't wind you up, do I? I pay when I can! I don't give you a hard time for being a raving bloody psycho!"

"Pay your rent, and I'll let you in!"

I could see I was getting nowhere. "Okay, okay! I'll fix you up later, when I've been back to the office."

I turned and walked back down to Cass's car. In a funny way I liked Sykes, even if he was a cantankerous old bugger. He was like this because he had to be, and because he needed the rent to play the horses. Sometimes he even won, occasionally quite big. He'd taken a cruise on the Sea Princess in the Caribbean on his winnings once. He called it "hobnobbing with the toffs." Any mixing of the classes was hobnobbing. He didn't get to hobnob much. Maybe next time he'd get to meet Cass's parents. That would make for interesting dinner table conversation.

But Sykes was like most gamblers, he was either a high roller, or practically a bum. I'd find him the money, probably get an advance from the payroll section.

It was turning out to be a bad day. If I'd known how it was going to turn out, I would have camped where I was and called it quits. On the car windshield a ticket fluttered in the dirty breeze. I had parked illegally for less than ten minutes. I was about to sling it, when I saw it wasn't a ticket at all, but a note. Typed. "Apartment 312, 44 Athlone Street, Brixton. 4:15 p.m. Very important."

Very doubtful. My instinct said I was being set up. I would make sure a few people knew where I was heading before I left. My finely honed preservation instincts were screaming out and telling me to make tracks in the opposite direction with all speed. Still, it gave me something to think about, apart from being locked out of my apartment. Perhaps that's why I swallowed it, though God knows, I've asked myself why a thousand times since.

I got on the cell to Cass, and explained I wanted to meet a contact. She was fine about it. She was too preoccupied with her mother's window boxes to be concerned about me using her car for an hour or so. She'd pretty well written off the day as far as *News* was concerned.

IT WAS AN UNASSUMING BLOCK of flats. Actually quite tidy for this part of town. Almost affluent. There was no security at all on the door, so I walked straight in to find an elevator that actually worked. I stepped out at the third floor. I noticed how quiet this building was. In most apartments blocks you can hear music playing, children crying or laughing, and televisions on too loud. This place was positively subdued. I found 312 easily enough.

The door to the apartment swung open as I knocked. A stale sweat smell hung in the air, like in a gym.

"Anyone here?" I called. No reply. There was no light on in the hall, but I could hear the sound of a radio, slightly off-station. I called out again. Still no answer.

My gut said get out, but I was drawn towards the light

seeping from beneath a doorway at the end of the hall. I stepped in cautiously. People were known to keep dogs, even in these apartment buildings.

I partially closed the front door. The first room was a living room, very nicely laid out. Spotless and comfortable. Two large sofas, leather, and a low wooden coffee table. The reading material on the table was not what I would have expected, but I am quite naïve when it comes to these things. *Big Girl*, and *Teaser*, and some others, heavier porn, too. Glossy magazines, fresh off the newsstand by the look of them. I flicked through one, then walked out into the hallway and checked another room. Kitchen, spotless, too. Nothing much to be learned here.

The radio still hissed from the room at the end of the hall. It was almost calling me to go there, but I thought it just possible someone was in there, asleep maybe. Best check the rest of the place first.

In the bathroom some sort of medical equipment hung on the wall by the bath, neatly and cleanly laid out. I don't know what the hell it was, but I didn't like the look of it. Too many tubes and stainless steel bits.

The door opposite the one from which the radio played was locked. Probably just a built-in cupboard. I left it and turned to the last room. I knocked first, then called out, "Hello." There was no answer.

I turned the handle, and tried it. It wasn't locked. Inside was a huge bed, unmade and badly ruffled. It looked like someone had been entertaining. The bed seemed to fill half the room, the remainder being taken up by an elaborate, black, built-in closet.

On the bedside table were a collection of sex toys,

oils, and the various accessories for what appeared to be a well-equipped professional. Chains and fur-lined cuffs hung from the side of the headboard and the foot of the bed. On the dressing table, amid the perfumes and makeup boxes, the radio played, and I noticed a half-smoked cigarette, stubbed out in a black enamel ashtray. The pack of cigarettes by it was my brand. Funny, that.

Something was wrong. Something I couldn't place. I was about to leave when I saw something seeping from beneath the door of the built-in closet and down to the floor. There, away from the black of the dark surface, the liquid slowly spread, red on the white carpet.

"What the hell ..." I muttered.

I didn't even think as I walked over to try the doors of the closet. As I touched the handle, the door sprang open, and suddenly someone seemed to leap out and smother me, surprising me completely.

Then everything seemed to happen at once. And that's how the whole mess started. Next thing I knew the cops were coming in, and things went downhill from there.

Chapter 3

My cell measured four paces by three. There was a window covered in frosted glass that would probably withstand a blow from a sledgehammer. I suspected the window faced into a light well or some secure compound. Either way, it provided a glimmer of natural light, if not a view. The door was heavy steel, painted gray (I was getting used to gray), which looked as if it came from an earlier time than the rest of the building. Perhaps government-issue strong-room doors were recycled from one installation to another. I've always approved of recycling. The spy-hole in the middle of the door allowed people to watch me as I wallowed in despair, sinking deeper into that seething, sucking pit so familiar to the truly depressed.

My personal effects and belt and shoelaces had been removed on my arrival. The government was so concerned about my welfare, it would not allow me to hang myself by my belt in the cell. The light in the ceiling had also been recessed, very helpfully, to prevent me from trying to electrocute myself. Presumably, someone in the prison system was under the impression that a criminal as dangerous as I would readily levitate to the light socket and then impulsively thrust his tongue into the exposed electrical contacts for some very good reason. And they called that taking the easy way out. It seemed an unlikely way to commit suicide to me.

As far as I could figure out, there was little that could actually make my situation worse. I had not been allowed to change my clothes, which were still covered in blood, and I was a mess. I had not been asked to give a statement. I figured the statement bit would come as soon as the crime-scene team had got me sized up for the court. I would be told that, if I showed remorse and made it easy for them, all being well, I might get out inside ninety years.

I was finding that, unlike the heroes of films, I was unable to sit calmly in a cell in the certain knowledge that I would be released. Being in a cell, with no watch and no diversions at all, I could only focus on one thing. Guilt. Even I was beginning to think I must be guilty. Only guilty people get locked up like this.

If I were taken to trial in the morning to enter a plea, there would be press boys waiting to nail me. That was an interesting thought. Then the boot really would be on the other foot. I didn't much relish the thought of hiding beneath a raincoat, stumbling into court – or down a manhole. Always assuming I got out on bail, of course.

Had I done anything wrong? I had been found covered in blood, sure! I had been at the scene of a crime, and I had maybe been in the girl's apartment under dubious circumstances, but I hadn't done anything to her. Had I? Perhaps I had. Perhaps, in the heat of the moment I had somehow forgotten what had actually taken place. I had heard of stranger things. Maybe I had had a blow on the head. Some kind of fall.

I recounted my movements since I left Cass, step by step. I could recall everything fairly clearly.

The difficulty lay in the fact that she was a hooker, and probably would let in a caller. That much seemed fairly safe to assume. There would be no need for her killer to force an entry. And she wouldn't need to know me. Except in the Biblical sense, she probably didn't "know" any of her clients.

I hadn't seen anyone since the two policemen had brought me in. I had yet to make the phone call I was allowed. I was technically under arrest, but as yet no charge had been specified. I even still had her blood on my face and hands. I was about ready to start hammering on the door to demand a phone call and a lawyer, when the heavy recycled door swung open. A portly, red-faced man with graying hair walked in. His sleeves were rolled up, and he carried a clipboard. He looked like a meter reader.

He sat on the bed, the clipboard on his knee. He tapped his pencil on it a number of times as he watched me, his small, intense eyes devouring every detail. He was not here to read any meter. Funny, though. You get a feel for faces in my business. Although he didn't seem to have a cruel face, I found being scrutinized like this quite unnerving.

At length he introduced himself as Detective Constable Van Allen and then cut straight to the point. "Mr. Sinclair, you are in a great deal of trouble. I suggest you call a lawyer. I can have a phone brought in if you wish."

"But I've done nothing wrong. Why would I need a lawyer?" I replied, rather weakly.

"You have done nothing wrong?" He repeated my words and then looked at the floor for a moment. Then he opened the file slowly, very deliberately.

"You were found in a prostitute's apartment, trying to clean up in the kitchen after apparently killing a woman named Kelly Watson. You'd agree, the appearance is one that suggests guilt, wouldn't you?"

"Well," I stammered, "when you put it like that...." They were simple words, but the way he said them left little room for doubt that I was a pathological sex beast, embarking on a sordid feast of sexual indulgence and death, whilst painted with blood in the image of my own lustful madness. I found this discouraging.

He looked at the floor, as if unable to meet my eyes. "The best advice I can give you is to call a lawyer," he continued. "You'll be needing one. A good one."

"Well, since you mention it, I would like to make a call."

He disappeared for a moment, returning with a phone on a long extension lead.

"May I ask the time?" I said.

He looked at his watch, then said, "It's 4:20. You've been here three hours."

"Thank you," I replied as I dialed through to the news-desk. I asked the secretary to put me through to Marlene. Our regular secretary was off, and I didn't recognize the replacement's voice. Probably a temp. Marlene's shift didn't end for another hour so she was sure to be in the news-room. There was a pause and then the secretary came back on the line and said Marlene was in a meeting.

"Would you like me to put you through to Marlene's voice mail?"

"Tell her it's Steve Sinclair, and I'm under arrest at Brixton nick, and I need to speak to her." She put me on hold for a moment before coming back to me. "I'm sorry, Marlene's not available, are you quite sure you don't want her voice mail?"

"Listen," I said, trying to sound calm, "just get her out of the meeting and tell her to come to the bloody phone. She'll understand, and with a bit of luck you'll still have a job in the morning."

Van Allen was still in the cell. I don't think he realized I was speaking to the newsdesk, not that it made any difference at all. After a moment Marlene's rasping voice came down the phone.

"What sort of trouble is it this time? Been caught sneaking pictures through people's windows again, Steve?" How Marlene managed to convey both contempt and pity at the same time I'm not quite sure.

"No, not exactly, Marlene. I'm being held for murder."

"Well, that's something, we might even get a story out of it!" She sounded more interested now. I heard the click of her cigarette holder on her teeth and the sound of a lighter. "You killed anyone I know?"

"Funnily enough, that's possible. Does the name Kelly Watson mean anything to you?"

"No, but I'll run it through the system anyway." Marlene was making out she was more interested in the news story than my welfare, but that was just her way of dealing with it. "Of course, Strathclyde'll be livid."

"If it makes a difference, I didn't kill her. She fell on

me out of a closet. Must have been dead when I got there." Van Allen was watching me intently. He was listening as though expecting me to say: "It's a fair cop, guv'na, I did it and them filthy coppers nicked me red-handed!"

"The cops have me nailed as far as they're concerned. Can you get someone down here? I could use a little support on this."

"Yeah, I can imagine. Why would anyone want to kill this Watson, though? You got any ideas?"

"No idea, not yet, anyway. I'm more concerned about getting out of here. Can you arrange for some clothes? I'm covered in blood. You might also like to get Cass to make a statement to the cops about my movements. I was only in the apartment for five minutes before they showed. I was in her car until then."

"Okay, she's here in the newsroom somewhere. I think she's working on some environmental stuff. Something like that." I heard Marlene take another drag on her cigarette, and then, as though summoning her strength for a great effort, she added, "I suppose this will have to take priority. I'll get things moving for you. I expect a serious lunch out of this."

"You got it, Marlene. Thanks." And with that, in spite of her unusual mannerisms, I knew Marlene would move heaven and earth to get me out of there. She was completely dependable.

As I hung up, Van Allen was on his feet. "If you don't co-operate with us, you'll be up for obstruction as well as murder, Sinclair." He was trying to rattle me now. I knew that game well enough.

"I'm co-operating. You had me here three hours, you

didn't even drop by to say hello. Now you get pissed because I wasn't there when the girl got stiffed. I'm real sorry I don't fit your version of events, but that's your problem. May I wash myself now?"

He hesitated. "So, do you know this girl?"

"Never seen her in my life," I replied.

"So how come your name's in her address book?"

"I don't know. But the Chief Constable of the Met is in my address book. Doesn't mean I have lunch at his house, does it?"

"That's right. You're on a local paper aren't you?"

"No, I'm on a national." I was always touchy about that and Van Allen was not exactly getting me at a good moment.

"Hmmm. Well, I haven't finished with you yet."

"Have you laid a charge?" I asked, feeling a little more confident knowing the paper was going to get me out of the mess I'd wound up in.

"I don't have to yet," he snapped back, looking a little more flustered. I got the feeling he knew there was something wrong with the whole picture. Sure there was evidence, but even he could see it all looked pretty circumstantial.

"Well, I should think about laying that charge soon if I were you. My paper's going to be really pissed about this if you screw us around, especially in the course of our work. The chief constable's not going to look kindly on the flatfoot that made his force look like a bunch of idiots, is he? You know bloody well I was there in the course of my work."

"Your work?" That took him by surprise, coming completely out of the blue.

"I was on a job. She was a contact. You'll be dealing with *News Consolidated*'s lawyers, not mine. Hope you've got some strong support from your boss, Van Allen. Our boys can make you people look really bad."

"You're in no position to threaten me – look at you!" Van Allen's face was flushed with anger. Here was his prime suspect, a homicidal animal in his eyes, chiding him as though he were a schoolboy. I was getting through to him. I decided to push it a little further.

"I'm not threatening you, all I'm saying is the lawyers will go after not you, but your boss. And he'll look for somewhere to pass the heat. Human nature, isn't it? Had your review this year, have you? Your wife think you're going to get a pay rise this year, does she? All the little Van Allens think Father Christmas might get them some extra presents come Christmas?"

Van Allen stormed out.

An hour later the door swung open and a constable entered with a young East Indian woman, carrying a small attaché case. She was tall and slender, definitely a corporate type of clean-cut legal eagle. If she worked as good as she looked, my troubles were over.

She extended her hand and said, "My name is Shandra Daliwal. I'm with *News Consolidated*'s legal section. I'm your lawyer."

"Am I glad to see you!"

"I think you'll be needing these." She opened the case and laid out some clothes on the bed. I waited for her to turn her back or leave or something, but she did neither. Fine. I can play games like this all day.

I stripped and changed. It was disconcerting having her watch me change in a prison cell, but this was a pretty weird situation, and I was in no position to complain about it.

"Shall we go?" she said, once I was dressed.

"What?" I said, surprised. "It's that simple?"

"Cass has given a statement putting you in her car at the time of the girl's death. It seems you were on a cellphone – we traced the position of the call to put you twenty-three miles away at the approximate time of death. Kelly Watson had been dead getting on for an hour before you even got to the apartment. They have no weapon, or anything to connect you to a weapon. Everyone's saying how sorry they are about this incident. You didn't think we'd leave you here, did you?"

"No! Not for a minute," I said, and then added, "Er, thanks."

As I walked from my cell, which had at least temporarily solved my accommodation problem, Van Allen walked down the corridor towards me. "Just a misunderstanding, Mr. Sinclair. You have to understand ..."

I cut him off, raising my hand and waving away his apologies. "It's all right, Constable," I said, using the wrong rank to rankle him further. "Anything I can do to help, you just give me a call." It's easy to be magnanimous faced with the prospect of not spending the next twenty years in jail.

"'Preciate that, sir. Perhaps you'd better use the washrooms, clean yourself up a bit." I could tell Van Allen was seething, but he was trying to hide it manfully.

Poor man, I actually felt a pang of sympathy for him in that moment. He had a tough job to do, and when something simple came along it must have seemed like a gift from the gods. Silly bastard.

Once I'd washed up we left. To my amazement and relief, I was free again.

SHANDRA DROVE ME BACK over the river. My mind was racing around in all directions. I had to sort out Sykes, just to get a place to sleep. I had not even begun to figure out who wanted me squashed by a dead hooker, and I was more than a little curious about who had sliced up Kelly Watson, and why. There were a few things out of place here, and they were running around in my head, not making much sense. Shandra asked if I was hungry.

"Sure, I didn't get to eat lunch," I replied.

"Okay, there's a Chinese I know on our way – you eat Chinese?"

"Sure, that'd be good," I replied.

"It's in Soho, and we can wait out the rush hour."

"Suits me," I said. One of the advantages of working for a national paper is that the accounts department is open about eighteen hours a day. I'd get an advance on my wages later. That would cheer Sykes up. I like to make people happy.

There was still blood on my leather jacket, so I left it shoved under the car seat. Shandra's little BMW was courtesy of *News Consolidated*. The serious in-house executives got well looked after. Still, I wasn't complaining. They were there when I needed them.

The neon of Soho was just beginning to flicker into life as we walked the crowded street between peepshow frontages to tiny Chinese eateries, packed, mostly with Asians. There was no way we'd be getting a table for a while. Well, that was a good sign.

Shandra cut through them – like a local. When you photograph things all day, you notice stuff. It's not like being judgmental. You just see things sometimes. Like, this person fits here, or, that person is awkward with such-and-such. And it tells stories. That's why I shoot, I guess. It's not even much of a skill. More like a gift for languages; if you have it, you have it. It's seeing light and dark, and people leaning into conversations, and seeing how far apart people are standing, and how they scratch their arm in a certain way when they talk about something, or lie.

And there was a puzzle in Shandra. She wore a neatly cut navy blue suit, and a hairstyle that probably cost more than I made in a day. She was nouveau Westminster in all respects and yet, here she was, slipping through the seedy crowd like a street slut from the Soho sidewalk.

Moments later Shandra was chatting with someone who looked like the owner or maybe managed the restaurant, as we stood in the doorway with others waiting to eat. She stepped past the queue with the man. He was Asian, busily overseeing things behind the scenes. It was a serious-looking conversation. Then she waved me over, and we were sitting at a freshly laid table. So she had some kind of pull here.

A few dishes were brought, and she spooned something onto my plate I had never seen before. Then rice and chow mein. She said something I couldn't hear and smiled a brilliant smile. There was a lot of noise in the little restaurant. Outside, people were hurrying by. I wasn't in jail anymore. Things were getting better.

"So, do you want to come?" The sounds of the restaurant were almost drowning her out.

"Sorry, what?" I said.

"Are you coming to the party?"

I had no idea what she was talking about. I had obviously missed something.

"Sure," I shouted back over the noise. "But you'll have to take me to the office first – I need to talk to someone in Accounts."

"No problem. I have to pick some papers up anyway."

After an excellent meal we stepped into the street to find it was raining lightly outside. Soho is a dump these days. But the neon still reflects nicely in some places. I guess it was better thirty years back. Or perhaps a lot worse.

I got the business out of the way quickly in Accounts. They know me well enough in there. Getting a few quid early was not unusual, but then neither was drawing US $3,000 and jumping on a plane for a story. I hadn't had one of those for a while, and was beginning to think it was a more appealing option than working London courts all the time. It amazed me how I could be so bad with money, and yet routinely handle quite large sums in cash, in the course of my job.

I waited in Photographic until Shandra called and said she was leaving. I placed my cellphone in the cradle to recharge as I left, and hurried down to reception. Shandra was waiting, holding a slim document file as I stepped out of the lift. Very Pierre Cardin. She drove swiftly through the now-empty city streets out to Notting Hill, where she had an apartment. She played Enya on the cassette player as she drove, and looked as languid as the music sounded.

Her penthouse flat was definitely at the top end of

the market. I smoked a cigarette on the balcony as she changed. Twenty floors below me, people came and went, unaware of the recently released felon above them. Not that I was a felon. Cop shops just make you feel like one, and it takes a while to wear off. Inside the apartment Shandra had lots of white furniture and low tables that were not much good for anything. I could imagine falling over those when I came in late if they were in my place. There were some pretty expensive but challenging pictures on the walls. They looked like original oils. Maybe they were her own. They gave me a headache if I looked at them for long. She had only one small bookshelf with a selection of travel books that looked like they'd never been opened.

I was wearing new clothes, so wherever we were going, I figured I'd be able to fit in. I'd have to thank someone in the office for getting the sizes just right. Someone was thoughtful.

When she returned to the living room, she appeared like some mystic apparition sliding in from the East, and I don't mean Stepney. She looked breathtaking. She wore a bronze-black piece of cloth that seemed to have been soaked and laid over her skin and then dried like a fine paint job. It clung like something alien and covered her, after a fashion. Her previously understated breasts were now substantial, her legs slimmer and longer, her entire figure somehow sharpened. She was about three inches taller, and looked the way Irish coffee tastes on a cool night.

I must have been staring. She said, "Well?"

"Nice frock, love!" I replied.

TAKING A BEAUTIFUL WOMAN to a party is quite enjoyable. Losing her after you arrive is not generally part of the plan. I don't really know how I managed it.

I can remember arriving at an impressive apartment in Dolphin Square. There were two heavies on the door who were classy enough to be called doormen, but were heavies nonetheless. Heavies who filed their nails, I suspect. It's hard to trust types like that. Not in one camp, and not in another.

Some guests were not finding it easy to gain entrance, but we swept through on a tide of confidence and Shandra's presence. I felt out of place from the minute we walked through the door.

If it started uncomfortably, it got steadily worse. Shandra introduced me to a couple of yahoos, whose names I forgot immediately, Simmington-Smythe, could have been. There was also a pretentious prat calling himself something or other the third. Maybe it's a reflex reaction, or maybe I seriously dislike the pomposity of someone calling himself after his father's father. Like somehow they were better than my father and his father. I wondered how my name would sound with III after it. Bloody silly, I thought.

Drinks appeared on silver trays carried by passing goons. Shandra drank from an impossible-looking glass with something colorful growing out of it. I grabbed a passing lager in a bottle with a top that looked like an engineering project.

As I looked about the place and Shandra chatted to the Updyke-Smythe twins I couldn't help noticing that most of the women in the room seemed to be barely nineteen. Shandra was definitely among the senior generation, and I don't think anyone could credit her with more than twenty-seven years. Okay, twenty-nine. The men ranged from about twenty-five to sixty, at a guess. Odd mix, but not so uncommon.

The apartment was on the ground floor and, outside a set of French doors, a small sound and light system was set up. There was a little dancing in the summer evening, which had turned out to be warmer than usual. I suppose things were only just starting, but a couple of teenyboppers were already dancing to a band I'd never heard of. Some kind of limp rock. Chewing gum for the ears.

True to form, the Upit-Smythes were laughing heartily at something Shandra was saying. It was that embarrassing type of laughter that onlookers can tell is forced. Insincere. She leaned over and whispered to me, "I was at Oxford with their younger brother, he was quite a scream." I liked having Shandra whisper into my ear. Her breath was soft and warm, almost a caress.

"How nice for you," I replied.

"He's in Bermuda now. Running his own bank."

"I see," I said, feeling increasingly out of place. " I'll remember that next time I'm there and need to get a payday advance."

"Come with me," said Shandra. Either she was oblivious to my discomfort, or she didn't care.

I followed as she cut through the crowd, thinking what a lovely shape her shoulders were, moving this way and that as she glided by people. A middle-aged fellow was getting a drink from a passing waiter. He was tanned, well-groomed and looked generally successful. If someone looking like that walked into a shop I was running, I'd switch all the price tags over in a second.

"Nigel," Shandra said, and he turned around. He must have recognized the voice, because he had a broad smile on his face, exposing a gold tooth. In the part of town I grew up in, they'd rip your head off for that.

"Nigel, this is Steve. He's on the *News* – in Photographic."

"Oh yes, you must be Steve Sinclair."

"Yeah," I answered, not that surprised that he'd seen my by-line around. It's always flattering to have someone remember it, but the trick is in being offhand about it.

He put out his hand, "Nigel Cummins, nice to meet you. How do you like the *News*?"

"Good paper. Nice team in Photographic. Better than most of the papers." I glanced around the room a little coolly, but Cummins continued to talk.

"Yes, it is a good paper. Pretty well the last in the Street, too."

He was referring to the fact that the major papers had followed Murdoch out to the Isle Of Dogs, and left Fleet Street. Most of the big boys moved out several years ago, breaking the unions apart as they did so. They installed badly needed modern printing presses, and fast-forwarded the technology by thirty years. The *News* had done all right, though, upgrading its presses to those left behind by the bigger companies as they departed. The machines that *News International* had installed in its fortress on the Isle of Dogs needed literally truckloads of paper, a logistical task of enormous proportions. Four million copies of *The Sun* a day is an enormous amount of paper, which then has to be directed onto the motor-way system of the United Kingdom and distributed throughout the country. The logistics of newspapers are mind-boggling. This was of little concern to the *News*. At two hundred thousand copies a day, it was a baby, albeit a highly profitable one.

Shandra chatted to Cummins for a little, and then moved on, sweeping me along with her. I suppose I was behaving badly, but Shandra was handling things very nicely. Quite a woman, all things considered.

"Well, what do you make of him?" she threw at me.

"Seems a nice guy," I said. "Nice jacket."

"Nice jacket?" she repeated. "He owns twelve percent of *News Consolidated*. It should be a nice jacket. When these guys pop out to buy a morning paper they end up owning the entire company." Shandra was looking around for the next point of contact. That's exactly what it was with her. It was a game, working from one contact to another. And she was good at it.

A voice called from behind and Shandra turned. A slim man, acting very casual – almost languid, stood there with a girl hanging on his arm. It took me a moment before I placed him, but then the cogs turned and I knew where I'd seen that face. It had been that very morning, in the news conference. He'd been the man talking so secretively to Strathclyde, the one who slipped out of the conference early. In this easy environment he looked slick and almost effeminate. A chameleon. But what I noticed most now was his eyes.

They were cool and bright, with an unmistakable trace of malice. I've seen those eyes in Africa, in Bosnia and in Romania. The kind of eyes that say something very bad. Some people totally miss it, finding nothing remarkable about them at all. But if you know that look, it is as if the man who carries it is branded on the forehead. And that usually means business for me, at some time or another. The reaper and I, armed with scythe and camera, respectively.

With him was a young girl. She wore her hair down, a tiny skirt and tight little jacket and seemed barely out of school. Someone could have told her how to do her face better, but maybe whatever school she'd just got out of didn't let their charges wear make up. She looked cheap.

I was not being quite fair. She looked expensive cheap. Expensive dressed-up cheap – now that's a trick! Either way, it was not a very attractive ensemble, and I could smell trouble. At least, that's what I think it was. I found her as disturbing as the man she was with. Particularly as she had made such a startling transformation from the previous time I'd seen her. Another chameleon. They move in herds, sometimes. It took me a second to make the connection, but it was definitely the same person. Her ears were now adorned with simple diamond studs – always a safe choice. But the piercing was clearly visible, and she had that strange imbalance, more holes on the left than the right. It was the girl I had seen in the press gallery at Hanson's trial. I kept my mouth closed and filed the fact away.

Her male companion was talking to Shandra under his breath. Very conspiratorial. She was looking uncomfortable – for the first time she appeared ill at ease. It was a new look for her and didn't suit the rest of her outfit.

I glanced about the place. In the space of twelve hours I had gone from renting, to being locked out; prison to freedom; and was now drinking some awful and expensive foreign lager in Dolphin Square. Not my average day.

Shandra was back. "Known him a while. First met him at university."

"Who is he?" I asked.

"Jeremy Carfax," she replied. "He's Nigel Cummins's cousin. He owns a good chunk of *News Consolidated*, too. He comes over as kind of arrogant. He's all right really."

"I saw him at the news conference this morning. What would he be doing at the news conference?" I said, voicing my thoughts.

"Oh, Jeremy's involved in lots of things. He pops up all over the place. I shouldn't worry about it."

I caught sight of Carfax looking at us. He was saying something to the girl. His eyes were fixed on me, and I think he must have known Shandra was telling me about him. The girl with him was looking away indifferently at something happening in the corner of the room. She did so with slightly too much purpose.

He whispered something to the girl, and they both turned away sharply. He giggled, and moved off. There was something very unnerving about him, the confidentiality he seemed to share with Shandra. I didn't think much of it at the time, but it lodged somewhere in my head.

We stepped through the French doors into the small walled garden. I lit a smoke and felt slightly more relaxed. We sat on a bench next to a struggling rhododendron. I thought we'd found the nicest place at the party. And here we were completely alone.

"So, how'd you manage to get yourself into that mess today?" asked Shandra. "You never did explain it to me."

I thought about it for the first time in a few hours. It

all sounded rather silly. "I got tipped to be there. It happens like that sometimes. You get the nod from someone, and just run with it. Sometimes it comes to nothing. Sometimes it pays off. You don't usually end up in the nick."

"Don't you ever feel like you're being used? When someone gives you a tip, you don't think the person has an ax to grind?"

"Sure, but so what. If the story's a good story, so what if someone hands it to you on a plate."

"You don't think there might be an ulterior motive?" Shandra was thinking like a lawyer. She'd make a lousy journo.

"Yes. But I don't care, why should I?" It was hard to explain. "People who tip us off always have a motive. What they don't realize is that we don't care. Their motive is usually so small and meaningless in the big picture, it just gets washed away with the tide."

I tried to put it in context. "Look at Watergate, and I'm not saying every journalist gets to work a story like that, but bear with me. You see, the point is that everyone remembers the President screwed up and got caught. Who remembers the name of the guy who was feeding tips to the boys on the *Post*? Sure, the guy had an ax to grind. So what? The bigger picture was more important. If someone comes along and makes the job easier, why stop him?"

"Interesting viewpoint," Shandra said skeptically.

"Most people want to be listened to. It's human nature. People love a good listener. Shrinks have been on that bandwagon for a while now. They'll listen to you, complete with caring expression, faster than a rat up a drainpipe and then slap a bill on you that you actually feel good about paying. Most of the journos in this city who are any good know the less they say and the more they listen, the better they'll do."

"So how come you do pictures?"

"Beats working for a living," I replied. "What about you, how come you got into law?"

"It beats selling cigarettes and newspapers," she answered. I thought she was being sarcastic. Then she went on. "My father has a shop in Stepney, he does okay. He takes home in a good month what I clear in a week. He opens up at 6 a.m., and closes at 10:30 at night. If West Ham or Millwall are playing that weekend, he shuts the shop and hopes they don't come and beat him up or destroy the shop. Believe me, corporate law really does beat working for a living."

"I see your point."

"My family has spent pretty well everything they've earned since they came here in '53 on an education that would get me this accent and my qualifications. The result is that I can afford to ensure they have a comfortable retirement, and that they won't have to worry about being victimized on home game weekends."

"That sounds pretty tough. Your father must be very proud of you."

She smiled. "I'd like another drink. You want another lager?"

"Sure," I said. "Why don't I get them?" I slipped back inside and joined a small queue to get to the bar.

I waited a while before being served the martini and a lager for myself. When I returned to the bench where I'd left Shandra, I found it occupied by the oil slick,

Jeremy Carfax. His companion was moving around to the music nearby. No one else was in sight.

"Lost your girlfriend?" he sneered. "Tell me, which does she drink, the lager or the martini, or do you like to swap around sometimes?"

"She was here a minute ago," I said, feeling like a trespasser who'd been caught crashing the party. "Did you see where she went?"

"No. She probably slipped off to be with one of her sort."

I was getting beyond uncomfortable with this, but swallowed it and turned on my heel. I wasn't going to let him provoke me.

"Probably having a quickie with our host," called Carfax, before he started giggling like a schoolgirl.

I swung round sharply and saw a look of surprise cross his face. Fear. Just for a moment.

Outside the apartment there were only the three of us. I walked back towards him, and his girl turned and watched.

"I say," he said shakily, rising to his feet. "I didn't mean anything ..."

"It's okay," I said calmly, and then slammed my clenched knuckles into his right eyebrow, opening up an inch-long cut. He didn't even see the second punch as it laid him flat out.

Cheap ran over to him, and I was leaving. The music was loud, and the place too hot for me now. Strangely satisfying feelings coursed through me. There'd be hell to pay when he came to, so a smart exit was called for. That'll teach them to let the riff-raff through the door. I wondered how tight he was with Strathclyde. Maybe I'd need to talk to someone on one of the other papers.

I slipped back through the French doors; no one seemed aware of what had happened outside. Over my shoulder I saw Cheap cradling Carfax in her arms. Inside, there was no sign of Shandra. I worked my way around the room a couple of times, scanning the faces. She must have left. I wouldn't be surprised if that was Jeremy's doing. She was nowhere to be seen, and it was time to get out, before I was thrown out.

I stepped out into the night, past the heavies. I was angry about Shandra. A light rain had made the pavements glisten.

It was about 11:00, and a warm breeze wandered down the road, pushing me with it. The yellow of the streetlights reflected from the clouds, and I was in no rush to be anywhere. In my jacket pocket I had the little Rollie 35mm I sometimes carried. It was small enough to fit in a pocket but had a very high-quality lens for candid work.

I walked the mile through to Big Ben, then over the footbridge towards Waterloo, the Thames a black, oily mass below. Tomorrow's paper was already on sale, and I shot a couple of frames of one of the newspaper sellers standing beside a fire with some homeless guys, chatting. That time of night, who else would be hanging around? Bums and the fourth estate.

I got on the last train running through "the drain," the dilapidated underground route through to Bank, one of London's oldest underground routes. It was built at a time when they were so wild about the system that experimental tunnels were being cut all over – or rather under – London. Raving high technology! Sometimes when the foundations are being laid for new buildings, the old workings surface, not on any maps, from the early twentieth century. No one knows where all the lines were. Half the builders were wiped out in the first war, at Ypres and Passiondale, taking their plans with them, I suppose. We will remember them, especially when their railway shows up under a subsiding tower block.

From Bank I strolled through to Fleet Street. It was one in the morning. The roar of a truck struggling out of the underground loading bay of the *News* and the slap slap of its rear shuttered door heralded another load of the second edition hitting the street. Then a couple more followed. The army of the press on the move. They were the only vehicles in the street.

Predawn is a magical time in a city. Stuff going on that no one thinks about. Streets being cleaned, papers being delivered, the first deliveries of the day going into Smithfield meat market. The way it has been for the last three hundred years, in London. It's the only place in England where some bars are allowed to be open after 11 p.m. The Smithfield Market pubs have a special dispensation to serve at unusual hours – some can be found open at 4 or 5 a.m.

As I walked into the building I could hear the sound of the presses, working on edition three – usually the last of the day. That would ship at about 3 a.m., carrying the latest news. The late editions were mostly distributed in the London area. They would be read usually only three or four hours after rolling off the presses. It was not unknown for a fourth to go to press, but it had to be a major late-breaking story.

It's always exciting to see the paper actually coming

off the presses, so I decided to walk down to the Stone, a special area on the pressroom floor. It has its own editor, who's a weird animal in the newspaper business. He's usually a printer but also a journo – sort of where pressroom meets newsroom. The Stone editor is the guy who signs the print run off and commits God only knows how many tons of paper per edition, the final check to make sure the paper looks right from a news perspective and a printer's perspective. In some ways he's the most important man on the paper. A good Stone editor will save your ass.

The last pages of the last edition were being signed off as I entered the pressroom. The size of the machines and their massive output of sound was overwhelming. Capable of more than 25,000 impressions an hour, the machines would sometimes take a couple of minutes to roll up to their full production speed before the enormous rolls of newsprint began their journey between the rollers. And at the far end of the press a minder would be checking the quality every few hundred copies, looking for a changing density in the ink, or shifting of the registration between colors. It was not unknown for a spelling error to go from a journo's laptop, past the sub-editors, past the Stone editor to the press and be caught by a printer checking something else entirely. If it was a serious or embarrassing error, the presses would be stripped of their plates, halted until new ones were made – with the error corrected – and the run restarted.

There was a coffee machine by the Stone, so I poured a cup and had a look at the pages laid out on a central table. Princess Anne was on the front page, without horse this time. It was not a bad looking paper. One thing the News knew how to do was use a picture. None of this "two inches by three" rubbish. Slap it on the front and take two-thirds of the page! Make sure the face is recognizable above the fold, so the guys passing the newsstand can see who is on the front, even with the paper folded. And big headlines! It may not be art, but it's News!

I passed a while chatting with a couple of the minders who were going off shift, and then went back up to Photographic. Pierre, one of the other photographers, was there, finishing some processing. He'd just got back from a job and had a couple of prints to make before leaving for the day.

"Heard you got arrested," said Pierre.

"Yeah, they managed to spring me, though."

"Someone said it was murder!"

"Murder? It was bloody awful!" I replied, laughing.

"I bet," he said. " But really, what was it about? The temp on the desk said it was a murder charge."

"It was – not me, though. Cops came in when I was there. I was the nearest person so they nicked me. I think they felt pretty silly about it by the time they really thought things through."

"Huh! It's not everyday you get nicked for murder, though!" Pierre seemed impressed.

"Well, for what it's worth, I don't recommend it."

I retrieved my fully charged cellphone and slipped it into my pocket. CNN was on in the background, another graveyard shift passing without much happening.

Some nights, when it was quiet, if there were a few of us around we'd play games with the other papers. It was not unknown to infiltrate their press room to retrieve an early copy of their first edition front page. Newspapers had been reprinted as a result of such escapades. One reporter, Tish, practically founded a career on such antics. All's fair in the Street of Shame. The *Daily Express* knows all about that. They were victim at least once, to my certain knowledge, while they were still in the Street. *Ah, Tish!* I wondered. *Where did you end up?*

But tonight was a dead one. Deader than Kelly Watson, poor girl.

I went to the terminal in the corner and checked my e-mails. The first was from Cass, and just said, "Where's my car?" The next, also from Cass, told me I was in for sixty pounds of parking fines but that she hoped I got out of jail soon, so I could pay her. It's good to have people concerned about one's welfare.

The last, Cass yet again, was marked Urgent. "Call me. We have to talk as soon as you get this." She had written "Urgent" three times at the foot of the message.

I guessed she didn't mean at 3 a.m. Whatever it was would wait until the sun rose. I left an e-mail for Marcel, the morning picture editor, explaining that I had been arrested while on a job, that Marlene had the details, and that I'd be sleeping late in the morning, unless he needed me. With that, I wrapped things up and left for the night.

Waking Sykes at 4 a.m. with the rent money was fine. He liked getting the rent money day or night, grunted his thanks and gave me the key to the Chubb lock on the door. I was asleep before my head hit the pillow.

I WOKE TO FIND MYSELF being dragged from my bed as my eyes focused on a face I had never seen before. Then I was hit by a freight train, as his fist plowed into my face below my right eye. The ceiling was sliding around in the wrong place and he hauled me to my feet again.

"What the hell do you want?" I managed to say. Was this Carfax's way of getting even?

He drove his fist into my nose, which immediately erupted in blood, warm and metallic over my face and in my mouth. I couldn't see much after that. My eye was swelling up already. I was on the floor, but he hauled me to my feet by my hair.

"Where's your computer, smartass?"

I mumbled through broken lips and teeth, "What computer?" What was the maniac on about?

"What computer!" He swung a backhand, nearly ripping my jaw out of my head with its force, and then slammed a punch into my solar plexus. I was trying to breathe when I vomited on his foot. The Chinese food wasn't standing up to this very well.

"Is it still 'what computer'?" he repeated, sarcastically.

He lifted me to a chair, slung me back in it, and then pushed my face back. Next thing I knew he must have punched my throat or something. It just felt like I was dying and I couldn't breathe or even scream, the pain was so fearful.

I was trying to say, "I don't know what you mean, you fucking deranged asshole," but the sound just came out as a stillborn scream. Try as I might, no words were coming. I kept thinking, *He's ripped my throat out. He's ripped my throat out.*

Then I began to hear what he was doing. I could see

a little out of my left eye. He was systematically opening drawers and flinging the contents across the room. One of my back-up Nikons was on a desk in the corner of my tiny apartment. He picked it up and came over to me.

"You're gonna tell me where it is, now start talking!"

I felt him take my left hand, slam it back against the wall, and then drive the camera into it like a hammer. I screamed in pain.

"I don't know what you fucking mean!" I tried to say – but my throat was stuffed. It didn't seem to open and I was suffocating. Getting dizzier by the second with pain and lack of breath.

"We know about your visit to Hanson's place. Where did you hide the computer you ported his disk to!"

The Nikon crunched into my broken fingers again. I wanted to say the computer was back at the office, but my throat was still blocked.

As he was about to hammer my hand again I saw the glint of something coming out of left field. There was a dull thud and he was still a moment.

Then he fell on top of me. I still couldn't breathe.

Sykes leaned over me, looking worried. He had forgotten to put his teeth in. He was a beautiful sight all the same. "Blimey! Don't know what you did to piss 'im off, son. I bloody hope you don't plan to do it often. Who'll pay the rent then?"

Chapter 4

S YKES HAD HIT MY VISITOR with a length of lead pipe, which had dropped him like a sack of potatoes. Whoever he was, he was a big man, and pinned me to the chair until I kicked his inert body to the floor. Finding myself under bodies was getting to be a habit.

He was breathing, and looked in far better shape than me. I was still in excruciating pain, my left hand swollen up like a melon, and my face looking like someone had used it as a football. Using my one good hand, I hurriedly searched him for some form of ID I found only keys.

"Jesus, Sykes, thanks, man!" I croaked, my voice sounding like someone else's, but no one I knew.

He prodded the unconscious form at his feet. "Don't mention it. I heard 'im sneak in a little while ago. I figured 'e was lookin' for you. There's been a car parked outside waiting, like. Then there's all these smashing sounds, and I figured he was robbing the place. And now you, looking like this!" Sykes scowled at the state of my face.

I thought about calling the police. Then I remembered he had mentioned the way I'd copied the hard drive. He might mention it to the cops, too, and then things would get a little complicated. That might be uncomfortable. Detective Constable Van Allen was one acquaintance I was in no rush to renew any time in the immediate future.

"You better get rid of 'im," said Sykes. "'E won't be very 'appy when 'e wakes up."

Pulling on jeans and t-shirt, I hurried down to the street and looked for a car that matched the keys. It took me three tries before I found a new Volkswagen Jetta, parked just up the road.

I moved the car down to Sykes's place, double-parking outside, struggling but managing to control the car in my weakened state. The quiet street was deserted. I would be all right for a few minutes. I opened the trunk and went back inside the house.

Upstairs I struggled with the dead weight of our intruder. He was out cold, but grunted as I hefted his body out of my room, the wind sighing out of him. Sykes tried to help, but was fussing and couldn't really do anything, being as frail as he was. He'd already done enough, thank God. I have no idea what would have happened to me without his timely intervention. The guy would probably have beaten me to death.

The unconscious form ended up half falling and half being carried. Worst of all, I could feel him trying to come round, almost ready to wake. Pushing my shoulder into his belly, I lifted him and staggered to the car, then dropped him in the boot and slammed it closed. I looked around to see if anyone had noticed what I was doing. With my current luck I half expected to see a police convention going on two doors up the street.

There was no movement in the street or from

neighbouring windows. I slid behind the wheel and drove the Jetta a hundred yards to the far end of the road, where the street bordered some waste ground. It would be undisturbed for a while here.

"What'd you do with 'im?" asked Sykes when I got back.

"He's comfortable for now," I replied. "I shoved him in the boot of his car and moved it up the road."

"He'll die in there!"

"No, just have time to think things over. I'll have a chat with him later."

It was hurting my face to talk and my throat was raw. I'd have to get myself looked at in the local hospital. Sykes obligingly called me a taxi. Our house not being on the main route, I was unlikely to hail one in the street. Soon I was on my way to Casualty, my right eye completely closed up and my hand clearly broken. I had washed thoroughly, trying to clean my wounds, but I was still a mess.

While I sat in the back of the taxi, I remembered Cass's message. It was 11 a.m. She'd be at work. I clumsily dialed her direct line, only to get the voicemail, so I called her at home.

Her flatmate answered the phone.

"Hello, is Cass there?"

"No, she's working today. Who's calling?"

"It's Steve Sinclair from the *News*."

"Oh, yes, she mentioned you might call. She said she'd see you at the office, or leave a message there for you."

"Thanks," I said. "If you see her, will you tell her I called, and that she can get me on the cell? She knows the number."

I dialed my own line at the office, and punched in the code to retrieve voice mail. There were two messages. I could feel my strength fading fast.

"Hi Steve, it's Cass." She sounded very excited. "When I got home tonight there were a couple of guys watching the house, at least I think they are. I don't know who they are, and it might be nothing. But I think maybe we should be a bit careful. I sent you an e-mail. We have to talk soon. I checked out that tape and the files we got the other night. *We have to talk.* Let's get together tomorrow."

So whoever we'd upset had made the connection between Cass and me. Interesting. That meant they must have some good information.

The usual bleeps followed, then the next message started. It was Cass again, sounding more agitated this time. "I'm on my way into the office, and I swear I'm being followed. I don't know where the heck you are, but we have to talk. I'll try your cell again – don't you ever answer that thing?"

I realized she must have been trying the cell as it had charged last night. Never mind. She'd try again. The taxi dropped me outside the hospital and I walked into the casualty department. I would have to come up with something more original than "I fell over."

THE CLOCK ON THE WALL was a regular Dali. It was melting and reforming. Was that music I could hear? Or a voice calling? It was Cass. What was she doing singing? I had no idea she could sing.

The clock sagged further, the numbers wavering and the hands bending like melted chocolate. I watched, fascinated. Then it was coming into focus. 3:27. Day or night? Government issue hospital clock. Cass wasn't singing, she was talking to me. No, about me.

"He's just waking up now."

I turned towards the voice. She was on her cellphone, or rather, just finishing a call, folding it closed. It was one of those expensive ones, so small it looked like you could inhale it into your nostril and not notice.

I was groggy. The nurses had given me something, and I was asked to lie down. That was before the examination, and now my head was bandaged. I put my hand up to feel it, and found my hand bandaged too. I felt my head with both hands, and supposed I must look like a mummy. Cass was looking at me like I was dying. Something to be pitied. The clock dribbled a little here and there. I was still very dopey.

"Hi," I said, weakly. My mouth hurt, and my throat was sore.

"Hi," she replied. "Nice mess you're in."

"Hmmm," I grunted. My lips were swollen and I was barely able to form words.

"Your landlord told me you were here. Said you had a little personal trouble."

"Some guy. . . ." I wanted to tell her, but it hurt too much, and I couldn't straighten out my thoughts.

A young nurse came in and looked at the chart at the foot of the bed. Redhead, Irish maybe. Why do people always think red hair means temper? She poured me some water and put it on one of those invalid tables that slide across the bed. It was beyond my reach and it hurt to move. She bent over me.

"Hello!" You'd have thought she was talking to a deaf

seven-year-old. I liked it. She adjusted some steel thing with an IV bag hanging on it. There was a tube. It seemed to come towards me, but I don't know where it went. I didn't care.

"You have a nice sleep?"

I nodded.

"Good! Doctor'll be along later with your X-rays. You got a lovely crack on the head. Don't worry, we won't ask how you got it just now. You have a rest till he gets here. Anything you need?"

I shook my head.

"If you want me to throw your visitor out, just let me know. If you press this button I'll be along in a moment." She glanced across the room at Cass, and then added confidentially, "And don't let your visitor keep you long. You need rest." With that she left me alone with Cass.

I tried to remember how I had got here. There was a phone message from Cass. I was meant to call her. There was the fight at my flat. My mind was sluggish and felt like syrup dripping off a spoon. I was hot. My head ached. I tried to talk to Cass.

"I called you. You were out," I mumbled. It was a half intelligible noise, but she got the idea.

"I wanted to warn you."

"Thanks." I grunted. It sounded ungrateful. "I mean, thanks for trying. Really." But my words were incoherent.

I could feel myself drifting away. The clock slid down the wall and spread out across the floor, and a rabbit hopped into the three-pin socket. I dozed again.

I WAS RIDING A SLINGSHOT probe out of orbit, skidding through the blackness of deep space. An armchair floated past me with Sykes in it, reading a copy of *The Sun*. I may have been dreaming.

Slowly the room came back into focus. There was a night-light. A soft yellow glow. Restful. There was a window, no curtains. It was dark outside. The moon was almost full. I turned and saw the clock said 11:00. The glass of water was still there. I reached for it, and, lifting myself up a little, managed to drink. Cass was still there, too. She was asleep, but woke as I put the glass down.

Not very coherently, I said, "Hi. Still here?"

"Yeah," she yawned. "I left when you fell asleep. I dropped in about an hour ago, and thought I'd wait. Can't exactly go back home."

"Why not?" I asked.

"They've got it staked out. Two guys in a car. They're not covering the office; I guess they figure I have to go home sometime. I don't want this happening to me."

I wanted to say something about not letting them in, or something witty, but I could hardly speak and my thoughts were disjointed. My head ached beyond belief.

"You have a concussion, a broken jaw, and your left hand has been pretty well rebuilt. They're keeping you in for a couple of days for observation."

"Nikon's a tough camera," I said, but she didn't understand the noises.

"Didn't get that. You reckon this was something to do with the Hanson stuff?"

I nodded. "The computer. They know," I said, very slowly and deliberately.

"I've stashed the computer. I had a quick look at it,

but couldn't make it out. You'll have to check it out. We must have something important, otherwise they wouldn't be so worked up about it."

"Is it safe, the computer?"

"Yes, they won't find it.

"Don't lose it. Nor the tape. Try to get the computer to Guy in IT." I mouthed the words slowly. "Tell him to copy the stuff. Tell him to hide it!"

"I will, I will. I didn't find anything odd on the tape. That's why I called you the other night. I wanted you to hear it, see if anything on it struck you as interesting."

"There'll be something there. These guys are rattled." I don't think she could understand what I said. It was a pretty one-sided conversation.

"I don't think you should go back to your place. I spoke to Marlene, she's pissed at you for getting beaten up. She's making sure Admin sorts all your health insurance stuff out. She wants a major story out of this. Hope there's something in it."

I nodded. "Me too."

"She's put it around that we're on a job in Scotland for the next week, chasing Royals. Just to make sure no one in the office mentions something by accident that gets us in trouble. Only Sykes and Marlene know you're here, so you should be pretty safe. I've told Sykes not to mention it. The fewer people who know what we're doing, the fewer can drop us in it."

I figured we were pretty good at doing that ourselves. And what did we really have? After Cass had left, promising to come back in the morning, I got to wondering where this was going.

I GOT MY FIRST NEWSPAPER JOB at fourteen. I wrote for *The Mercury*, the local paper where I lived in the Isle of Wight, and then I'd help deliver them too. *The Mercury* had a circulation of about 2000, and used the hot lead process on a press that was a museum piece, not to mention a deathtrap. It accounted for plenty of serious accidents and not a few deaths over the years – the result of burns from molten lead.

The editor, Mr. Waring, shut up shop one day when the advertising was not selling well enough, and never re-opened. Newspaper Lesson Number One: newspapers are about advertising, as well as news. Forget that, and you go bust. Whether it's *The Mercury* or *The Times*. Murdoch or Waring.

Before moving to the island, my parents had built their lives up from nothing to being owners of a number of local papers in the East End of London. The island was attractive because it was a better place to bring up kids. A better place for their business to grow. A good place to develop an accent one didn't have to be ashamed of. A place to farm.

I was only fourteen when I got a call from someone who didn't like something I'd written. I told them I was sorry, but that wasn't enough for them. They made me feel like a rotten little shit. I still feel like shit about that story, a poor review of a choral performance. But it taught me a lesson I never forgot. Think before you write, because you'll almost always upset someone, however unintentional – and is it worth it?

Now the stories are bigger, and the people involved are more powerful. But the rest holds true.

I'm not afraid of upsetting people. I sometimes take

great pleasure in it, to be absolutely truthful. As long as there's no real danger to myself. Nail the bugger, and make sure there's a good clean path to the emergency exit. When I frame something in the viewfinder I am not a judge, or anything like that. I'm just bringing in what the desk wants. Oh, sure, there are some snappers that make a song and dance about doing it for the good of mankind, and changing the world and all that bilge. They make such a big deal about it, you could set it all to music and play it on the sound system at the Lutheran church on Sunday and dance in the aisles to celebrate their righteousness. Personally, I'd rather make the shot and get the hell out in one piece.

Having said all that, the words of the great press photographer, Juhan Kuus, stay with me, buried very deeply under my concerns for the sanctity of my own personal security: "Hold the mirror and let the world see its reflection. But do only that."

The reflection is there in the paper the next day. The readers do the judging. But when someone gets that upset before you go to press – then you're on to something. You'd better hold on and expect a bumpy ride.

BY THE TIME I WAS DISCHARGED I was practically dying of nicotine withdrawal. Cass drove while I smoked a head-spinning cigarette, worrying about the growing mountain of unanswered questions in my life. What happened to the guy I stuffed in the boot of the car? What was so special about the material we lifted from Hanson's computer? Where did the girl called Kelly fit in? It seemed fairly safe to assume the people watching

Cass's place were the same ones who sent the heavy to my place, but why?

I wasn't very clear where we were going, until I recognized the corner where I had dropped Cass earlier in the week. "Your parents still away?" I asked.

"For another six weeks. We can crash here till the heat blows over. I figured it was a good idea. I don't want to end up looking like you. You weren't much to start with, but what good looks you had, you lost back at your place." Cass was being unusually forthcoming. She had a point, mind. I've never been what you might call distinguished looking – kind of light brown hair, average features. But I prided myself on what my mother would have described as "a nice open expression, an honest, pleasant face." A girl could do worse – or so I'd thought. I looked harmless enough.

"Thanks for letting me know that," I said. "It makes me feel so much better."

She punched in an access code to get through the main door, and stepped into the ancient elevator in the foyer. It was one of those aging contraptions with a gate affair that looks like a prison door and has the capacity to snag fingers. It groaned up four flights in the time we could have walked with ease.

The place had the look of being very upmarket in 1927. There were four other apartments on this floor, quiet and discreet behind heavy, black doors. The landing was opulent with a deep red carpet, and rich wood paneling. Cass had a key for her parents' apartment, and as she unlocked the front door I noticed one of the other doors open a fraction.

"The old lady next door's a bit of a busybody," Cass

said, as we entered. "She keeps an eye on comings and goings. Has done for years, I'm told. Don't mind her."

The décor of the apartment was 1920s with touches of Ikea and Laura Ashley. Cass's parents liked tiffany lamps and art deco pottery. That was fine by me, though I hoped they didn't have those weird square teacups. They look okay, but I always dribble the tea down my chin or in my lap when I drink from them.

Cass made a cup of tea in the kitchen as I sat down and tried to get my thoughts straight. I noticed my camera bag and the laptop in the living room. She must have brought it from the News. I opened it and checked my gear. Lenses, cameras, aspirin and a few first aid supplies, as well as a ragged teddy bear. It's amazing what I keep in there. "Smut" the bear turns up all over the place in news pictures; in the arms of a child leaving his burned-out house, in the hands of little girl who wasn't allowed to school because she shaved all her hair off – it makes sure the picture gets good play. Works every time. Everything was there in the bag, including the little Rollie and a note from Pierre.

> Dear Steve,
>   Cass said you needed your stuff, so I packed it up for you. L is in the secure locker. Otherwise all in here. I put some 400s in your stock, as well as a 100 and a couple of 1000s. Bring us back some haggis,
>
> Pierre.

I couldn't figure out the part about the haggis until I remembered that Cass had told people we were going to Scotland. Fair enough. Pierre had kindly stocked me up with our usual 400 ASA film as well as a slow one and the 1000 ASA stock we used for night photography. With film technology where it is, many photographers can shoot without a flash at night if they are careful. This makes a huge difference if you don't want the subject to know s/he is being photographed and is a useful trick to have up your sleeve.

Pierre had also put my Leica gear in the secure locker, safe from light fingers. That was a blessing. My entire worldly goods were wrapped up in the camera bag and the secure locker.

The living room was like a library. Books on every conceivable subject lined the walls. There was a computer and a stack of CDs, mostly reference material.

"Nice library," I called back towards the kitchen, glancing through some of the books.

Cass's voice drifted back, "That's all Mom's stuff. She used to be a sub on *The Standard*. She's retired now."

Sub-editors on British papers are like miniature editors, and have enormous influence over how a story looks and is used. Unlike other countries, British papers have always made the sub-editor role critical, far beyond mere layout issues. On a British paper a sub can not only cut stories and write headlines, they can tell the journo to rewrite it from a different angle, get a whole new set of quotes, or insist on documented proof of all references, before allowing it near a page. The sub can also tell a photographer to go and get a better picture. Or a differently shaped picture. Or just prevent the photographer from getting any decent play. Subs have generally come up through the ranks of journalism, and know their stuff. They always pick a story to pieces, drawing on their vast general knowledge to verify and quantify the story. The result is that British national papers are technically unrivaled by any other national media. Four hundred years of practice pays off.

Cass brought the tea in on a tray, a delicately crocheted mat covering the dark wood. Very domestic. Not really Cass, though. She placed the tea on a low table and we both sat down.

"What do we do from here?" I asked.

Cass sipped her tea and looked thoughtfully in the direction of the laptop. "We have to work out why these people are so mad."

The guy in the boot of the Volkswagen would be pretty mad by now. It had been three days.

"I think I should check something out. The guy who did this," I gestured to my bruised face. "He's in the boot of a car in Hampstead."

"You killed him?" Cass looked more than a little concerned. I don't think she minded playing with the big boys, but complicity in a murder was a little out of her league.

"No," I said reassuringly. "I just dumped him there after Sykes slugged him. I was planning to pop back and ask him a few questions, but the next thing I knew, they had me under some sedative in the hospital. He's had three days to think things over. He'll be feeling quite talkative about now."

At first Cass looked quite taken aback, but then she agreed. "He might help us get somewhere!"

"We should take a look at that computer," I glanced

at the laptop. "There's something on there that's upset someone pretty badly."

"I got your friend Guy to look at it," Cass said. "He copied the files you got from Hanson. He said he'd try to check them out soon."

I plugged in the laptop and set it up on the coffee table, then scanned through the directories copied from Hanson's machine and clicked into the Exchange folders, looking for an address book file. There seemed to be two distinct sets of directories. One wouldn't let me open any folders. Password protected. The other was more what I expected. From these it took only a second to get a list of contacts. I scrolled down them, while Cass read over my shoulder.

"Anyone you know?" she asked.

"No … ," I said. I read the names one by one, moving down the list until I got to K. "Wait a second. We have a name."

The cursor rested over the name Kelly Watson.

Chapter 5

LOOKING THROUGH THE CONTENTS of Hanson's hard drive was an exercise that met with mixed success. I found I could jump in and out of some sections with ease, and yet one section remained locked up tight, hidden behind passwords. I knew Guy kept a database of articles written for the *News*, published and unpublished, going back several years. If he did a search for names in that, matching against the names I could extract from the address book on Hanson's hard drive, perhaps I could get a lead.

I zipped the Exchange files together, took a cable from my camera bag and ran it from the phone socket to the laptop. A moment later I was on the Net and sending the zipped files to Guy at the *News*.

I included a quick message: "Guy, can you run a check on all the names in this Exchange file? Do so without letting on to anyone you are doing it for me. Then let me know what you find, soon as you can. Thanks, Steve S."

"We might get something out of it. Or maybe nothing." I said to Cass.

Next, I found the appointments manager. Plenty of entries here, but only with numbers next to them. I tried getting into several other directories, only to find them password protected. All I could tell about them was that they were large. Most of his hard drive, by the look of it.

I took a closer look at the appointments. "What do you make of this?" I asked Cass. "Gotta be code…."

"He doesn't look the sort who would be smart enough for that."

"Maybe he didn't make it up. Maybe someone set it up for him," I mused.

"That sounds more like it. That says he's part of a group. Just guessing, but maybe he's in some kind of organization."

We listened to the tape Cass had lifted from the answering machine. There were no messages, just a couple of fax transmissions coming into the computer. The tape was a dead end.

I turned to her and said, "You remember the first time we talked about him? I said I thought he had been in court before – looked like he was familiar with the setup. I'd really like to know if he's got form. I mean, a guy like that just has to have a record, right?"

"Yeah, but how are you going to check that out? It's not like we can just hack into the Met's computer and download the file."

"No, but … there may be another way. You ever heard of Dirty Harry?"

"The film?"

"No, not the film."

THAT EVENING AT 7:40 I introduced Cass to Dirty Harry in the public bar of the Landogger Trow, a small pub east of the city. His leer, as he looked her up and down, went part of the way to explain how he got his name. I had phoned earlier to set up the meeting and asked him to check out Hanson.

Dirty Harry was a tipster. He made a good living giving tips alternatively to the media, to my certain knowledge, and to the police, if my suspicions were correct. For these tips he was paid according to the accuracy of the information. Where he got the information was a mystery. But it always checked out. He had been a policeman at one point. I found out by accident once, seeing his real name on an old court document in a file at the *News*.

He was known as Dirty because he was, well, dirty. He looked it, and most of his news was dirt. He knew who was having nocturnal liaisons with whom (a very lucrative tip angle, especially if a love nest was involved for the media to stake out), and which celebrities were spending just a little too much on the horses. When a minor Royal checked in to a rehab center, Dirty Harry would be close behind. He also had an ability to leer at women that bordered on the frightening. His lazy left eye would twitch in a suggestive wink, intentionally or not – who could tell?

"How lovely it is to meet a lady such as yourself, Miss," simpered Dirty as he fawned over Cass.

Cass nodded hello and sat with half a pint of lager in front of her. Dirty was my contact, and she was leaving me to deal with him.

I placed a pint in front of Dirty and lit up a cigarette. "Well," I said, "you got anything on Hanson?"

"Interesting man, Hanson," said Dirty, looking at the surface of the beer-stained and dented wood. He was almost talking to himself. "He's gotten hisself in a lot o' trouble. Upset people. Powerful people."

"What makes you think so?" I asked.

"Well, he's been in bed with some big boys for a long time, see. Only now he suddenly seems to have no friends."

"What do you mean?"

"Well, this bigamy charge for a start. He could have ducked that with a good lawyer. But he hasn't got anyone, least not anyone who's "known," if you know what I mean. He's just got some brief who does a bit of criminal work on the side. He's been up on plenty of charges before. Assault, handling stolen goods, all sorts. He was part of that protection racket going on in Southwark ten years back, remember? No, I guess you don't."

I didn't want to get Dirty reminiscing about the past, but I needed the history lesson. I listened and drank a lager slowly.

"See, all that time he had a top brief. Kept him out of the nick and doing his job, whatever that was. Someone was looking after him, he was part of something. Must've been to have help like that."

"And now?"

"Now he can't get off a bigamy charge. He's about to get into things a whole lot deeper, too."

"Like what?"

"Tomorrow morning he's going to be brought in."

"Arrested?" I asked.

"Yeah," said Dirty, adopting his most conspiratorial tone. "Mind you, you're not to let him know, or I'll be in trouble."

"That's understood, Harry. I wouldn't drop you in it."

"They're upgrading the charge. It's gonna include fraud. They'll also make sure he don't get no bail. Truth is, he's probably safer in the nick, if he can stay in solitary."

"What do you mean?"

"Someone wants Hanson nailed. Word is, if you help him slip over in front of a truck, you can pick up a useful cheque. Five thousand at least."

"Who would be behind something like that?" Cass cut in, her curiosity getting the better of her.

"I don't know. I'm working on it, but it's someone high up. Someone who won't make it easy to find out." Harry handed me an envelope. "That's a copy of his record. He's had some interesting friends. Have a read of it. You'll find it useful."

With that he turned to Cass, leer in place, raised his glass and said, "So, love. Do you come here often?" Cass was about to get the lowdown on the real reason Harry was called "Dirty".

To SOMEONE SITTING in a car watching an apartment, there are few things more obvious than another observer arriving. The way they usually drive past once to check the situation out and secure a good line of sight for their observation is all pretty obvious. How many times have I doorstepped a place only to see another journo cruise by to check it out? Plenty. Doorstepping, or being a "milk-bottle," is a regular practice. You sit on a house and wait for anyone to go in or out. You shoot them when they do, and try and get a comment if you're a journo. Eventually someone coming or going will talk.

Sometimes it is intimidating. It's meant to be. When you have the front and rear covered, you'll get the person eventually. Everyone has to eat – sometimes they'll get someone to come by and bring food, or supplies. Only a few really tough ones just draw their blinds and sit it out. More often than not the subject cracks before you do. I doorstepped a place for six days and nights on one occasion, before being asked in and getting the story. That was a lousy New Year. Just me and a coffee in the car.

I was thinking as we headed towards my Hampstead apartment. It was time to take care of the body in the boot of the Volkswagen, without tipping off anyone watching my place. It would not be easy. However, if I let it go much longer I might have a corpse on my hands. While some people may consider me callous in my work, I have a reasonably pure heart, and murder is not something I wish to practice. Besides, I had already bucked a murder charge once this week. I might not be so lucky a second time.

I called Sykes on the cell as we waited in traffic on the Finchley Road. "Hey, Sykes, how are you?"

"Is that you, Steve? You still in hospital?"

"Yes. Kind of …"

"Well, I suggest you stay there. There's some new fella parked outside just waiting. He probably wants to see you about his friend."

"Hmmm. Has he given you any trouble?" I asked.

"Nope. Just sits and waits. I think they must have found 'is mate in the other car. It was gone yesterday morning when I walked up on the 'eath."

"You be careful, Sykes. They put two and two

together and they might suspect you were the one who put their friend to sleep."

"Nah, I doubt it. 'E didn't know what 'it 'im anyway. But I don't care. I'm going down to see my sister Eth tomorrow morning. She's in Bournemouth. Haven't seen her in thirty-two years."

"That'll be nice for you both."

"Yeah, and convenient, like."

"Thanks, Sykes. You be real careful."

Sykes was turning out to be smarter than I had thought. Ducking out of this was the best thing he could do. We wouldn't have to go cruising by my apartment, which was a relief. They were sure to be looking out for Cass's dilapidated old Ford and would probably recognize us. If they had found their friend, then they would know I was in the hospital. They would probably also find out I had a visitor. There were sure to be some very upset people around.

Even a capital city can seem like a very small place at times. As we drove towards Cass's parents' place, I said, "You're sure there's no way they can find out about your parents' apartment?"

"It's not listed in the phone book, and it's owned by their management company. I can't see anyone going to all that trouble, can you?"

I was skeptical about that. We'd already seen our antagonists make a link between Cass and I. "What about your roommate?"

"She's used to me going on stories. She thinks I'm in Aberdeen."

"I don't feel good about this. What about you?"

"Chicken?" she asked.

"Kelly Watson's dead, and we don't know why. Tomorrow morning Hanson is being taken into custody, and there's a chance he'll be iced before getting anywhere near a courtroom. Yeah. I'm chicken. If you were half as smart as you think you are, you'd be chicken." I was growing increasingly uncomfortable.

She pulled off the road a block before reaching the apartment. "We have to go back there sometime," she said.

"I know. Funny. It's like being on the other side, isn't it?" I lit a smoke and blew it into the rainy evening. The gray-blue smoke was whipped into the evening air.

"What do you mean?"

"Like they're stalking us, instead of the other way round," I murmured, looking out at the passing pedestrians. "I prefer it the other way round."

"Oh, God. They could be out there now. And they'll be wound up about their friend." Cass looked like she was beginning to realize how serious this thing had become. It had crept up on us, slowly at first. A court story, then a scam of some kind, and then a body. Now we were being stalked and we still knew nothing about the people interested in us.

I reached into my camera bag and brought out a telescoping umbrella. If we were going to be on the receiving end of this stuff, we needn't make it easy. I would walk past the apartment block, umbrella down, and check for anyone doorstepping the place. They wouldn't expect anyone on foot. Who walks anywhere these days?

My jaw was painful. My throat still rasped and my face was purple and yellow from the bruises of my last visitor. Cass had those fine features that wear bruises very badly. I didn't want another go like the last one for either of us.

Two people, probably returning from offices in the city, walked by, chatting to each other.

"Hang on here till I get back." I said and slipped out of the car and fell in behind them. They probably didn't even know I was there, and to an observer it would look like a group of three friends walking down the road. If anyone was watching, they weren't looking for a three-some. As I neared the apartment, I checked both sides of the road. I thought I saw someone light a smoke in a nearby car, a flaring match. I glanced in their direction and they pulled out and merged into the traffic. Not a watcher, just someone going somewhere. Probably.

The path to the apartment was clear so I doubled back and climbed into the car beside Cass. You can never be completely sure, though. People get into apartments and watch, and do other things. They aren't always dumb.

"It's clear," I said, trying to sound confident.

"You've got your camera gear, haven't you?"

"Yeah," I replied.

"I have the computer," she said, and then bit her lower lip. Quite suddenly she sounded decisive. "Okay. Let's fuck off out of here."

"Yeah." I said. "Glad you said that."

She pulled out into the traffic and swung across the road, heading south.

A SMALL BED AND BREAKFAST in the New Forest, a couple of hours from London. Far enough away to be distant, remote even. We would be accepted as lovers looking for a quiet retreat, or birdwatchers or some-thing, by the locals. It was for a few days only. Fine. Letting the dust settle seemed like a good idea.

Rose Cottage, just like on the chocolate boxes, was owned by an aging Polish woman. She showed us the room, pointing out the view of a nearby clearing in which red deer had been seen some years before. Possibly in the reign of William the First. A clumsy but entertain-ing nude adorned the wall above the head of the bed. I looked at it for a while before realizing it was our host-ess. A fine, healthy-looking woman in her youth.

"I painted it myself," she said with exaggerated modesty. I suspected she had done this before.

"A fine work."

"You're very generous. I am a hopeless painter – but enjoy it. And that is what it is for, yes?"

"Of course," I replied. True art is still alive in the remote corners of the English countryside.

Our hostess had lost her Polish accent almost totally. Funny how stories fall at one's feet sometimes. A young woman conscripted into the war effort, she had worked in the docks in a port the Allied ships managed to get into.

After meeting a young British sailor on one of the merchant marine convoys, she kept up correspondence with him, and after the war, came over when he asked her to marry him. They married, on the strength of one meeting and five years of letter-writing, and enjoyed thirty-five years of happy marriage before he had a stroke and died peacefully. This sad occurrence left her with Rose Cottage and a living to make.

Tea and scones, cream and jam. How very English. Just right for the tourists. Cass disappeared to walk some paths in the forest. I returned to the tiny room to switch on the television and catch the early evening news. I get withdrawal symptoms if I miss it. Even when I traveled overseas, I caught the World Service news, in the 6:00 evening ritual of sitting down and hearing, "This is the BBC, in London."

The day's stories were unexciting – a football scandal and some stockbroker caught with his hand in the till. I was about to turn it off and put the radio on, and was reaching for the remote, when I was surprised to see a shot of three or four MPs leaving Parliament. A reporter stopped them and asked about a controversial revision to the Immigration Bill. So the political analysts had got it right.

Some talking bald head spouted his point of view in a five-second sound bite, and the scene cut to the studio. I had barely heard the story – I was still staring at the screen. Behind the sincere and impassioned voice of right-wing extremism in the government was a half-hidden face that I had seen very recently. The cogs turned in my head. They had all walked out together; the body language was there in spades. Why was Jeremy Carfax hanging out with the lunatic fringe of the ruling party?

Thinking about Carfax had me wondering about Shandra. I had left that situation a little up in the air, to say the least. I thought about e-mailing her, just to let her know I had had to duck out of town for a few days, but in the end decided to just let it slide. She'd probably not be interested anyway. She was doubtless walking her own path at the moment, whatever that might be. I wanted to know more and would like to share something of it – but she was of a different world. Her friends, the Carfaxes and Smythe-Prostate the Thirds of this world, were not my people. They never would be. Still, maybe I should phone her.

I was just getting ready to go and find a phone when Cass's footfall graced the wooden staircase. She had her combat boots on. She clumped up the old stairs and opened the door. She was soaked. I hadn't noticed when the rain had started.

"Nice walk?"

Silently she dripped rainwater in the doorway.

"Raining?" I asked. Her hair was straggling down her forehead, black hair painted to her noble brow. It suited her, in a dramatic sort of way. Very summer rain-washed. Wholesome, even. Like a hair-care product advertisement.

"I reckon his wife would talk," said Cass, pushing by me.

"What do you mean?"

"We know he's been abandoned, right?"

"Sure. Dirty Harry swears by it," I replied.

"Well, maybe his wife will talk. She'll be feeling let down, her husband's just been taken in, and she must know he's in trouble. She also probably knows he's been dropped by the big boys. She'll be sweating bullets, and might give us the break we need."

"You may have something there."

"I'll give her a day more to brood, and then give her a call." She was talking a lot harder than she looked.

She slung her raincoat on a radiator, and sat down in an easy chair. "What shall we do about food?"

"Let's drive into Brockenhurst and see what we can find," I said. "What do you think about me calling a friend? Someone I meant to talk to before we left."

"Forget it. Don't be so daft."

That was as far as our discussion got. She walked into the bathroom, and I heard the shower start to run.

I lay on the bed, looking at the much looked-at cracks in the ceiling. It was not long before I dozed and found myself dreaming of Shandra. She was driving her BMW and laughing, her long black hair streaming behind her. It would have been a nice dream, but then I realized what she was laughing at.

She was laughing at me.

Chapter 6

I WOKE WITH A START to find Cass asleep beside me, beneath the covers. She was glowing and scrubbed like a fresh virgin delivered for some pagan rites. There's a pagan in me – or is animal the word I'm looking for?

Her chest rose and fell in untroubled sleep, and her Victorian nightie wrapped her chaste breasts disappointingly thoroughly. I looked away, wondering how I could think such thoughts of my colleague, and then watched again as the moonlight caressed her cheek.

Outside the night was clear and moonlight streamed in through the window. I looked at my watch, surprised to find it was 3 a.m. So much for dinner. I went to the window and looked out at the trees swaying in a light breeze outside. It was a lovely night for a walk, and there was no sleeping now – not with her installed like that. And the sofa was too unwelcoming after the comfort of the bed.

I pulled on my jacket, picked up a camera, and carried my shoes silently down the hall to the stairs. The creak factor was low as I sneaked down the stairs to the front door. I stepped into the night, and felt the bite of the deceptively cool air on my face.

I walked through the deserted street, eventually turning away from the sleeping village, and made my way deeper into the forest. From a distance I looked back. In the deepest night a sleeping hamlet is a beautiful thing. It is so easy to imagine it a hundred, or even five hundred years earlier. The houses, the thatched roofs unchanged. And the black and white of Tudor buildings. Take away the marginal street lighting and this could be a country living in Henry VIII's reign.

Trees sighed in the distance, and somewhere I could hear a brook. No cars. This was a different kind of nighttime from that of London. Altogether more silent. I walked into the woods and followed the sound of running water, untill I came to a small river, where I sat and looked at the forest night. The silvery waters hustling by, the trees whispering. Only in the darkest recesses was there the menace of silence.

I sat beneath a tree on a damp patch of forest floor. I lit a cigarette, momentarily blinding myself in the flare of phosphorous. Sucking hard, I felt it bite my throat. Why did I do that crap?

I decided to take an inventory of the people about me. Hanson was a crook of greater or lesser accomplishment, depending on whose lawyer you chose to believe. Cass seemed an idealistic young journalist, who was probably a bit naïve for the job. Shandra was rolling in money, probably someone else's, and drove the kind of car no one in my family could have afforded at her age, if ever. Dirty Harry was just Dirty Harry, and Guy was, well, just buried in his technology.

And then there was Carfax. What was he doing tied up with the raving loony right wing, anyway? And to be fair to the right-wing loonies – what did they want to be tied up with a shit like that for?

How the heck had I got involved with such absurd people? I was about ready to go back to shooting belligerent defendants outside the Old Bailey. I slung a couple of pebbles into the brook. The silvery gray shape of a badger ambled by in the darkness. He paused and looked at me before hurrying on. I lit another smoke. There was a rusting tin can nearby that I used as an ashtray.

"You can never find a florist in the middle of a forest, but you can always find a cigarette machine." I mumbled the rhyme and wondered where it came from. The sun was edging daywards, and it was time I started walking back. I pushed the two butts into my pocket and walked back towards the cottage. The cold damp of morning was creeping inside my bones now.

BACK IN THE LOUNGE of the bed and breakfast, I hooked up to the Net and pulled in an e-mail from Guy. Although he had no idea where I was, he knew I'd be checking the e-mail every day.

> Your message arrived safely. We should talk. You've got an extensive data source of some kind – but fairly sophisticated encryption techniques. Seems to float and adapt to the person trying to access it. If the reading device doesn't emulate a specific identity, it sets off a batch process to first erase the data and then format the computer's hard drive. Quite a

sophisticated deterrent. I have isolated the executable parts to stop it wiping my drives, but have not yet managed to read the data.

A few questions you might set your mind to:

1. Who do you know capable of this sort of sophistication? It is beyond your average computer hack.
2. What would they be trying to encrypt so thoroughly?

Just so you are aware, this does not look civil – possibly military. Call mid-morning. I have to talk to you about some of this stuff urgently.

Guy was never much of a letter writer. There was obviously something there that had booted his hard drive. He didn't usually get so excited about things.

As I unhooked the modem Cass came downstairs. She wore a pair of tight jeans and a heavy pullover. She looked quite desirable in a wholewheat biscuit sort of way. The sort of girl my mother would approve of. I couldn't help but think she would be a great woman to marry. Not for me, of course. But for someone.

"Morning," I said.

"You snore like a fucking walrus. And don't try and pull the bed stunt again. I only let you sleep there 'cause I was too knackered to kick your tobacco-stained ass out of there."

I looked at her quizzically. "It's a lovely day out," I said.

IN THE PUBLIC BAR of The Huntsman I waited for the two pints of bitter I'd ordered from the strapping barmaid behind the heavy oak bar.

"There you are, dear," she said, placing the two large glasses before me. I handed her a fiver and she returned a few moments later with a fistful of wet change. I carried the two brimming glasses to where Cass and I sat by the glowing embers of a fire. "Something's been troubling me," I said.

"Really?" said Cass, in an imperious tone that made me wonder if she wasn't being just the tiniest bit sarcastic.

"Yes," I replied. "I was wondering about how this whole thing got started. I just got handed a slip from Bonnie, and told to go and shoot Hanson."

"That's normal, isn't it?" she asked.

"Yes, but I never checked who originated the request. Usually it says something on the slip. Marlene usually requests the jobs, or the acting news editor, but not this one. It was left blank."

"Didn't that strike you as odd?" said Cass, idly inspecting the detail on a card coaster on the table before us.

"Not at the time," I replied. "Sometimes people just forget. What about you, how did you get instructed onto it?"

She thought for a moment, and sipped her drink. "In the morning news conference. Marlene was assigning stories in the normal way, and I didn't have anything special. As the meeting broke up Marlene came over and briefed me on it, confidentially. Then when you were in the newsroom you came over after talking to Marlene and gave me those shots, remember?"

"Sure, but, that's unusual, isn't it?"

"Yes. But like I said at the time, it was a special instruction from Strathclyde. He was trying me out. At least, I think he was." Cass looked very thoughtful. This was something she was having second thoughts about.

We waited for our lunch. Scampi and chips, and a piece of limp lettuce. It was a sign of things to come. Over the next few days our lives slowed to a crawl. We remained out of sight, biding our time. My face and hands slowly recovered. And all the while I wondered what lay ahead on our return.

Chapter 7

THE BLACK WATERS OF THE CANAL were spotted by the light rain falling from the Amsterdam sky. I flicked my cigarette butt into the road over the bridge, hitting a cyclist by mistake. It bounced unnoticed from his knee and hissed in a puddle on the cobbles. The neon reflections of the street lights danced on the wet road, and I pulled my coat collar a little higher. The cyclist pedaled on into the night, huddled in a heavy black coat, hat pulled down over his face. In my present frame of mind, a perfectly innocent person on an innocuous personal mission could seem sinister. I think his mudguard was loose. He clattered over the cobbles, heading away from the city center.

The bridge I was standing on was off the Prinzengracht. In the canal below, a barge was tied to an ancient iron post set into the dockside. An old man was doing whatever barge people do with ropes. The smell of cooking in the galley drifted up, carried on the smoke from the stove that heated the interior. His cargo was anyone's guess. The canvas cover, pulled tightly over the freight hold, sparkled in the rainy night. It was a fine night for a killing.

Three weeks had passed since I had slipped quietly out of sight. An e-mail from the desk, a quick trip to pick up a transmitter from the office, a ferry ride later, and I was in Holland to cover probably the least exciting economic summit of the year. Still, it had to be covered and someone had to do it.

It was a good excuse to stay away from London, and that was my prime concern. Another beating like the last one and I would be ready to quit. Cass was holed up in her parents' place on leave, last I'd heard – smart woman.

I was killing time in a strange capital. The week-long summit might make the paper a couple of times. My assignment was to sit on it, get everyone who mattered and be at the press calls. File a few pictures, and bring in some decent library material. A week of that and then back to London. Whatever heat there had been would surely have died down by then.

My company credit card was letting me spend money again, *News Consolidated* having credited my account up front with expense money. That was a nice touch. The boys who administered my card would no doubt be amazed to find it back within its limit. I was staying in a modest guest house on the Prinzengracht, near the Amsterdam Marriott Hotel, the location of the summit.

It was not only cheap, but also comfortable. I would come out well ahead on my expenses. My only complaint was that I was getting bored. It was approaching midnight, and I was feeling the emptiness of being a stranger in a strange town. There wasn't much to do in the hotel, and I was trying to avoid the rest of the news crowd on the grounds that the fewer people who knew my whereabouts the better.

Getting bored is something I just don't generally do. This is the result of a childhood experience that left an indelible mark on my mind, if not my body. I was five years old when I made my fateful mistake. I became bored, and voiced the fact. At that time we were living on the ground floor of a dilapidated house in Stepney. It was part of a building that had been subdivided and condemned by the council. Because of the demolition order, the rent was low and we could just about manage. There was no rush for people to move in to this part of the street. The wall nearest the railway track at the back of the house would shake with passing freight trucks every few minutes, day and night. I have no fond memories of the place. Living in a dump is still living in a dump, whether you laugh about it or not.

Upstairs, there was an old woman who used to play the piano at night for her amusement. She had no television, and was slowly drinking herself to death. I liked her, and she used to teach me a few chords on the enormous black wood piano in her living room. Her name was Madame Lisokova and she was what my parents called a white Russian. An émigré. She would occasionally be visited by someone my mother told me was a count. I understood that a count was like a king but not so important, and that Russia had been full of them at one time, until they all moved to London or Paris. This count was a friend of Madame Lisakova's, and would talk Russian with her. Sometimes I overheard them, of course without comprehending.

There was nowhere safe to play when it rained, and on this particular day I had exhausted my repertoire of mischief. It was wet as the Thames in the street and my mother was busy. I shouted from the living room: "Mummy, I'm bored!" She called me from the kitchen and I came running to be scolded. At that very moment, the rotten floor of the room above the living room gave way, and the piano fell through our ceiling. It landed where I had been playing with some plastic soldiers on the carpet. I have never dared be bored since.

I was lucky to get a warning. Madame Lisakova was less fortunate, falling with the piano and breaking her back. She was confined to a wheelchair for the rest of her life, which I believe was considerably shortened by vodka. The count never ventured to visit again.

The upshot was that, in my teens, when my friends were all moaning, "Nothing ever happens to me!" I just kept my mouth shut and checked the ceiling periodically for signs of structural fatigue. After many years, the absence of boredom ceased to be an act of suppression and became second nature. Which was why I stood and watched the surface of the canal, concerned at the return of this emotion so thoroughly banished by my own strict conditioning.

Trouble was, hanging around the Marriott after the summit delegates had entered for the day was all that there was to do. I had to shoot them on the way out – unless the organizers decided to have a press conference – in which case we might get to shoot some talking heads and wire them back to London later, with the day's entrance and exit shots. Not exciting – but that was what I was being paid for. Sometimes you just shut up and take the money. It beats digging roads.

I strolled along the Prinzengracht, passing coffee shops and alleys of bookshops. I was looking for the right picture, something elusive, and yet I knew it was there somewhere. Now and then I paused to shoot a frame, using the Leica. I was relaxed, not trying too hard.

There is something about the Leica. I am not into comparing one camera to another – the one that a photographer is most comfortable with is usually the best for that particular person. However, the Leica stands alone. It is simply the finest press camera ever to have been crafted in the history of photography. Nothing less. It fits the hand like a writing instrument. Its action is one of sliding metal, hand-formed by engineers who are passionate and painstaking craftsmen. It feels solid and reassuring. It feels Germanic and precise – because it is. Many photographers use the M series Leica devoid of any electronic metering. The camera has changed little in the last fifty years. It is still essentially mechanical and steel, crafted with the precision of a Swiss watchmaker.

I know I am no exception when I say I feel that this camera is more than simply a machine. My Leica was not bought – it was part of a complex synthesis. First I chose the model I wanted. There was never any hope that I would be able to afford to do something as extravagant as buy one outright from a dealer. But that is part of the process. Next, I found out which photographers had that model. This process was almost as subjective as selecting the model in the first place. Some press photographers abuse their gear. They are usually the ones with limited talent and dubious motivations.

My choice was not only a photographer I respected and liked, he was later to become the picture editor of the *Sunday Independent*. In fact Dave was a bloody godsend to me in a lot of ways. I let him know I wanted his

Leica. We made arrangements and when he was finished with it, it became mine. That took about a year. That was how long it took for him to find the one that he was after – as he went through much the same process I did.

And so I came to own my dream camera. The previous owners were nothing less than a pedigree. It stays with me still and remains the safeguard, the tool and the trophy of my work. It is worth more than any cash value a dealer could place on it. What price those years, the sweated blood, the fear, elation and success?

I prowled, and shot some silent black and white pictures for myself. I've seen other photographers who forget to do this. They lose a love for the art. They end up shooting purely for the wage. This is the prostitution that turns a good photographer into a cheap snapper. When the magic goes out of it, it's time to take a break and shoot for yourself. I hope I never stop.

My meandering had brought me back to the bridge. I framed the rain-spotted canal under the cold white light, the moon's silvery reflection on the surface of the disturbed water. Below me the bargeman was loading wood into the potbelly stove in his cabin. I could see his wizened features clearly through the open doors as he worked at the foot of the companionway of the little cabin. The texture of his jacket, the stubble on his face and the black depth of the canal, it was almost right.

As he relit the stove the fire flared a little – illuminating him and giving his darkened shape the form I was looking for. I had my picture. It had been there all the time.

MORNING DRIZZLE AND A BREEZE off the North Sea. A small contingent of mixed European press hanging out outside the Marriott watched the endless black Mercedes ferrying delegates to the morning session of the economic summit. A few finance ministers were vaguely newsworthy, the German and the Italian notably, and we watched the diplomatic plates on the cars to work out who was who.

One of the biggest challenges was being sure who you were photographing. I spent the previous hour scanning pictures downloaded from the Net, making sure I knew at least approximately who I was shooting. I would not have been the first photographer to get a perfect set of prints of a bodyguard and completely miss the person I was supposed to shoot. That wouldn't happen this time. The one nice thing about these summits was the fact that, generally, the subjects did not make it hard for the press to get at least something. In many instances they were quite pleased to be given some attention.

At 8:30 precisely the cars started arriving, and the delegates made the brief walk to the front of the building. About six paces was all we had, but it was plenty. A good shot in this case was simply a matter of eye contact, and an expression for the camera. To get Thatcher was more difficult. Outside Number Ten you rarely had more than three paces before she disappeared into the government Jaguar.

This one was a piece of cake. Once in, the delegates would be seated until 4 p.m., unless a major announcement was to be made. The press liaison guys were pretty helpful, and if the British delegate were going to say anything noteworthy, one of them would leave a note for me in the hotel. After the daily arrival pictures, a few of the press guys meandered over to the restaurant and ordered coffees.

I made my way through the luxurious hotel lounge to the restaurant with a radio journalist I'd met a few times. Her name was Stella, and she could easily have been a television anchor, judging from her looks. The big eyes and expensive hair were a dead giveaway that she was on her way to greater things. As the sole representatives of the British press, we found ourselves a quiet table and ordered some breakfast. Several groups of journos and photographers were sitting around in the restaurant. Small enclaves of French and German mostly.

Stella was on the political beat, and did some financial coverage. She'd started as a freelance with Independent Radio News, but was on the BBC payroll now. "It's just my luck to get stuck here!" she moaned.

"What's wrong with it? I like Amsterdam," I said.

"Are you crazy? I got sent over yesterday at lunchtime, just when the call about Notting Hill was coming in," she said.

"What happened in Notting Hill?" I asked, my curiosity growing.

"You didn't watch the news last night?"

Strangely enough, I actually hadn't. I'd been on the ferry at the time and I'd forgotten to turn on my radio. My only lapse ever except for a few weeks when I was out of range in the Sudanese desert. But that's another story.

"We're missing the biggest riots in London since the poll tax," said Stella. "And I'm stuck here for another four days. By the time this wraps up, it'll all have blown over and we'll have to wait another five years for footage like we saw last night."

"What happened, exactly?" I asked. It was not unusual to see some rioting on the Notting Hill annual carnival weekend, but that had come and gone weeks ago.

"Some communist group had a rally in Hyde Park, and the right-wingers pitched up and caused shit. They started working their way through Marylebone and set a few cars on fire. The footage was pretty impressive. It happened on the Broadwater Farm estate too – some community leaders' houses were firebombed, and everyone turned out into the streets. Of course, the cops then turn out in full force and gave the mob something to throw stones at. Really nasty fighting."

"Anyone hurt?" I asked.

"My desk says someone was killed by a brick that came through a window. Plus there were about fifty hospital cases. So far that's the only fatality, but there's a heck of a lot still happening. There's a whole section of Notting Hill the cops can't get into. It's part of a council housing estate. It's practically a no-go zone. The right-wingers went in there, but the local kids sealed it right up behind them." Stella clearly wanted to be back in London. She added, "I don't think they'll be coming out, if it's the part of Notting Hill I think it is. Lots of radical unemployed kids. They've got nothing to lose."

"It's odd, isn't it?"

Stella looked at me as if I was daft.

"I mean, why didn't this happen at the carnival? That's how it happened last time, remember?"

"When did it happen before?"

"Back in '85, I think." She was pretty young. Perhaps

she wasn't in the business back then. I remembered well enough. There had been rumors at the time about the unrest being coordinated, and that there had been an underlying group of right-wing activists organizing it. They'd make sure that if a union march or a left-wing demonstration took to the streets, their boot boys would be on hand to make trouble. They were said to be smart, though. Sometimes they'd set up a counter demonstration. On other occasions they'd mingle with the crowd, and at an opportune moment lob a brick at a police car, or a constable, before quietly disappearing. The cops would then get understandably pissed at the marchers. Of course, nothing was ever proved.

Stella shrugged. "Heck, I don't know. That's ancient history. Aren't you just starved?"

Our coffees arrived with some rolls and croissants.

"Weird," I muttered. I would have liked to have been down there to cover it, because something just didn't sound right.

"Still," said Stella. "The Party must be loving it."

"What do you mean?"

"You know, they're trying to push the revision to the Immigration Bill through. A race riot here and there won't do any harm to their cause."

"I'm pretty out of touch, Stella. I've been on courts for the last month or so."

"Oh. You must have been living at the foot of a mine-shaft to have missed that little gem!"

"Hey, you're the political reporter, not me!"

"Sure. Anyway, they're pushing the immigration issue harder than ever. Closing our doors to a lot of the Commonwealth – the old colonies. It's probably the nastiest piece of right-wing legislation since Hitler gave nationalism a bad name."

"I see. Will it go through?"

"I bloody hope not. If they do, we'll have race riots all over! Half the people they'll be locking out are already in Britain on temporary visas."

"Is it that radical?"

"It's pretty heavy. Cuts a lot of people out. I can't believe it'll go through. Sanity usually prevails, even in politics."

Our breakfast arrived, honey-smoked ham and eggs as only a really fine hotel can provide. We chatted and decided to take a walk, before the morning session ended. There might be some pictures to shoot around midday, and if there were to be a press conference the liaison guys would know by then.

The conference area was off limits and sealed with security. Lunch came and went. By the end of the day a few media types were grumbling about the lack of opportunities and, after the last shots were hurriedly taken and the delegates had left, most photographers headed back to their hotel to process their material and wire it in. I arranged to meet Stella later for a beer in one of the little cafés off the central square, and hurried back to The Rembrandt Hotel.

IN MY BLACKED-OUT ROOM in the guest house, I pulled the film from its light-proof casing and placed the film end on the processing spindle. Working by touch, I loaded it into the reel and slipped it snugly into the developing tank.

Once it was in the tank, I sealed it and turned the lights on. I had already mixed some chemicals, and they were sitting at the correct temperature on the bedside table. I poured them into the developing tank and tapped it lightly to dislodge any air bubbles that might mark the film surface. After three minutes I flushed the tank with water several times, and then added some fixer. I had mixed the fix up at double strength to push in a little extra contrast and fix the film quickly. As the film began to fix I turned on a portable transmitter, a Leafax, and waited for it to warm up. By the time it was ready I would have the negatives dry and the images selected.

A few minutes later I was drying the film with a portable hairdryer. Then I loaded a series of negatives into the Leafax. Captioning took only a minute. I dialed London direct and waited to be put through. Someone answered on the picture desk.

"Hi, it's Steve in Amsterdam. I have a transmission for you."

"Okay, hold on a sec." There was a pause as he switched the call into a different circuit.

His voice came back sounding a little tinier.

"Okay, Amsterdam, what are you transmitting on?"

"It's FM, 256."

"FM 256, how many images?"

"Four images – all color. All captioned."

"Okay, come ahead and then stay on the line after completion of your final transmission."

"Starting now," I said, and entered the "send queue" command.

The high pitched whistle started and I hung up the

phone. The Leafax would hold the line until I picked up the handset or killed it. It was not unusual for transmissions on bad lines to take several attempts and sometimes several hours. European lines were excellent, though, and this would probably be done in ten minutes. Most of the lines in Amsterdam seemed to be digital, which meant that the digitized images simply flew through.

I watched a progress indicator and saw that the first image was complete after three minutes. This was going to be nice and simple. I made a cup of tea as the images continued to send. In the tiny guest house room I was quite self-contained and effective. By the time the last image was complete, the entire elapsed time from beginning process to ending transmission amounted to no more than thirty-five minutes. I picked up the phone and spoke to the London desk again.

"Hi, this is Steve."

"Right, thanks for hanging on. Just a couple of things. I have a note to tell you someone called Shandra was looking for you. We gave her your e-mail address. Also Cass Collingridge was trying to reach you. Don't be surprised if you see her in Amsterdam."

"Okay – is that it?"

"That's it."

"Great – thanks for holding on to the messages. Speak to you tomorrow night."

"Right."

The phone went dead and I powered down the Leafax, folded it closed, and slid the briefcase-sized machine under the bed.

I released the blind I had rigged over the window, and

looked out over the evening skyline. The view from here was of the back of a row of houses and a few backstreets, the unseen face of the city. Being in quite a tall building, with my room on the top floor, I had a good view behind the façade of the city. Not very inspiring, but I opened the window to clear the smell of the chemicals, and sat smoking my cigarette, looking out over twilit Amsterdam. The last few bicycle commuters were heading home, their lights weaving along the roads.

I finished my cigarette and hooked up to the Net. Downloading three messages took only a moment and then I disconnected.

The first e-mail was from Cass. It simply read, "See you soon."

That was meaningful.

Next was Shandra. "What happened to you? Hoped to see you but you've been away for a while. Please call me, love from Shandra." More surprising, but promising.

Next was Guy. "Cracking this hard drive is not so easy, but I think I'm getting somewhere. Contact me on your return. Guy."

I typed out a reply for Guy and sent it immediately, asking him to make a backup and let his team have a go. I sent Cass an e-mail containing just the seven-digit local phone number of the Rembrandt Guest House. Anyone else seeing the message would not even know the city it was in.

I was beginning to think that maybe the whole Hanson thing was turning into a dead end. Plenty of stories just get dropped and labeled as mysteries. Maybe the situation with Hanson would be one of them. Still, Cass was evidently on her way out, or at least had something up her sleeve. That was all quite intriguing. With luck it would cast a little light on the mystery of Hanson and why I ended up under the body of one of his acquaintances.

I left the guest house at around 10:00 and wandered into the central square to meet Stella. As I walked I developed the uncomfortable feeling that someone was watching me, following at a distance.

I glanced over my shoulder and caught sight of a young man with a shoulder bag behind me. Probably just a tourist. I took a left at the end of the bridge, away from the city center, and quickened my pace a little, then paused to look in the window of a jewelry shop before doubling back.

The young man walked smartly past. I made my way back towards the town center, obviously mistaken in thinking anyone would follow me. I was hungry and a beer would go down well. At the canal edge I lit a cigarette, casually glancing around as I did so. In the distance a man seemed to be struggling to roll up an umbrella. Apart from that the street was deserted.

I found Stella sitting at a table on the pavement outside the café, reading a wire report. She handed it to me and said "St. Pauls …"

"Bristol?"

"Yeah."

"It's just like '85. It'll be Harmsworth next," I murmured as I scanned the AP report. More arrests, two dozen hospitalized. No deaths.

"Interesting?"

"Very …," I replied. "They don't mention that bunch of right-wingers you said were in Notting Hill."

"No. Not a word. I noticed that," she added.

"Very strange." I would have thought that was the strongest story, but then I was just a photographer. I stopped a passing waiter. "Hi, you got a beer?"

"Sure," he replied in perfect *90210* American English. "You English?"

"You got us," I replied.

"You guys eating?" he asked.

I am always amazed at how the English don't go to the trouble of learning other languages, yet most Europeans speak English as well as many English people do. This young Dutchman was talking fluently, and I could manage about three half-formed words of his language. "What do you have?"

He rattled through the list of specials and we ordered.

Stella sipped her wine and asked, "Is the *News* leaving you out here all week?"

"I think so," I replied. "I really don't know. They've just asked me to sit on it for the moment. If anything else comes up I'm sure they'll call."

"This summit's as dead as a doornail for me. I have a few comments already, but they want me to hang around in case anyone says or does anything unexpected – which they won't."

"What makes you so sure?"

"We have elections in three European countries in the next three weeks. These guys are fresh out of surprises. The others are all secure and just marking time. Maybe if something happens back home, one of them will say something out of the ordinary – but not likely."

"On the other hand, someone might blow the building up tomorrow."

"Right," she said sarcastically.

"I think you're just sore at not being there to cover the stuff going on back at home." This hit home, and she started playing with the salt cellar, radiating tension.

"Why do you want to be back there so bad?" I asked.

"These stories don't come along every day. I'm here and some young trainee will be out there scoring points. My luck's not running so good right now." The way she was talking I suspected she knew very well who was out there scoring points.

"You'll get your chance," I said. "It doesn't always do to chase it too hard."

"What makes you say that?" she asked, as she removed a speck of cork floating in her wine glass.

"Chase it too hard and you might not find it. Believe me, just relax a little and let it come to you."

"That sounds like good advice," she said – then added, "but I don't have that kind of patience. Heck, look at me, I'm twenty-seven years old."

"That's hardly retirement age," I said.

"No, but I planned to be in television news by now. I should have made the transition last year."

"You sound like you've got it all planned out." I said.

"You probably think it's silly!"

"Not at all. These days you need a plan."

"I sure do. I'm a good reporter, but look at me. I'm no oil painting. I'll have to make up for it by being bloody good. That's why I started in radio. It wasn't my first choice. Nowadays the big breaks all happen in TV."

My eyes wandered to the pavement opposite. A man stood in a shop doorway across the road. It was the same man I'd seen behind me on the way to the café, fiddling with his umbrella.

There was quite a noisy crowd in the café. Some college kids were laughing loudly and getting rowdy nearby. I had the horrible feeling they were laughing at me. Someone sure as hell was.

The café was quite busy now. There was noise and smoke, and the shadowy lighting offset the roughly plastered walls and their clumsily framed paintings. It was a café scene worthy of Monet. Some press guys I recognized from outside the Marriott had arrived. Music crackled out of a speaker that had clearly fallen from its wall-mount bracket some time ago, and I was being watched by a figure in the shadows across the road.

Our meal had been excellent. Veal. Nice and light. I paid with my freshly recharged credit card, and suggested to Stella that we should go and chat to the other press guys. I said I was going to the gents and slipped out to the rear of the café.

On the way I saw our waiter. "Hey, mate. I need a favor."
"Sure, what is it?"

I slipped him a generous tip to show me a back way out of the restaurant. Past the gents, the corridor did a little dogleg, and then a door was wedged open onto the alley behind the row of shops and restaurants. If that sucker standing in the street wanted to tangle with me, he'd have to try a little harder.

I slipped into the alley and hurried cautiously away. A drunk in a pile of trash groaned – it could have been Waterloo on a quiet night. The alley emptied out into a backstreet. I walked quietly along, and got about thirty feet before a large overcoat – with an even larger man squeezed into it – stepped out of a shadow and blocked my path. I heard an engine start and a large, burgundy,

Volkswagen Synchro van pulled alongside the curb to my right.

Before I had time to think, the side door slid open and a pair of arms took hold of me and pulled. I was propelled into the van and maneuvered into the back seat by strong hands. I struggled to free myself, and shouted out, in the hopes a pedestrian might hear me, but the only result was a stream of Teutonic oaths being hurled back at me. Unable to free myself I stopped struggling, and desperately tried to think of a way out of the speeding vehicle. It raced through the streets and, as I tried to fathom what was happening, I heard the engine note change as we moved onto a major highway. I tried to reach the door handle, before being roughly pushed back into my seat, told to stay still by voices in the darkened vehicle. As my eyes became accustomed to the gloom I got my bearings.

I was in the rear section of the van. Besides the driver and someone in the front passenger seat, there were three men seated in the row of seats before me. In the rear seats with me there was a body, I hoped merely sleeping, huddled under a blanket. I noticed the van was towing a small trailer. These guys came well equipped.

"Wait a minute," I said loudly, to anyone who would listen. "Hey, I said wait!" I was shouting this time. I smacked the shaved head of the biggest of the men in the seat ahead of me. He was the sitting in the center, and his head banged against the guy on his right in a satisfying way.

"Just what the fuck do you think you're doing?" I was pretty pissed now. I put on my best "I'm gonna smack you around" face and stuck my face an inch from his.

Being kidnapped on top of the events of the last month was not my idea of a happy ending. If I were to end up face down in the Amstel with a chain around my legs I wanted to know why.

The guy I had pushed looked round indignantly, rubbing the side of his head. His friend was looking pretty sore too. I'd have to remember that trick.

"What you want?" he said, the only Dutchman I had come across so far who had anything but flawless English.

"I want to know what you think you're bloody doing, you raving Dutch bastard! You can't just kidnap me!" I made another desperate attempt to open the door, but found myself pressed back into the seat again.

"Firstly," he said, "I not Dutch. I Danish bastard. And, second, I not kidnap you."

"Well, what the hell do you call this?" I gestured at nothing in particular.

The blankets stirred beside me. Cass's face emerged. My jaw dropped, then hung limp like a ventriloquist's dummy resting. "Steve! Would you shut up and let me get some sleep? I've been on the go since 5 a.m.! And show some kindness to your hosts, they went to a lot of trouble to find you tonight." She muttered something about bloody photographers, and disappeared beneath the blankets again.

I was too surprised to speak for a few minutes, unsure whether to be grateful or outraged. By the time I had thought of the questions to ask, I was the only person in the vehicle still awake except the driver. I decided it might be wise to wait until we reached our destination before asking too much of anyone.

Chapter 8

THE BEACH AT DAWN WAS A PLACE OF GHOSTS. Mist hung low over the coast, swirling like a ghostly veil for a headless bride. I stood on the beach by the parked Synchro and watched the man who had been sitting in the front passenger seat as he busied himself a little way down the beach. We were the only two people awake. The driver slept wrapped in a blanket behind the wheel.

A light breeze blew ashore. It carried the sound of a bell on a buoy, warning shipping away from this coastline. The sound hung in the air for a few moments, then it was gone. We stood in soft, loose sand, which the wind swept along the beach in great eddies. There was a muted, otherworldly quality to the light. I had shot models in this light for the fashion pages. Mist dissolves the harshness – blows the shadows clean away. A bit of work in the darkroom and you can make the girls even more pale and wan. Sight, sound and touch. I suspected today's work would be rather different.

I had no idea when we had arrived here. I had been woken from my crumpled sleeping position by the sound of the passenger door closing. I'd edged forward until I could climb out. Cass was still sleeping.

A seagull materialized out of the grayness of the sky. It saw the VW Synchro and dodged away seawards. I got the impression this was a very remote coast. Certainly I could see absolutely no sign of habitation or even roads. Our tracks were still visible in the sand.

I climbed to the top of a dune amid pathetic clumps of grass fighting a losing battle with the wind. It was the only vegetation. From that vantage point I found another higher dune behind. I struggled down the soft sand and climbed another, hoping for a better view. From atop the second I could see more dunes. They disappeared into the mist; it seemed they went on to infinity. To seaward the beach stretched away, the tide far, far out.

The sea wasn't visible, but I knew it was near. Its sound was there beyond our vision. The salt, sweet smell declared its presence too. I slid down the dune and made my way back towards the Synchro. I had my first smoke of the day going, biting me in the throat. I looked up the beach and watched as my companion set up some sort of aerial. It seemed quite sophisticated, requiring some kind of footing, and three stays to support the thirty-foot-high mast. A wire ran back to the vehicle, which I guessed was drawing power from the battery. He knelt and held something to his ear. A moment later he spoke into a mike and wrote something on a pad on his knee. I could hear the crackling reception, but the words were foreign and unknown to me. He finished writing and slipped his pad back into a pocket. It was a neat field radio setup. Very simple. Once he had his message he hurriedly began gathering driftwood and brought it nearer the VW. I gathered some bits and pieces from nearby and added them to the pile.

He lifted a box from the trailer hitched to the VW and pulled out a can of lighter fluid, which he poured over the driftwood and a few pieces of cardboard from the trailer. It flashed and flames flared out as he flicked a match onto the piled wood. In a moment we had a fire going. This was done in complete silence, with a few grunts in my direction and awkward glances. He seemed a bit of a knuckle-dragger, so I chose not to press for too much information, though my curiosity was eating me up. Cass would be awake before long, and I wanted to hear her story.

I gathered plenty of firewood, took it to the pile and warmed myself by the fire, as he pulled a kettle from the trailer and filled it from a jerry can of fresh water. There were stirrings coming from the Synchro and gradually the lure of coffee drew people to action. The door slid open and the three passengers from the row of seats in front of me tumbled out and looked sleepily around.

The early-rising radio operator unloaded cooking utensils to get breakfast organized. I offered to help and tended a pan of bacon and sausages. The fire cut the damp of the mist from me and warmed my face. The smell of sausages wafted among us.

Cass stumbled from the sliding door of the Synchro, a blanket still wrapped about her. She looked like an Eskimo. It suited her.

"When you're good and ready, I'd just love to hear some kind of explanation as to what this is all about."

She grunted. I didn't think she was being deliberately obstructive. That wasn't in her nature.

"Shall I fix you a coffee?" I offered. There was another

grunt. I took it to be affirmative. Cass was not really a morning person.

I poured two coffees into two dented tin mugs that were laid out for us, and spooned an unhealthy level of instant coffee into them. I threw in too much sugar for mine and added boiling water – before finding some milk and richening it all up. The coffee was great. It burned all the way down and warmed my stomach.

I handed a cup to Cass. She sipped it, winced, and sipped some more. "Not bad," she mumbled.

"Any idea where we are?" I asked.

"None at all," she replied.

"Great," I muttered. "Miles from anywhere, hardly any cash and no bank machine within a hundred miles, I'll bet."

Our host had set up a folding table on the sand and laid out various dishes. Cass and I walked toward the dune and sat apart from the rest of the group.

As I sat and began to eat, she told me what it was all about.

"Ever heard of Green Rage?" she asked.

"No. What is it, a mutation of mad cow disease?"

"Keep the smartass comments to yourself. It's an environmental pressure group. It hits the big industrial concerns that do more extreme forms of environmental damage."

"You mean the oil companies?"

"Oil, mining, nuclear, sometimes the factory ships." She paused to savou her sausage. Sausages are one of the few foodstuffs I cook to perfection – unlike my eggs, which come out deader than shoe leather. "You have the pleasure of being their guest."

"Oh," I said, in mock surprise, "and there I was thinking I'd been kidnapped. Easy mistake to make! Perhaps later we'll have a light supper and all play charades. But I was forgetting, the game's already started!"

"Shut up, Steve." Cass's irritation was thinly veiled. "They've never brought a journalist along before, or a photographer. You have to remember that most of these guys are wanted in several countries. They're considered terrorists in Germany. Especially after the airbase incident last year."

"I remember that. The F-16 they painted pink! Great stunt!"

"The German security forces didn't share that view. The one member they caught is serving three years for breaching the security of the base. And their prisons are no fun."

I sipped my coffee. The caffeine coursed through my body, the effects heightened by the fresh sea air.

"They don't usually bring journalists along, for fear of someone leaking word to the police ahead of time. When they went up Nelson's Column so many press came running up from Fleet Street, they got the publicity they wanted. Same with London Bridge, and Big Ben. The banners made great pictures.

"Anyway, they contacted me about a year ago, asking if I would be available for an action if the chance came up. I've been standing by for this since. I got a call late last week asking me to wait outside *Consolidated*'s office at 10 a.m. on Tuesday, and to wait to be met. They made me promise no one would to know about the meeting. Next thing I know I'am on my way here. I managed to get a quick message off to you, but that was all I could do." That made sense, at least. "I'm not sure what they've got planned, but whatever it is, it's remote enough not to have many passing press taking an interest. Anyway, judging by their past performances, you won't be disappointed."

"So how come I have the pleasure of doing the pictures?"

"Simple! They wanted a discreet and very good snapper. They told me it had to be someone quite tough – we may have a bit of a journey. Someone who really knew their business. I did my best, but you were all I could raise."

"Very funny," I snapped back. "It sure beats the economic summit. I figured I was being followed last night and couldn't work out who the hell it was."

"They've been checking you out for the last couple of days."

"So why didn't they just ask me to shoot their stuff? Why follow me around like a bunch of eco-Nazis, and then seize me like a bunch of kidnappers? And what about my gear? I can't shoot anything without my gear!"

"Relax, Steve. Cool it. They had to pick you up like that. They couldn't very well tell you about the job. You'd be on the phone to Marlene and then half the world would know about it. D'you suppose the security at the *News* is so tight that this job would stay under wraps for long? No way," she said, answering her own question. She had a good point there, too. "Besides which, I'm told that in this case, the less anybody knows before hand the better for all concerned."

I didn't like the sound of that at all. It was the kind of

suggestion that means there's going to be an inquest afterwards, and you're going to want to say, "I knew nothing about it."

Cass carried on, "As far as your gear goes, it's all taken care of. They picked that up about five minutes after you left for your date with Stella."

"It wasn't a date."

"Looked like a date. Candlelit dinner on the pavement. Very cozy."

"I didn't notice any candles." I replied. "So, apart from kidnapping and abduction, not to mention breaking into my room, what else has this band of merry men been up to?"

"Come on," said Cass sharply. "Your gear is in the trailer, along with a set of wet-weather clothes they've put together for you. We're going for a little boat ride." There was a look about her that I found disturbing and ominous.

If there's one thing I hate it's an offer I can't refuse. "Great," I said, uneasily. "Nothing quite like messing about in boats, is there?"

"Just take it easy. You'll have a blast," she said, easing the tension a little. I didn't believe a word of the "I know nothing!" and "The less you know the better," story she was spinning. That ranked up there right along with, "This isn't going to hurt." I had the distinct feeling she knew a hell of a lot more than she was saying and was hiding most of it.

BREAKFAST WAS ALMOST DONE, smokes being lighted. Some of the assembled group laughed together;

others looked more concerned and preoccupied. Cass and I watched until the Dane I had insulted the previous night came over to chat to us. Judging by the way the others were avoiding talking to us I figured they'd been told to keep their distance.

Cass did the introductions. "Steve, meet Bruno; I never got the chance to introduce you two last night." Very sarcastic. As it was, I felt awkward about the way I'd acted the previous evening.

"Hi," I said. "I'm sorry about my behaviour last night. It wasn't necessary and I'm sorry."

"It's okay. You feeling a little better today?"

"Yes," I said "It must be the sea air."

"Good. You like sea, *Ja?* That is good, very good. You will enjoy today if you like sea."

"Oh, what do you have in mind?" I asked.

"We going on a little trip." He was thickset, very blond and had bright blue eyes. He was Danish to the rind, and seemed to have a strange enthusiasm for the cool morning. The day or two of facial hair was catching the mist and glistened with dew. He was grinning as though at some private joke.

"We're going on a little trip by sea?"

"*Ja, Ja.* And you will be able to do some nice pictures. We have been exactly right with the weather. It has taken a lot of planning, but our forecast is holding up well. Everything is going exactly to plan."

I said, "Where are we going, and what kind of boat?"

"You see in a minute," said Bruno, and walked away toward the radio operator, down the beach a little way.

Bruno and the radio operator chatted for a moment and then Bruno started talking into a small handheld radio. Holding it close to his face, he talked rapidly and then looked around at the group of us. He ended the conversation abruptly and called out to everyone to get their gear and prepare to get moving. For our benefit he repeated the instruction in English, and motioned for someone to bring Cass and me a large backpack.

I opened it, and found inside my camera bag, and two sets of full wet-weather gear. It was Helly Hanson gear and looked brand new. Someone had spent serious money on seeing we stayed dry. Thoughtful.

Bruno walked over to us and said, "Good gear, *Ja?* We don't want you to catch cold and die! You have to bring the pictures back!"

"*Ja,*" I replied, as I handed Cass a set of the water-proof and extremely warm trousers. I pulled mine on and then the jacket and boots, before stashing my shoes and leather jacket in the holdall. The clothes were a perfect fit. Someone had really done some homework.

The others of the group were kitting out too. Quite suddenly they changed from what looked like a motley crew of rabble-rousers into a uniformed and efficient team. The transformation was a little disturbing. The driver and a young woman were apparently staying with the vehicle, while the rest of us were making ready for what was apparently going to be a cold journey.

The jackets had built-in buoyancy and life preservers, as well as superb insulation. I shouldered my gear, and followed Bruno as he headed down the beach. He shouted something to the driver and waited a moment as the radio operator and another joined us, and we began walking seaward into the mist. The dunes were lost in a moment as the weather swallowed us.

Bruno was clearly the leader of the group. He introduced us to his colleagues as we walked.

"This is Ingmar, who you saw working the radio earlier, and this silent fellow is François." Cass had already been introduced, probably before I was picked up. Ingmar, Bruno and François carried heavy packs on their backs. They looked uncannily like a trio of commandos. Ingmar was also carrying several coils of rope, and some elaborate clips and harnesses. The equipment looked vaguely familiar – in fact I'd last seen something similar when I was shooting a climber some months previously in Scotland.

We did not seem to be moving "down" the beach, this beach was actually very flat. It reminded me of parts of the Essex coast. It was one of those rare areas where the tide would race in, easily outpacing a man as it rushed up the shallow and almost imperceptible incline of the shore to the high water mark. Bruno told me this area was the edge of the Wadenzee, a stretch of water sheltered from the North Sea by a string of islands; Terschelling, Ameland and Schiermoonikoog were among the few romantic-sounding names he mentioned. It was blessed, or cursed (depending whether your vessel was deep or shallow draft) with silted-up sand channels, which dried up at low tide, leaving stretches of sand like the one we were walking over. At low tide there were channels, but one needed to know the lie of the land and sea. At high tide this piece of land was about two metres under water. We walked for probably half an hour before I heard a radio crackle and Ingmar pulled a radio handset from his pack. He held it before him and moved the aerial to and fro for a moment, then pointed into the distance, away to our left. I realized he was using it as a direction finder, and as we walked into the gray distance, I began to hear more clearly sounds of the sea, faintly at first and then the rhythmic brushing of the waves on the sandy beach.

We saw them like shadows at first. Pulled a little way in from the waves, two large inflatables were beached on the sand. They must have been twenty feet long, each manned by two crew, waiting for us. One of the crew shouted over for us to hurry, we had to move fast or lose our catch.

When we stepped into the inflatables their crews dragged them back into the waves. I said "Hi" to our crew, but got only a friendly grunt in return. As one manned the center-mounted wheel, the other moved to the stern and lowered the two enormous Johnson Seahorse engines over the transom. He did a quick check of the cabling and then moved forward. The helmsman, a gaunt-looking German named Johan, pressed a button and the engines coughed into life. Cass and I sat tight and waited.

I shot a glance across at Bruno, now busying himself in the other inflatable. I sure hoped he knew what the hell he was doing. This didn't look like the kind of gear you use on a pleasure cruise.

The boats were a dull gray color, perfectly suited to disappearing into the weather. The other inflatable was already nosing along the shoreline, the waves barely ripples on the morning tide. Bruno and Ingmar talked to their helmsman and looked at a map. Ingmar delved in a bag, and then began erecting a small stand in the boat. I watched as he assembled a small radar unit, of a kind used on small fishing boats and yachts.

From the activity around the viewer they could apparently see something out there, and the inflatable quickly picked up speed and began to plane. The breeze was now a cold wind as we moved smartly along. The sensation of traveling quite fast in the mist was unsettling. We followed about thirty feet behind Bruno and his group, barely able to see their craft, but following a bright light they had attached at the stern. I could see it was shielded so that only someone following close behind could make it out.

Then the fun started. The lead boat rose higher in the water, its muted engines assuming a higher note, and she flattened out and surged ahead. We followed and picked up speed, passed thirty knots, then hovered around forty. The waves out here were more noticeable and soon were long and rolling as we cut out deeper heading west. Behind each craft a wide white scar sliced the surface of the sea as the wake formed a "V" lost in the mist behind us. It was pretty clear we were heading into the North Sea off the coast of Holland. We seemed to be doing so blindly as well as at great speed.

"Cass, these guys are nuts. What if we hit something?" I shouted to make myself heard over the rushing wind and the engines.

"It's okay. They've got radar in the other boat. They can see everything, and besides they've done this plenty of times." Her words did nothing to reassure me.

The waves deepened and we began to make long surging movements, the hull lifting clear of the waves as we forged ahead into the deeper water. As we crossed a particularly choppy section of the sea, a brief deluge of spray soaked us all. My gear was safely stowed. It had been through worse than this.

Then we were into a new swell. It was a long sweeping movement – I guessed it must be part of a different, deeper channel. The inflatables raced through the long seas like thoroughbreds stretching their legs in a full gallop over the South Downs. The sound was largely left behind us as both Cass and I held tight to the bucking craft. Around us now we were seeing the sea break in spats of white, here and there. The horizon was lost in the monochrome of the weather, and we flew blindly onward, the passage a complete test of faith in radar and Ingmar's ability to read it. I would not have been surprised in the least to find we were piling into the steel wall of a tanker at forty knots at any moment.

After about fifteen minutes of this the fog seemed to thin a little and we could see the inflatable ahead more clearly. The guy on the helm motioned me over, and held out the radio. Apparently Bruno wanted to chat. The boats were slowing a little.

I took the handset and spoke into it, saying, "Hi Bruno."

"Hi, we are nearly where we should be. You will have to be ready. If you get some good pictures you just tell Johan to get you back. We want those pictures to get out, no matter what. I don't want you to hang around and get arrested with us, that would do us no good."

"What are you going to do?"

"Ah, you'll see. I'm not going to broadcast it over this radio, but all you have to know is, when I jump you'll have to shoot to get the banner. Okay?"

"Sure. I don't know what the hell you mean, but I'll do it. And by the way, good luck."

"Thanks. We'll probably see you in London. If I don't get another chance to say it, thanks for coming along."

I looked at Cass and she took the handset.

"Thanks Bruno, good luck!" She handed the set back to Johan, and I began to make out the strangest of shapes in the mist ahead.

A little way ahead a concrete pillar seemed to rise from the sea and disappear into the misty sky. It must have been thirty feet around and was painted brilliant yellow, muted by the half-light of the morning. "Cass," I said, as I stared into the gray distance. "Just what the fuck do you suppose that is?"

Both the inflatables had slowed to what now seemed a crawl, only about eight knots. We were separated by about forty or fifty feet and I could see Ingmar gesturing to our left. I shifted my gaze in the direction of his gesture but could make nothing out.

There was sound though. The deep ominous resonance of large diesels. They were invisible, yet not distant.

And then slowly I began to see a form there. It was another yellow column, the same as the one ahead. Then it began to dawn on me. Above us the grayness was slightly more dense than it had been. And the columns were moving.

"Holy Christ, Cass! We're underneath a rig." I glanced over at Johan, who was carefully monitoring his speed, holding position. "I think it's being towed. And we're right under it." The platform towered high above us, lost in the weather.

"Wow, that's a neat trick. The people towing it don't even know we're here," she said.

"I guess not. Why would they? After all, who would be stupid enough to get this close to a rig being towed?

They'll probably realize soon. They have to be using radar in this mist. Someone will notice us."

"I read somewhere that rubber leaves almost no trace for radar," said Cass.

She was right. I remembered now. The rubber of the inflatables would be almost undetectable.

I GRADUALLY BECAME MORE AWARE of a low throbbing in the distance. The sound, at first sucked up within the mist, was louder now, and coming from two different directions. It seemed to echo around my body. It was the sound of the large diesels of the tugs pulling the rig. A tow of this sort would take, I guessed, three or four, maybe more tugs. The weather hid us from their sight.

As we watched, the rig steadily marched northwards, moving up a channel. Its stately, menacing movement seemed as unstoppable as the rising of the sun. A light breeze sprang up, and the mist began to thin out a little. I thought of the planning for this operation and it dawned on me how detailed they must have been. The way things were coming together was the work of someone methodical and fastidious. Even the weather was doing exactly as they had hoped. The enormous rig was now exactly where they had planned it should be, and their interception of the vast structure had so far gone unnoticed.

Johan passed Cass an envelope. Inside was a laminated sheet of paper. It was the specification sheet for an oil platform. I read the details as best I could. The structure was to become a part of the Ekofisk group, another drilling point on the already extensive network of rigs arranged in a hub of twenty-seven installations. It would be towed by tugs until about 180 miles west of the coast of Norway, far into the North Sea. There it would be sited and anchored to work for an expected lifespan of thirty years.

As a part of the hub, this rig would have the oil it drilled piped directly to Teesside, on the northeast coast of England. The diagram showed the towering structure and detailed the scale of engineering. The rig had been assembled in Holland and was in the early stages of its journey, which is where Green Rage had seen an opportunity.

The shallow water here forced the tow to be done with minimal ballast. This meant the rig would float very high, and had to be handled very slowly and carefully. Later, when the legs of the structure were flooded, and more of the structure below the surface of the water, they would be able to step up their progress and move at greater speed. But for now their pace was slow, and they were vulnerable to interception. Which was precisely what had happened.

"This is going to be a hell of a story," said Cass.

"What are they going to do?" I said, a growing sense of unease filling me. "They can't exactly steal it."

Far above us, eighty or ninety feet, was a dark shape that must be the base of the platform. I strained to see it, but the mist was still too dense. From ahead I heard the engine note of Bruno's inflatable suddenly climb and the craft rose up in the water to race fifty yards to the foot of one of the great legs.

I watched amazed as first Bruno and then the diminutive figure of François stepped from the inflatable ahead and clung to the leg of the platform. I raised my camera and focused on the end of the 200mm Nikon lens. Through the telephoto I could make out a series of rungs on the platform leg. They were using these to make their climb, burdened with heavy backpacks. If they fell in with weight like that on their backs they'd sink like rocks. I shot a couple of frames as they began climbing, and was then forced to grab a rope on the side of our craft, as suddenly the two Seahorses roared and took off. We pulled a tight U-turn, the boat leaning perilously into the seas, and then headed away from the rig.

We flew over troughs and hammered into the growing waves, leaving the rig astern, racing almost alongside the inflatable Bruno had just left. We clung to the ropes on the side of the craft to steady ourselves as we shot away, bouncing and tossing us around.

"Are we leaving them to it?" I called to Johan, unable to believe it was over.

He eased the power off and let the craft settle back to a drift. The other boat raced off into the distance to take up a new position. If these two teams knew what they were doing then they were very good at it. I had trouble keeping the other craft in sight.

"We're just standing off for a while," said Johan in his clipped accent. "Ingmar picked up a signal on the radar; they are sending a boat back to investigate. It might be a routine check, or maybe they picked us up on their radar."

"What about Bruno and François, won't the people towing the rig see them?"

"No, they'll be halfway up by now." He held the radio to his ear. "Ingmar says their escort boat's heading to the rig, but it'll still take a while to get there. Bruno just said they are almost out of sight of the surface. They climb fast! If this weather holds for five more minutes it will give them time to set everything up."

We listened for the sound of approaching engines. Cass asked, "Do you think they saw us?"

"I think not. They would have sent out someone for us by now if they thought there was anyone trying to get aboard. It's more likely to be a routine check," said Johan, peering into the mist.

His radio crackled into life again, and he held it up to his ear to hear better. "Looks like the boat's taken up station just astern of the tow. That's normal. We were lucky he wasn't there an hour ago. It would have been trickier to make that drop-off."

"Won't he see them when the weather clears?"

"Yes, but that'll be fine. It'll be too late to stop them by then."

We were moving slowly forward, matching the course and speed of the rig, by now half a mile distant, hidden in wreaths of mist. Yet even as I thought of the effectiveness of the misty curtain, a freshening of the wind seemed to draw the veil away for a moment.

I could see Ingmar in the other boat talking quickly to the climbers on the radio, and looking into the radar's viewfinder. The boat sent back to check would be under them by now.

Johan listened with his radio pressed to his ear. "They're on the main platform now; they can't be seen from below."

Cass leaned across and said, "This is where it gets interesting." I had been right when I guessed she knew more than she was saying.

"You better hold tight. If this wind keeps up we'll have to act in the next few minutes," said Johan.

"What are you going to do?" I asked, trying to make out the activity on the other inflatable. They were rigging some sort of flag.

"You'll see soon enough."

The gusts that had come earlier were gradually growing to a steady blow. The mist was thinning, and the legs of the rig were now visible. As the swell lifted us I caught sight of another craft ahead, watching the progress of the rig. It was a small tug of some kind. Its heavy shape was probably fine in a choppy sea, but in these waters it was ungainly and clumsy.

Our engines were set to idle and we lay dead in the water for a moment. I watched as Ingmar finished raising a brilliant red, white, and green banner, with the Green Rage logo and the words "Dismantle Ekofisk!" emblazoned across it. The bright flag streamed out over the stern as the wind caught it.

"They'll see that any minute!" I said to Cass. "What's he trying to do?"

"Oh," she said calmly, as she watched the other inflatable through a pair of pocket field glasses, "I think he knows what he's doing."

"I bloody well hope so," I said. "I think piracy still carries the death penalty in England. Isn't that one of the laws they never got around to repealing?"

"You could be right." It didn't seem to trouble Cass very greatly.

The last wreaths of mist disappeared as the wind whipped the surface of the sea into whitecaps and a cold steel-gray swell. Quite suddenly the tug ahead seemed to see the Green Rage banner, and swung round hard to starboard to intercept them.

I realized the other inflatable had been closing quite quickly on the tug, as we had sat dead in the water. They were trying to get attention. I steadied myself and shot a few frames of the tug now closing on the Green Rage inflatable, both vessels in the frame, with the rig in the distance. They'd make great front page shots, strong vertical pics with the seas looming huge in the foreground. I kept shooting as the two craft closed on each other, then the Green Rage vessel swung round and began to make its way off to the west. The tug took up the chase, squeezing an extra couple of knots from its laboring diesels, clearly audible in the distance.

We crouched, waiting. So far we were undetected. Indeed, seeing anything as small as our inflatable in that rising and falling seascape would have been difficult. It dawned on me that if Ingmar had wanted, he would have left the tug boat far behind by now. Instead, he was just steadily drawing them off. Then word came over the radio, and we surged forward.

The acceleration that accompanied the rise in pitch of the big Seahorses was breathtaking. In moments we were hammering across the troubled gray surface of the sea towards the rig. About a mile away the tug was still pursuing Ingmar and his flag, leaving the back door wide open for us.

We took up a position two hundred yards behind the rig.

Johan turned to me and said, "This good for you?"

I sized up the rig in the viewfinder, not knowing what to expect. I could get the whole thing in nicely, so

I was happy. "Sure, this looks good."

He spoke into the radio, then shouted across, "You'll only get one try at this. Bruno says you have to get it right first time. We have to leave any moment. The tug's turning back. If they can stop us they can arrest us – and then you don't get to do anything with the pictures. Even if they see us it'll complicate things."

"Okay. Let's do it."

He spoke into the radio, then shouted over to me, "Ten seconds."

I framed up the shot, counting down the seconds. "Five, four...."

"The tug's close, I can hear it," said Cass.

"Two, one...."

Exactly on time two bodies fell from the rig. Behind them an enormous banner streamed out, unraveling as they fell headlong.

I hit the trigger and the Nikon dragged four frames a second through its spinning gears as the two climbers hurtled towards the sea. Their fall took five seconds, twenty frames – "Green Rage! Dismantle Ekofisk!" streamed out behind them.

I watched the two bodies hit the water, immediately swallowed in the depths. I barely had time to shut my gaping mouth as the engines gunned again and we swung away heading east. The movement nearly pitched me into the sea, it was so sharp.

From the bow the other crew member, who up to this time had been little more than a passenger, was now galvanized into action. Taking a pole from the floor of the craft, he mounted it into a purpose-built footing, and then pulled the distinctive Green Rage banner. He prepared to rig the flag as we swung off to starboard, and I realized we were moving in a huge circle. In a moment we would be coming back on the towering rig.

The flag blew back between us and over the transom as we sped out of the west towards the rig. The tugboat and her crew came in sight. A white-haired man was on the foredeck, a bullhorn in his hand. A crew member on the tug saw us and he shouted, and then pointed in our direction. The tug spun round on a dime, churned white water erupting from its spinning screws, and headed straight for us. We made directly for the rig, and then eased away, as if being headed off by the heavy craft. Very smoothly Johan eased the inflatable round, slowing speed to just a little more than the tug, and moved ahead of it, just out of reach.

Again the tug began to follow, trying to match our speed. There couldn't have been more than twenty feet between us. The Seahorses were barely turning over, but the tug was straining to meet us. Through the telephoto lens I could see the white-haired captain of the tug, in the wheelhouse now, shouting, enraged at our insolence. I managed to squeeze off a couple of frames of him, just for posterity.

To the best of his knowledge we were the same inflatable that had disappeared off to the west earlier. How the banner had got onto the rig he had yet to figure. I could see the crew's confusion. Some pointed to the banner on the rig, perplexed, while others threw insults in our direction. They tried hard to squeeze a couple more knots from the diesels pushing them along.

"But what happened to Bruno and François?" I called to Johan. "They seemed to go down like lead!"

Johan shouted above the noise of the engines, "They're fifty feet under with breathing gear on."

"They can't stay there for long, can they?"

"This guy's taking the bait beautifully," he yelled. "You see," he pointed back at the rig, "I've drawn this guy off far enough for Ingmar to recover them." He looked over the stern and, sure enough, the tugboat was following dutifully. If anything it was gaining a little. Our engines slowed a little more, teasing him.

The radio was going again. Turning to me with a smile, Johan said, "Ingmar has Bruno and François aboard. They're fine. It's time to go home." With that the engines roared, and from thirty yards behind us the little tug saw the awesome power hidden at the stern of the inflatable.

It was no more than two minutes before the rig and the tug were lost to view, and we swung slowly round onto a course set for home.

As we sped back to our launch point ,I remarked to Cass that I could see no sign of the other boat.

"They'll head north. I expect they'll hide somewhere in the islands. There are loads of tiny passages in there, many too shallow for anything but the smallest craft," she said, pointing towards the northeast.

I said to Johan, "Will the rig owners try to chase them?"

He shouted back, "They have already called the coast guard. They said it was an act of terrorism." For the last few minutes he'd been listening in on the rig's radio frequency as they regrouped and discussed what to do next. "We should expect they'll have a helicopter up here before long, maybe twenty minutes," he added.

"How do you plan to dodge that?" I asked.

"You'll be on the road to Groningen by then." He motioned to his crewman. "And we'll be laid up under a camouflage net, same as Ingmar. They'll probably lay low on one of the islands till nightfall, and then head further up the coast. Those islands have scrub and grass and plenty of places to hide. They were great for the resistance in the last war, now they serve us just as well. We are carrying provisions for at least five days. I'll head south for a couple of days. Then slip into a harbor somewhere. It'll have blown over by then."

The engine was slowing, the hull settling to a lower profile and then coasting towards the shore, now visible in the distance.

Johan was chattering into the radio, and with a roar the Volkswagen Synchro suddenly roared into view. It raced across the flat beach, sand flying from its four spinning wheels.

He called back to us, "Get your stuff ready, there's a helicopter about ten miles south of here coming up fast. It's going to be close."

He gunned the engines and the inflatable slid up the beach a little way, the impact throwing us both forward. Grabbing our bags we rushed to the burgundy van, and jumped in through the sliding door. We were barely in as the van sped off up the beach, the engine screaming, before exploding into the dunes and heading inland.

Far behind, Johan and his crewman dragged some netting over the beached inflatable, brushing away the tracks of the Synchro.

We crested a huge dune, the front wheels of the Volkswagen flying into space and then sinking into soft sand. Cass and I were hurled about, luggage flying everywhere inside. For a moment the van foundered, digging itself in to the loose sand. Then the four-wheel drive seemed to find some purchase and the vehicle lurched forward. Quickly I fastened my seat belt, my wet hands slipping on the fittings. I was damned if I was going to be put through my seaborne ordeal only to be hospitalized and unable to file my pictures because of some mad Dutch driver.

Then, suddenly, we were on tarmac. A small coastal road, with traffic coming towards us. Our driver was moving smartly along, inside the speed limit. Just another late summer touring party. There was no reason for anyone to be interested in the vehicle.

Through our rear window, I saw a speeding helicopter sweep across the road at about a hundred feet and head seaward. The van's driver picked up a mike and spoke, presumably telling Johan the coastguard helicopter had just cleared the road. By now he would be invisible to the fast-moving chopper. He'd relay the message up to Ingmar, and there would be no clue about how the rig had been bannered so blatantly.

Our driver was laughing at something that had come over the radio. He turned and said, "They haven't a clue. Ingmar's monitoring their radio. Apparently they're searching the rig for intruders – they think they're still aboard!"

Cass, stripping off her wet gear, added, "They won't know how it was done until they see your pictures."

"That's pretty cool!" I laughed. I felt giddy with

excitement. Under the gear I was damp where water had trickled down my neck. Cass and I both shed the wet weather gear. The young woman I'd seen earlier that morning handed us towels, two thick wool pullovers and some heavy trousers.

"Get into these clothes," she said. "You'll be freezing in a few minutes. Now the rush has gone, you'll feel the weather!" She was smiling and we shared her infectious sense of elation. What had happened today had been really important. We had been part of something.

I was stripped to my underwear and began to shiver, suddenly cold. Cass was down to bra and panties, and was fiddling with her bra, about to remove it. I glanced out of the window, and cursed my ridiculous sense of decency. She looked pretty damned good about now.

I pulled the thick wool pullover on, its coarse fiber rough against my skin, but already warming me. The trousers were a little large, but dry and warm. Cass slipped into the same kind of clothes, shooting me a quick look.

Our friend in the passenger seat handed over tall cups of hot chocolate. I felt the burn of a brandy stiffener. That was perfect. These guys were really good.

I drank the hot, sweet liquid and felt my body infused with warmth and a sense of well-being. Settling back in the roomy seat, I gazed out the window. This was what it was about. Sticking it to the big guys and getting away with it. Better than that, I credited my job satisfaction to the fact that these guys at Green Rage were not the "terrorists" people made out; they were highly organized and effective people. They were sincere. Hell, they were right! If the Conservative Party looked after the media as well as Green Rage did, that happy band of pilgrims would have fewer troubles.

I saw the ramp onto the motorway signed for Amsterdam, then began to drift off into a doze. I'd file the pictures later and the desk would be wild. They'd go all over, under the syndicate agreement *News Consolidated* had with Associated Press. I had good cause to feel content.

Chapter 9

WE HEADED FOR THE TOWN OF GRONINGEN, moving along in light traffic. The town rested quietly amid a flat landscape punctuated by dikes, villages marked by church spires, and canals running back towards the Wadenzee. The land stretched out into a flat pan of rich grassland. It was dairy country, the black and white form of Friesian cattle in every field. The cows, named for their origin in this the Friesland coast, were returning from their milking, commuting back to their fields. The villages sat like islands on this green sea of reclaimed land. It was not hard to visualize the waves breaching and flooding this area.

The sun had broken through, and the flat light of this region and the windswept landscape combined to lend a dynamic, sculptured quality to the scenery. Even the small trees that clawed an existence out of this environ-ment looked permanently at the mercy of the sea and the weather. They seemed to be windswept even on a day like this, when the wind was little to speak of. Still their branches reached downwind, after years of expo-sure to the blast. Some grew so contorted they might have been bewitched, or cursed by the elements. Tumbledown stone walls lined the cemeteries and the older houses we passed as we worked our way east, back towards the main highway.

When we reached Groningen we pulled into the car park of a modern hotel, cheap but functional, and excelling at being unremarkable in every aspect. This was the end of the road for Cass and me. A train would take us back to Amsterdam either later that day or the following one, whichever we chose. Our priority now was to file the story and transmit our pictures.

Using my credit card we paid for two rooms and unloaded the Synchro. As the vehicle pulled off, the driver waving goodbye, I felt a touch of sadness. I didn't know who he was, or the woman with him. Come to that, I knew absolutely nothing about the people I had just spent the last few hours with, except that they had given me the chance of what promised to be some great pictures. I'd have to remember to write to them and thank them. First, though, I had to get the pictures sorted out.

The standard bathroom in most modern hotels has one distinguishing feature press photographers know about. It has nothing to do with the design specifications that a team of architects doubtless arrives at after many months of deliberations, formulating the most effective design for the space concerned. It has nothing to do with recessed soap dishes, or toilet roll holders.

The single factor that endears bathrooms in Holiday Inns, Trust Houses and Best Westerns throughout the world to the press photographer is that in recent years they have done away with windows in bathrooms. This means they make excellent darkrooms. A towel to line the door, a lock on the inside, running water and a shower rail on which to hang the processed negatives.... it all goes to make the perfect process setup. Most also have a socket for a hair dryer — which few photographers travel without — for drying the roll of film after fixing and a final rinse.

I left Cass in her room, setting up her laptop and going through the notes she had made as I dozed on our return journey. My place at this time was in the bathroom. I locked the door, and slid a small wedge I kept in my camera bag beneath it. There must be no chance of an accidental entry, or any other kind. I took the pre-measured powdered chemical developer, added it to a quart of water mixed at exactly the right temperature, and placed it to the right of the sink.

I turned off the lights, and let my eyes adjust to the light, or lack of it. All points of light were smothered, but there is always something. Slight light leaks are tolerable, if not actually desirable. Working by touch, I cracked open the three rolls of film I had shot, and loaded them onto the three-roll spool. I placed it on the surface by the basin, then sealed the top onto the canister and felt it slide home.

I double-checked everything before I turned on the light. The empty film canisters were there. Their spools were in the bath where I tossed them. The lid of the developing drum was snugly right. Next I ran a burst of lukewarm water into the drum to rinse it and make it ready. Once emptied, in went the developer — three minutes timed to the second, then another rinse, and another really cold one. Then the fix. As I opened the drum and ran cold water in I checked the leaders of the films. They were nice and clear. There were precise images there, crisp with just the right edginess and contrast.

Without good contrast the images would be flat and lacking in precision. In a gray light achieving the right strength where light meets dark is the greatest challenge. In bright sunlight it can be an enemy, but in flat lights it is something to strive for. It adds harmony to the image, and lifts it off the page.

I washed the strips of film thoroughly and then hung them, glancing briefly at a few of the better frames. They were good. As I lit up a cigarette and opened the door, I felt the satisfaction photographers chase well up within me.

I NEEDED SOME CAPTIONING INFORMATION and knocked on Cass's door. She had changed from the heavy clothing and wore a long skirt that swished about her ankles, and a white loose blouse. She was barefoot, and looked extremely relaxed. She had found a bottle of red wine somewhere, and it stood open on the coffee table, along with a little basket for her earrings, necklace and bracelet, and a mug for her toothbrush. Her makeup bag was there and a bottle of perfume that looked expensive.

I never really thought of Cass as having things like that. Looking round I saw that she had makeup on, something I had never really noticed before. The more I thought about it, the more I thought I'd never seen her wear it. There was a nice smell too.

"You filed yet?" I asked.

"I called it in about twenty minutes ago; want to read it?"

"Sure," I said. I sat in front of the laptop and scrolled up to the tagline.

She wrote well; she wrote with a committed fluency. She had a sincerity that marks strong journalism. And yet there was something about it.

The rig was apparently an accommodation rig, being sent up to Ekofisk to increase the capacity of the field. The older rigs were at the end of their useful lives and were being prepared for sinking in deep water. This was central to the issue. The sinking of redundant rigs meant waste seepage into the local marine environment, six thousand feet down. Green Rage wanted the rigs to be brought ashore for dismantling and responsible disposal. This sounded pretty sensible, if considerably more expensive. Disposal in deep water cost about $18 million, but dismantling and scrapping a rig on land would cost around $125 million. Still, last time I heard the oil companies were not short of a few bucks. Besides, they put the stuff out there – they should clean up the mess.

Green Rage was of the opinion that the companies should not be allowed to station new hardware in the North Sea without a commitment to reasonable dismantling practices. After all, a company would never be allowed to construct a factory in the United Kingdom, or the States, without a full environmental impact statement, which would include wind-down information.

There was definitely something not right here. She knew too much.

The article described the entire expedition, yet managed not to name anyone. It also failed to mention any distinguishing details about our Green Rage colleagues. I guessed that was because Cass had agreed not to. How she had suddenly become so informed on the rig issues, I was not sure. Maybe before I joined her in the Synchro she'd got a briefing.

"Great story," I concluded, nodding at the screen. "Very well informed."

I was about to light a cigarette when Cass placed her hand on mine, and said "Light that and I'll kick you out of this room." She removed her hand slowly, and went to the wine, pouring a glass for herself, and then looking over at me.

"May I try the wine?"

"Of course." She took a wineglass from beside the bed, and filled it with the languid rich hock.

I sipped the heavy German wine, lost in thought about the story. I would have to file shortly, but could enjoy this breather, while the negs dried. Too little drying and the surface of the neg would be delicate and susceptible to scratching. That was not a problem on quick jobs never to be used again, but this one would be used time after time. I wanted the negs to be in good condition. A little time now would ensure that. Besides, this wine was good, even to a palate as hardened as mine.

Having taken a hearty sip, I eyed my wineglass and said, "Nice plonk!"

She rolled her eyes in contempt.

I said, "You didn't mention any names in there, I noticed."

She lay across the bed, propped on one.elbow "No, I didn't want to say anything that might identify them."

"I see." It seemed reasonable enough. "Did the desk say anything about it?"

"The desk wanted names, but I said I wasn't given any. They want that protection – they can have it. Besides, they gave us a damned good story."

"Marlene okay with that?"

"She's cool with it. She knows I had to make agreements to get this one." She threw her head back and laughed, then added, "They're wild about this story. Apparently Green Rage faxed a press release while we were out there to most of the papers and TV stations saying what they were doing, and everyone thinks it's a hoax. The Dutch coast guard's saying nothing."

"So the first time anyone will know about it is when we hit the street?"

"You got it!" She emptied her glass, and reached over to fill it again. She looked at me with a hard gaze and smiled. "We beat everyone! They could hardly believe their ears when I told them we were right there. Marlene practically gave birth."

"I can imagine. I'd better get my pictures over there," I said, and sipped the warming wine. "They'll be wanting this stuff badly."

"You bet."

"I was going to ask about names for captions, but I guess we drop that this time."

She nodded, then said, "Hey, you'll do well with this. AP wants the pics and words, and will run it as soon as the *News* goes on sale. London's pretty happy about it all."

Cass looked unlike I'd ever seen her. She was positively glowing, lying back on the bed, a glass in her hand, her skirts scattered around her. I thought she looked a little gypsy-like, a little wild. Heck, she looked dangerous.

"I'll get this stuff off. Then shall we think about lunch?"

"Yeah, don't be long. I'm famished."

The negs were dried and ready to be edited. I found three suitable frames, two verticals and a horizontal, and prepared them for transmission. Front-page pictures always look better as verticals.

I dialed the London line reserved for transmissions. "Hi, it's Steve Sinclair. I'm in Holland. I have three images to transmit. FM 256." I switched over to transmit, and replaced the receiver.

The images went through while I smoked a cigarette. After the transmissions were complete, I called in to the desk to get some feedback.

"I'm looking at them now," said Vince, the number two on the desk. "I think Bonnie wants a word, Steve. I'm gonna put you on hold a sec."

She came on the line. "Hi Steve, where you been, man?"

"All over. Seen the pics I filed?"

"I have. Most of the newsdesks figure this is a hoax. I had the *Mail* earlier trying to get pictures out of us. They heard we had something. We should do well with this."

"AP's in on this one?"

"Sure, and they're putting a bonus in there for you."

"I could use it," I replied.

"So how'd you get this thing?"

"Cass set something up; I just got pulled along on the job. I'm not complaining." I said. "She had some connection in the group."

"Whatever gets the picture," she said, just happy to have it. "You heading back to the summit?"

"You want it?" I asked. I didn't want to hurry back to London just yet.

"I think it's a dead dog, but go and sit on it anyway. London's slow this week. Sit on it till the end of the week and then check in on Monday."

"Okay. That sounds good. Do you need my number here, in case there are any questions? I'll stay here till tomorrow morning and then head back to Amsterdam."

"Probably don't need it but give it to me anyway."

I read her the string of numbers, and said I'd be in the hotel most of the day.

"Okay, and well done, the rig pictures will be on the front of the next edition. You done good."

"Thanks Bonnie. Speak to you Monday."

I hung up and turned the Leaf off, its fan winding down in a subdued quiet whine. I would pack things up properly later. I wanted to eat and then have a doze. The early morning was catching up with me.

In Cass's room a platter of cheeses sat on the coffee table, and two bowls of chicken soup, and bread rolls. The freshly-baked rolls were still warm and gave off a tremendous smell that stoked the hunger pangs in my stomach to a full flame. "This looks great," I said, sitting down and helping myself to the food. The soup warmed me through. "Damned if I'm not still cold from this morning. That mist just gets right inside you! It didn't seem too bad at the time, but now I can feel it," I said, as I swallowed the steaming soup.

"Have some more wine," Cass said. She leaned over and poured the last of the bottle into my glass. "I know what you mean. I'm only just getting back to normal. Just think of those poor devils out there on the islands. They'll be freezing."

"I get the impression they know what they're doing. They did a good job today. I didn't see a single hiccup. That's something for a small outfit like Green Rage."

She got up and walked over to the bedside cabinet, and drew out another bottle.

"Blimey, you have quite a reserve," I laughed.

"Well, we're done for the day, so we might as well crash here for a while."

I thought about that a second. "Sure, sounds like a good plan." Cass seemed unusually friendly suddenly. This was quite unexpected, but welcome all the same. She was relaxing at last. Come to think of it, I'd never seen her at rest.

She drank her wine and buttered a roll, then placed an enormous piece of Brie on it. "These Dutchmen know a thing or two about cheese. It has to be the perfect food to eat with a good wine."

"Yeah," I said, trying a piece of the creamy white cheese. "The desk was pleased with the pics. They're pretty strong." I understated it intentionally.

"I spoke to the newsdesk just before you came in," she said. "Marlene has practically had an orgasm over this thing. First in a while, I suspect. She's a very happy lady. They're wild about the pictures. They were just coming into the newsroom as I was talking. I could hear them calling across the room to come and look at the screen. I think they half thought I was pulling a hoax until she saw them."

"They would never think that of you," I said.

"No? Just remember the Hitler diaries. Okay, this isn't quite the same, but there are some weirdo ways to get attention out there."

I drank more of the wine and told Cass about the pictures we received every week on the picture desk showing alien space ships. There were some excellent examples of ships over Hampstead Heath, always very good fakes. I supposed. Maybe they weren't.

We were well into the second bottle when Cass dozed off. We were both exhausted from the early morning and the rush of the job. Had it been otherwise I might have been offended. Now the fuel cells were low, and the wine drained them finally. She lay there gypsy-like on the bed, quite beautiful to look at. She should try and relax more often, I thought. She almost looked like a real woman.

I was stretched out on the couch at the time and ready to doze too, but thought better of it. After the last time I had fallen asleep with Cass, I figured I was better off going back to my room. My head had barely hit the pillow when the wine and tiredness overcame me. As I slid into sleep I saw the slow heavy waves around the rig and the banner waving in the wind.

I woke to the sound of hammering on my door. I looked at my watch. It was 6 p.m. and I had slept most of the day. The banging on the door was more insistent, and then I heard Cass calling, "Steve, open up. God, man, what's wrong with you?"

"Okay," I said, wiping the sleep from my eyes, "I'm coming." I opened the door and she rushed past me to the television in the corner. She turned it on and scanned through some stations till she found the BBC transmission on cable. "In the lead-in they showed pictures of the rig," she said, staring at the screen. A story about riots in Birmingham was just finishing, and then one of my images came on the screen. White writing on the bottom right corners credited the picture to the *News*.

"Nice picture!" she said.

"Hmmm," I agreed, "not bad."

The newscaster was leading into the story, saying, "And in foreign news, London-based resources company Allied Resources was subject to a demonstration by environmental group Green Rage today."

The screen switched to another of my images and zoomed in on the banner, the figure of Bruno falling, and then to the inflatable nearby. Bruno was unrecognizable, as was François, their faces covered behind dive masks.

"Protesters managed to board an accommodation rig, and fly a banner from the rig whilst it was being towed to a location in the Ekofisk oil field. The demonstrators then dived off the rig, and disappeared, leaving their banner behind. The group then harassed the efforts of a vessel sent by the company to remove the banner, for safety reasons, before making off and avoiding arrest by the Dutch authorities."

Some film of an Allied Resources tug steaming out of a harbor followed, though it was not anything to do with the rig we had been involved with. I assumed it was lifted from a corporate video produced by Allied Resources.

"A statement released by rig owners, Allied Resources, said: "The protesters failed to do any lasting damage to the structure, although there would be some extensive refitting required to repair damage caused by the intruders, who appear to have vandalized the structure whilst aboard."

The camera switched to a corporate headquarters in London, where a spokesman in a Saville Row suit was speaking before a crowded press conference. There was a crowd of journalists and reporters asking questions simultaneously. I recognized several of them.

The spokesman tried to keep to his prepared statement. "The company has been embarrassed by this act of wanton vandalism, and will be making an insurance claim to rectify the damage done by the intruders. We think they probably got aboard before the rig was launched, and that somehow they avoided our security in the docks.

"Obviously this is an area we'll be looking into in the immediate future. Our greatest concern is actually what else they did while they were there. We have to ask ourselves if they carried out any activities that might prejudice the safety of our staff once the accommodation rig is in place on the Ekofisk field."

A journalist asked, "What sort of threat might you be looking for?"

"Well, we don't really know. What we do know is that these people have shown us time and time again that they are not interested in reasonable discussion. They seem to want to disrupt our efforts in the Ekofisk area regardless of our efforts to discuss the issues, even resorting to unlawful means."

"Are you suggesting they may have tried to damage the rig permanently?" asked the reporter.

"That would be hard to say, but we can't rule it out."

A reporter at the back of the group, off camera, asked, "Is it possible that the group could have left some sort of explosive device aboard?"

"At this stage we are not ruling out any possibilities." The spokesman was acting defensively, and the journalists were latching onto anything he waved in their direction.

The first journalist, one of the television news regulars, got the next question in: "Are you saying that you suspect the group has left some sort of booby trap, or a bomb?"

Cass muttered, "Oh my God!"

I glanced at her. She was very pale suddenly. She slumped into a chair, her eyes fixed on the screen, her mouth open.

"Allied Resources has a duty to protect any staff using this accommodation platform. The lives of our staff are our greatest concern."

Another journalist cut in, "How are you preparing to do that?"

"We have a team aboard the platform at present scanning the entire structure for explosives. We will reroute the rig into Stavanger for further tests if we should find anything untoward."

Questions were now being shouted out from the journalists, baying for angles on this new twist.

The spokesman, not so defensive now, wound up: "I'm sorry, that's all we have to say at this time. Thank you, gentlemen." He turned on his heel and retreated back through the reflective glass doors of the office behind him, though not before I noticed a hint of a sneer on his face. The remaining reporters and journalists called questions out after him. The news cut back into the studio, and the anchor moved on to the next item.

I turned to Cass and saw she was stunned. This wasn't how things were supposed to play out at all. It was probably a good moment to make a cup of tea. I went to the bathroom, which still smelled slightly of fixer, and filled the kettle.

It took about two minutes before the hotel phone was ringing. I picked it up and heard the friendly voice of the night picture editor, Stewart.

"Hey, Steve!" he cried. "Long time no hear!"

"Hello, Stewart. Why do I get the feeling I don't like what I am about to hear?"

"Okay. Let's cut to the chase. First, speak to Marlene after we finish. She wants to talk to you and Cass pronto – but it's good I got to you first. She doesn't know I have your number yet, but I'll have to give it to her in a couple of minutes; she's bound to ask."

"Fine. Next?" I said sharply.

"We've had the Filth all over this place all afternoon." Stewart always called the police The Filth. It wasn't exactly a term of endearment, though as he talked he sounded quite pleased. A little activity must have brightened things up in the department for a while. I could imagine the boys in photographic helping the police look through an endless supply of meaningless material from the last twenty-five years. They would take the cops for a ride without their even knowing. There was no chance they would do anything that might compromise me. Of that I could be certain.

Stewart went on, "They want to know who shot the

pics and how we got them. They were anti-terrorist unit. Serious boys."

"Oh, great!" I groaned. "What did you tell them?"

"Bonnie was on the desk at the time. She said the pictures came in without a credit over the dial-in line. She said that the transmissions often come in like that, and that the desk sometimes didn't know who actually took the pic for days."

"They swallowed that?" I asked.

"Sure, she showed them stuff coming in like that, and they were happy. Liked the toys too, all those noises and lights." Stewart could be very condescending.

"But we never send without crediting the photographer."

"Mike was transmitting from the next room. Quite a good setup really. Nearly fooled me, but I saw him on the way to the coffee machine."

"I owe you guys," I said.

"Now, here's the good news. You don't have to go back to Amsterdam to cover the summit." He was positively excited about it.

"Oh, joy!" I said sarcastically.

"No, we have another assignment for you. You'll have to handle it very carefully."

"I can hardly wait. What is it?"

"We want you to find Green Rage. If they're screwing with us, you're going to nail them!"

When I got off the phone, I placed a cup of tea in front of Cass. "Well?" I said.

"That's not good." she replied. "Not good at all."

"We're supposed to contact Marlene. I hear she wants to talk to us pretty badly. Maybe you should tell me a little more. I get the impression you've been holding out on me." I lit a cigarette, and drank my tea.

"Why would I do that?" she replied petulantly.

"You mind if I smoke in here?" I asked, not waiting for her response. I wanted her to start talking. It would be easier that way. I was only guessing, casting around in the dark. I had no idea what game Cass was playing. I waited, and blew smoke in the direction of the half-open window.

"Okay," I said, "let's try it like this." I didn't want to sound too much like a schoolteacher, but it didn't do any harm, if it got a reaction. "The police have been all over the *News* today. They've been in photographic and they're almost certain to have been in with Marlene. If we're going to be hung out to dry, it would at least be nice to know why."

She shifted uneasily, her hands clenching each other. It was obviously news to her that the police were taking such an active interest in the matter. I'd never seen Cass look so uneasy. It wasn't as if she was usually intimidated by them. I wondered what was so special about the whole Green Rage business.

I went on, "Would you at least tell me this, did they leave a bomb?"

"No! There is no way they would do that."

"Are you sure?"

"Yes, I'm positive. There's no way they would endanger anyone's life!" She was angry now.

"You can't know that. They might not tell you, have you thought of that?"

"No!" she cried in exasperation. "They'd never do that!"

"They may have planted something, without even telling their friends in the inflatables."

"They didn't do that. They didn't vandalize anything either."

"Come on, Cass, what makes you so sure?"

"How could they? There was no time to. These idiots think they boarded the rig in Rotterdam; they have no idea. Don't you see? Those bastards at Allied are trying to fool everyone, including you. It looks like they're succeeding! Don't you realize, you idiot? They always win because of their lies, and they're winning now! Believe me!"

"I'm just trying to work it through Cass, that's all! What about the vandalism?"

"There was no vandalism, at least not when they left. The company could have done it. Must have done it! Remember there was only them and us out there. They'll probably trash the thing and then make it look like us, and get an insurance claim in as well, no doubt."

"I don't think Bruno and François had time to do anything much," I said, trying to be reasonable. "Also, it just doesn't seem to be like them. But, look – really – I don't know them!"

"Of course they wouldn't!"

"What makes you think they can be trusted like this?" I was exasperated. "We could have been accomplices to something we're not even aware of! It's not like it would be the first time the press was taken for a ride!"

"You're wrong!" She stormed across the room and stared out the window. The wind was rising outside.

"Really?" I shouted. "So how come you know so damned much about them? And this rig story, you got that all from a short release about the launching of a new accommodation platform? And how did you come to be so informed about Ekofisk?"

"I checked my facts …," she blustered.

"And what the heck kind of story was that about being called and told to be outside the office? Come on, Cass! You've been lying somewhere along the line, just tell me where, so we can work it out together!"

I paused. She'd clammed up. If she was going to spill, she'd do so soon or not at all.

"And Bruno, how come you knew so much of what his plans were?" I remembered how she had needed no introductions to anyone, and how she seemed to know more about things than any reporter would. "It's like you've met before or something. …"

She looked at me, a tear in her eye, and then said, "Yes, we've met before. Of course we have!" She was weeping freely now, the tension adding a razor edge to her voice. I was starting to feel sorry for having pushed her so hard.

"Well, tell me about it," I said, reassuringly. "I just want to know where we stand."

"There's not much to tell really," she answered slowly. Her voice softened. "You see, he's my husband."

Chapter 10

"HOW CAN YOU BE MARRIED?" My head reeled. "I mean...." I was searching for words.

"People do get married, you know," she replied. "We've been married for two years. And we've known each other since childhood."

I thought about this for a moment. "It makes things a little difficult, doesn't it? I mean, how can you be a journalist on a major newspaper if your husband is what Marlene would call a 'raving enviroterrorist'? It doesn't do anything for the impartiality of the media, if you see what I mean...."

"Listen, Steve, I know that. That is why I've always kept it very secret. I work under my maiden name, I even pay tax under my maiden name."

"Is that legal?"

"Not exactly."

"But how did you manage it? I mean, surely someone must know?"

"I am every bit a part of Green Rage as Bruno is. We started the operation five years ago. Since then we have placed a number of people in media positions. I am one of," she hesitated, "well, several."

"Wait a minute! You can't do that."

"We already did. Took some work, but we did it."

"But," I clutched my head, "you're one of us — aren't you?"

"Sure. But I'm also one of them — if that's the way you like to think of it." She went on in a calmer vein, "There's nothing illegal about what I'm doing. Nothing at all."

"But why?" I said. "Why this elaborate charade?"

"Because it's the only way. Bringing about change is about public opinion, mass media, and making people take notice."

"So hold a demonstration in Hyde Park, like anybody else!" I snapped back at her.

"Yeah," she sneered. "Wander round in circles with a banner while no one takes a blind bit of notice? No thanks. Hit them in their pockets and they take a lot more notice. Their shareholders give them all kinds of shit when this sort of thing happens. That makes them squeal."

"Look, you might as well tell me everything," I said with growing unease, "I mean, you've totally blown away any faith I may have had in reporters or the pressure groups." I shook my head to try to rid myself of hundreds of questions. "Jeez, I don't know which is worse, you or those buggers at Allied Resources. They've turned the thing round on us completely!"

"Us?"

"Yes, us."

"So you consider yourself with us? You won't blow the whistle?" She was looking relieved and in spite of these unexpected developments I never even contemplated the idea of shopping Cass. As far as I was concerned, we were in this mess together: just her, me, Bruno and a bunch of wild foreigners who may or may not have placed an explosive device on a deep sea oil platform. What company I keep. This was meant to be a simple job covering an environmental action. Instead, I found myself being nosed around by the cops in London, and Interpol wouldn't be far behind. The image of Clouseau in the uniform of a gendarme was already hunting me down. I was beginning to think that Hanson and his friends in London were preferable over Interpol. It was only a matter of time before they got involved, too.

"I would never give you away," I said. "Besides, heck, I agree with most of what you say! I just hope Bruno didn't leave a bomb on the rig. And I don't like the way you did this. I don't like any of it." I dragged heavily on my cigarette. "We have to find Bruno, and see what he has to say about it. There may be a way to come out of this thing clean."

"Should we call Marlene? What do we say to her?" she asked.

"I don't know. I suppose we could tell her that you and half her newsroom are deep-cover political plants, but she may not buy that one. Come to think of it, our credibility there at the moment is probably so low she won't believe anything we say anyway. You can be sure Allied's working hard to discredit our story, and us along with it."

"We have to say something."

"I know." I stubbed out my cigarette. "I'll call her, and play it by ear. I hate this, though."

I reached for the phone and dialed the newsdesk direct line for Marlene. A curt voice answered, "Newsdesk ..."

"Hello, Marlene, it's Steve."

"Well," she said sarcastically, "hello sailor."

"I saw the news at 6:00."

"Oh, I'm so glad. And what did you think of it?"

"They're lying. I'm sure of it. I saw the climbers go onto that rig, and there's no way they could have done any damage, they were on it less than ten minutes. Maybe less than five. The guys at Allied Resources are just adding some spin."

"You think so ..." She didn't sound convinced.

"Very clever spin, but just spin." I hoped she'd swallow it.

"Well, I'm glad you share my suspicions about that little press conference. I get a particlular feeling when I'm being fed a line of crap. I had it listening to that press conference. Now, in the meantime, you have to turn this thing around."

"Yes," I said. I wasn't going to like what followed.

"You know there is only one way to do that," Marlene carried on. "You will have to find Green Rage, and get a full explanation of how they pulled this thing off, and what they did while they were on board."

"That won't be easy," I muttered. I knew the futility of protesting, but also knew she was right. "We can try. Can I make a suggestion?"

"Of course, what do you have in mind?" I could tell by her tone that she was open to it, but surprised at a mere photographer throwing in his own initiative.

"I was watching that news conference. About the

third or fourth question threw in the possibility of an explosive device. I just wondered if you had anyone at that conference, and if they happened to catch the voice on tape. It was the first time the idea of a bomb was mentioned, and I sure didn't recognize the voice. I wonder if it was a plant."

"Oh, Steven," I hated being called Steven. Only my mother is allowed to do that.

"Is that too far-fetched for you?"

"Steven, Steven, do I seem so gullible?" she paused. I wondered if I really seemed that stupid. Then she continued, "We've been on that since the news conference, and — for what it's worth — I think it was a plant."

"The whole conference swung around at that point, as far as I could see, and that reporter was pretty quiet after the question. It smells bad. ..."

"Well, you leave that to me." I heard her lighter, and the sound of her drawing on her cigarette. I could almost see her sucking on the long black cigarette holder. "In the meantime, you and your pretty little friend Cass had better get something concrete. You have about twenty-four hours. Tomorrow we're leading on your pictures and we'll be annihilated for co-operating with these people. The following morning we'd better do something to make ourselves look very, very good."

"I see." Twenty-four hours is nothing. Twenty-four hours is just not possible. "That will be plenty. Marlene. I'm sure we'll be fine."

"Good. I knew I could rely on you. Now, there's the matter of the police."

"What?"

"Yes, they may be wishing to talk to you and Cass. So

far we've told them nothing. They're only sniffing around at present, and I've refused to tell them who wrote the story or shot the pictures. So they don't even know names. Yet. I don't think they'll arrest me, as they don't even know if there is a charge to be brought, until they inspect the rig. They can't get a warrant to search us if there's no charge, so they'd rather we co-operate as much as possible. I can stall them for a while. When they inspect the rig the chances are that things'll change radically."

"When'll that happen?"

"Well, if my information is right – which it always is – the rig will be diverted to Stavanger. The police will probably then be given the guided tour by Allied Resources."

"By which time they have had plenty of time to do whatever they like aboard that rig!"

"Quite."

"We'd better get moving."

"Can I speak to Cass?"

"She's gone out for a while," I lied. I felt like a three-year-old who has just been asked what he's doing and said "nuffing."

"Hmmm . . . you have work to do. Brief me in the morning. Now get on with it."

The line went dead. It could have gone a lot worse. We could have been hauled back to London to explain ourselves. We could have been dropped and assigned to financial coverage of the London Financial Futures Exchange.

I turned to Cass, who was still looking worried. "It could be a lot worse," I said.

"What do you mean?"

"Well, all we have to do is find Bruno, prove he's a

good guy and get that story into a credible form and over to London in the next twenty-four hours.... "

"I've no idea where Bruno is or how we're going to find him. He'll be lying low trying to avoid being spotted by the authorities. Exactly how could it be worse?"

WE SAT IN THE HOTEL restaurant staring into our seafood soup. It was beginning to get dark outside and we were no further forward. Cass had tried calling a phone number in Stockholm which Bruno had given her for use in an emergency. An answering machine took her message and that was the end of the trail. Cass said the number in Stockholm was a message centre for the group's operations. She didn't know any more than that. The calls might be checked every few hours, or once a month; she simply didn't know.

"You two certainly have a strange sort of relationship," I said.

"Of course," she replied. "But it's what we chose. We knew what we were getting into. As it is, our little operation is becoming very effective. We have influence far beyond what we originally set out to achieve. We've managed to really make a difference. Most of the targets are not quite as nimble as Allied Resources."

"But don't you find it difficult? I mean, you must hardly ever see him. That's a high price."

"But I can manage it. Besides, we have a job to do."

Cass was beginning to sound like a zealot. Now the guards were down, I could see it more clearly. Or maybe she was just incredibly focused and committed to her cause. Part of me admired her for having the courage to do what she was doing. In the meantime I began to wonder if I should remove myself from the situation with the least possible complication, and get as far away as humanly possible, while leaving her to carry the can.

"Don't get me wrong," she said. "I love him as much as any wife loves her husband. We just have a different way of living. He travels a lot. He's out there on actions in France, Germany, Holland, and in the UK. I'm working on a longer-term project, looking at ways we can extend the organization's influence."

"How nice," I said. I could almost hear the strains of a violin playing in the background. I felt I'd been duped. I was beginning to feel the whole readership had been duped.

"I know what you're thinking, and you're wrong."

"What do you mean?" I doubted she had a clue what was on my mind.

"You think I'm like a spy or something. I'm not. I'm a genuine journalist and I always cover stories as fairly as possible. When an issue comes up that I have a strong view on, I write what's on my mind. Of course I have strong views on the environment, and anything I write reflects those views. But those are the views of society in general – instead of 'industry' or 'Big Business.' Our work with journalists is simply to help those who share our views, give them a little edge. We try and get them the better jobs, make sure they're aware of the right opportunities, see they have excellent references – things like that."

"That doesn't seem so bad," I said, humoring her.

"It isn't. Remember how most jobs used to be filled? Nepotism and self-interest. If you shared the same view as the owner of the company, you were in. If you were for 'the establishment,' part of the old school-tie network, then you had it made. We're creating our own networks. We're getting our own people on the inside. And it works."

"Anyone I know?" I wasn't sure I wanted to hear her reply.

"I can't give you names, but yes. Several. One of which you see every night reading the news."

"You have to be kidding."

"Not at all. You see, our little organization has a good funding base. There are supporters out there who believe the only way is to take a radical approach. And they come to us!" She added in a more somber tone, "Though if we don't keep our image clean they'll drop us like a hot potato."

"I see your point. You get a bad image and the funding dries up. And this business with Allied is a threat to that."

"I'm not in it for the money, none of us are."

True lunatics never are, I thought. "But you still need the funding."

"We need money to put on stunts like this. You know that." I wondered how much the organization needed to carry out its activities. There were vehicles, boats, communications, accommodation, food and salaries to think about. Probably a lot more besides.

"That's all right, I can see it's a necessity," I replied.

Cass sipped her wine and played with her soup. We were losing time and there was no progress. In a few hours we'd have to report back to Marlene and we'd have nothing to appease her but a few notes and suggestions.

Reluctantly I began to admit to myself that perhaps she

was right. Perhaps Bruno hadn't done anything serious to the rig. If that really was the case we had to find him somehow and prove him clean. I was beginning to think it was a hopeless cause, when a voice came across the hotel intercom and asked for Cass Collingridge to come to the front desk to take a call. At least this might be a break.

Several minutes later Cass returned. She looked agitated but excited as she sat down. The call was from Stockholm. I could tell she had the feeling we might be in with a chance.

"They're trying to raise him on the radio. They think they have a good idea where he is, and they hope to make contact later tonight. If they reach him, we'll be given a place to meet him in the morning. I hope you can read a map, because it'll be in the middle of nowhere...."

"If they reach him." I completed the sentence for her. I was skeptical. "It's probably doubtful. And who are 'they,' anyway?"

"Stockholm's a liaison point for all our actions. It's like a clearing center, for radio, e-mail, and telephone messages. It's not a part of the organization I've been involved with. Ingmar and Bruno take care of all this stuff.

"You see we have to have our own security measures. The fewer people who know about these arrangements the better." She sounded exasperated. I listened patiently and let her go on. "We don't want to be infiltrated the way we infiltrate others, so we have a very low profile and very precise rules about contact. Half the people you were with this morning are wanted in several countries for their activities. They are brave people. We have to protect them."

"Well, I'm in your hands." Now it was just a matter of waiting. I get used to it, but never enjoy it. "So, what now?"

"They'll call, like I said."

We struggled through an uncomfortable dinner and coffee. I left Cass outside her room and went back to my own. I settled down with the radio on, listening to the reports on the BBC World Service about race riots in Birmingham for the second successive night.

I turned on the laptop and dug out a copy of the computer game "Myst" from my supply of entertainment CDs in my camera bag. These were specifically for burning off hours when I could not sleep, or for killing time. Before long I was relaxed, struggling with the problems of the D'ni civilization in an Age far off. Perfect escapism. I dozed off with the laptop beside me, a cup of tea going cold on the bedside table, and the radio talking to itself.

My sleeping thoughts slid into a dream of Cass, a blushing bride, walking up an aisle in the newsroom, with reporters and photographers tossing confetti. All the reporters wore evening dress, as did the photographers, and the assembled news staff. Cass wore a dress that was cream, but as I looked closer at it, I could discern words on it. I stared and realized the dress was made of newsprint, but had the texture of silk.

She clutched a bouquet in her hand, which on an impulse she tossed over her shoulder. I couldn't see who caught it at first – her back was to me. Then she turned and I saw it was Shandra. She shouldn't be there. She's not news staff. She came towards me, holding out the bouquet. I felt it in my hand, but there was something wrong. It was heavy. And it was ticking. I held it up to my ear, and realized it was a bomb. I tried to throw it far away, but my arm was weak. Try as I might I could barely move it. It fell to the floor at my feet. Shandra was laughing, giggling a little way off

That was when I woke up, dazed by the ringing of the telephone. The unfamiliar long ring of a continental telephone is even more intrusive than the double ring of British Telecom. The phone by my head rang so loudly I would have sworn it was inside my cranium.

"Ahhhh...." I said despairingly into the phone.

"What?" said Cass.

"Ah, Cass," I said.

"Are you awake?"

"No," I replied, and hung up.

It was only a moment before the phone rang again.

"Listen, Steve, get dressed and get your gear. I'll be outside your room in five minutes."

"Not again! We had an early one yesterday. What is it now?" My memory was slowly de-misting the picture of yesterday's events. Yes, I could remember now – we had to find Bruno.

"Just get dressed," she said, "I'll explain when I pick you up." She hung up.

Pick me up? I lay still for a moment before I rolled off the bed, and crawled to the bathroom. I managed to slide into the bath and turn on the shower. It woke me in an instant. By the time I was pulling my leather jacket on, Cass was knocking on my door. I had had the good sense to put the coffee on as I dressed, and as I opened the door, I placed a cup in her hand.

"Well, that was quick," she said. She looked like she

had been up for hours. She drank some coffee and sat down.

"We're in luck," she declared confidently. "I've spoken to Bruno."

"How'd you manage that!"

"I got patched in over the shortwave. We've some ground to cover, but we're going to see him in the next few hours."

"That's great," I said as the coffee began to clear my head. "Did you have a white wedding?" I asked.

"What?"

"Where are we going?"

"Ameland. Come on…."

"Coming," I said. I picked up my gear and my ruck-sack. Where the heck was Ameland?

"It's okay, you can travel light this time. Just take your photographic gear."

We walked through the sleeping hotel. It was just after 5 a.m. A sleepy night porter said something in Dutch, and we said we'd be needing the rooms for at least two more days. This seemed to satisfy him, and he returned to his dozing. In the car park in front of the hotel, we got into a Toyota Cass had hired. She took the wheel and I was asleep again shortly afterwards.

I woke as we drove up the ramp of a tiny ferry and Cass parked the car neatly in the dead center of the craft. We were one of only two vehicles on the ferry. The other was a postal truck carrying the morning mail. It was too early for any sane traveler to be moving around, that much I was sure of. The throb of the engines moved us off, and out into a misty seascape.

Cass stepped from the car, and disappeared into a

room at the side of the car deck. She returned a moment later with a steaming hot coffee in a tin mug. It was black and just what I needed.

I gathered my wits and asked her, "How did you finally get hold of him?"

"Bruno? I spoke to him on the phone, which was patched in to the shortwave. He's camped on the coast of this island, not far from the port on the other side. He made touch with the radio operator about midnight. I spoke to him at one this morning. It took me two hours to get hold of a car, but I managed to get Avis to open up for me."

"So what do you think we'll get from this?"

"Well, we have a plan."

"Great," I said. "What is it?"

"Oh, I think you'll like it," she said, a smile on her lips. It was good to see her looking a little more hopeful than I had left her last night. She got out of the car and went over to the postal truck behind us. A moment later she returned with a newspaper.

"That was a good guess," I said.

"How else do you suppose they'd get the papers?"

She opened the paper, and there on page three was one of my pictures. We couldn't read the story with it, but the picture was well used, and credited to Associated Press. "That's nice. They gave us some good coverage," I said, optimistically.

"I just wish I could read what they said!" Cass retorted. "They're quoting that Allied Resources spokesman, I can make that much out."

Before long the ferry approached a low-lying island, and pulled in to a modern dock. It looked very recently built. The dock facility was out of place among tiny cottages and shops of the tiny port town. It seemed to be the only building in the town less than a hundred and fifty years old.

We pulled away onto a country road that clearly saw little traffic outside the tourist season. A few minutes out of town Cass stopped where a track went off to the north. It was barely more than a sand path, but after checking a road map and some notes, she decided this was where we should head.

The track deteriorated rapidly, giving way to sand dunes that drifted across the road, if such a sand track can be called a road. A broken-down wooden fence lined the side of the route and then disappeared, and after another half-mile the road ended in a cleared area surrounded by dunes.

Cass turned off the engine and stepped out of the car. "Come on," she said. "We have to walk about a mile up here, if I'm in the right place."

I grabbed my gear and followed. The wind was fresh on this side of the island. I hadn't really followed our track, but to the best of my reckoning we were on the west of the island, the seaward side. There was no morning mist here, and the wind had a bitter edge to it. As we stumbled down the sand dune and onto the beach, I looked out at the troubled sea.

This was a very different sea from that of the previous day. The surf came crashing in, and the waves were capped in angry white horses, with spume blowing from many of them. This was the North Sea of books I had read. This was the North Sea of exposure and tumbling, mountainous waves piling in from the Atlantic and crashing in to smother a windswept shoreline. Thank God we'd done our marine exercise yesterday, and not today in the maelstrom before me.

We walked up the beach against a steady wind, leaning into the blast. I guessed it was blowing force six or seven. Our ferry crossing had been easy, as the channel lay to the lee side of the island, and so was sheltered. The next dry land to the west was probably northern England. There was plenty of room for the waves to build, plenty of room for them to become the angry gray sea before me.

We almost missed him entirely. Cass had walked past, and I was glancing at some driftwood that lay on the high water mark. As I looked at it I got the idea it was freshly burned, and walked over to it. Kneeling down, I felt it. Sure enough it was warm. That was when Ingmar stepped out of a dune further up the beach, dressed from head to foot in an all-weather survival suit, and waved, calling me over.

He wore a cap under his hood, and the ocher-colored suit look like something that might be worn by the Afrika Corps. Others appeared, dressed identically, and stomped down the loose sand of the dune. They were almost invisible, and only as I crested the dune did I see where they had dug in.

It was an extensive camp. Beneath a netting cover draped with scrub, the inflatable was covered with a sand-colored nylon cover. The same material was stretched over a wire running between two scrub bushes, and made a shelter. Beneath this was a large tent, and two smaller ones close by, all in Desert Storm camouflage. It was perfect, and to all intents and purposes invisible. Even if a helicopter had passed directly overhead, it would have had a hard job noticing the camp.

I called after Cass. "Hey," I shouted, "they're over here."

She turned, her hair wild and swept like the branches of those trees that tried to eke out a lifecycle in the dunes. As she headed back I could see concern on her face.

Bruno headed out of the camp, intercepting her and motioning her to come with him further up the beach. Well, I thought, a husband should have a few moments with his wife. Doubtless there would be some recriminations. By telling me about her involvement with Green Rage she had probably broken all their vows of secrecy. On top of that Bruno had a bit of explaining to do.

Ingmar came up to me and said, "Come, let's get under cover. There have been a couple of patrols up the coast already today."

We moved under the netting, and he stepped into the tent, after removing his shoes. I did the same, and Ingmar zipped the door closed. Inside the wind didn't seem quite so loud.

There were a couple of portable tables set up, covered with maps. A powerful shortwave radio sat in a stack of electrical equipment, including a satellite dish and a small portable television. CNN was on in the background.

"This weather's bad news," grunted Ingmar.

"Looks pretty dirty out there, but it could be worse," I said cheerfully. "It could be raining."

Ingmar looked skeptically at me. "It will be shortly," he said. "Schipol weather is broadcasting rain advisories for this area within the next thirty minutes."

"Oh well," I said, trying to lighten things a little. "Just

as well you were out there yesterday, hey?" I laughed, rubbing my hands together.

Ingmar's two crew were in the tent with us, one listening to a radio broadcast, the other looking into a device I recognized as the radar from their inflatable.

"Hey, that's cool," I said.

"Yes, we can see any traffic coming this way long before they see us. But we have to be careful with it. If they are military they can pick up our radar signal and home in on it. We have to watch out for that, so we just check it every few minutes. The weather is closing in, though. No one will look for us in this."

"There," I said, "every cloud has a silver lining!" My efforts to raise the glum mood seemed to be falling flat. In fact, Ingmar looked at me strangely. There was an uncomfortable gap in the conversation. "Actually," I said nonchalantly, "I find this weather quite bracing."

They were all looking at me. "Is there something you're not telling me?" I ventured.

"She didn't tell you already?" said Ingmar.

"What do you mean?" I laughed nervously, "Tell me about what?"

"She didn't tell you where you and Bruno are going today?" Ingmar sighed and then a smile spread across the broad face. "I think you had better sit down."

"CASS!" I SHOUTED. "Cass? Are you there?" I saw her on the sand up ahead, sitting with Bruno, a regular pair of lovebirds. "Cass, I think we should have a chat," I said, flushed with anger. "I just want to say, that if you think I am going out there in that sea you're bloody mad. You can forget it!"

She didn't say a word. Bruno had the somber look of a St. Bernard. How is it that the Danes always seem so damned strong and silent?

"Anyone who goes out in that needs his head examined," I concluded. "And you won't get me out there. Not now, not ever. Forget it. Not a prayer. No way, José!"

The rising wind almost carried the words away, but she said, "I see."

"Never!" I said with finality. She looked back at me blankly.

"Good," I continued. "Now that that's settled, when do we get out of here?"

"I was going to ask you, but I just didn't get the chance," she muttered.

I sat beside her. Bruno was making me feel guilty. Guilt I could live with. Drowning in the icy North Sea I could not.

"I can't do it," she said. "It needs a photographer. It needs someone impartial. Truly impartial. If it ever comes out that I'm involved, it would discredit us."

"But why do you have to put a photographer aboard? Haven't we got enough pictures!"

"You don't see, do you? Oh Steven – you can be such a clod!"

"What?" I spluttered.

"You see, we have to put you aboard. We have to have pictures showing that no damage was done. Don't you see, if they're going to trash it, they'll do it just before they arrive in Stavanger. It would be too suspicious to do it now, while it's still under tow. They'll wait until there are no contractors around towing it. They'll wait till no one can verify anything. It'll happen just before Stavanger."

"But you want to put a team aboard while it's under tow?" I asked. "You must be bloody mad."

"No one would go up those rungs, unless they really had to," said Bruno. "Least of all for the sake of a few bucks." He let out an exasperated sigh, "No one would risk that climb. It's bloody hard, and the rungs are cold and wet. One slip and that's it. With a pack on your back the next stop would be three hundred feet down on the seabed."

"How high is it?" I asked.

"We climbed about a hundred feet. But it was in shallow water," Bruno explained. "They're now in deeper water, so they've probably flooded the ballast. It would be less, but they won't flood more than they have to. It needs more pulling, the more they flood. That costs more in diesel and towing time. But this weather, it might make them flood deep. We'll have a full gale in the next six hours," Bruno stared at the growing sea. As if on cue, the first spots of rain began to spatter my face. They were not so much raindrops as lines of water blown flat against me in the climbing wind.

"You think, even if I was stupid enough to come with you, that you'd be able to board the rig in this?"

"I don't know for sure," he said frankly looking at the gathering storm clouds. "But I probably can. We know where it is now. We could rig the radar – which you can probably operate. Two of us might just make it. More, and we wouldn't have much chance. Fuel is the biggest issue. We just about have the range if we move about now. But I guess, if you're not going to do it, then we don't have to worry, do we?"

"You think I'm chicken?"

"God, is that your problem?" he sneered.

"What do you mean?"

"Chicken? Anyone would be chicken! That I can understand. No one would do this unless he really had to. So, no, I don't blame you if you are chicken! I think that we have trusted you and gone out on a limb for you. We went to a lot of trouble to put you in front of a great scene and you pressed the trigger – like you said yesterday, you owe us. Still, it's not your fight, is it? Why should you get involved?"

I stared at him, and then Cass.

Cass said, "It's payback time, Steve."

"Oh, God!" I groaned. How the hell do I get myself into these positions?

I STRIPPED DOWN and changed into wet weather gear Ingmar had arranged. I could hear the grunts and groans of the others dragging the inflatable to the shore, and then struggling to load it. The rader was dismantled and moved out of the tent, then reinstalled into the inflatable. As I pulled the last of several layers of clothing on, Cass came in to talk.

"You see it has to be you, don't you?"

"Yes," I muttered. I tried to smile but hiding abject terror has never been one of my strong points. "It's all right," I said. "You can't blame me being a little nervous. I know we'll be fine."

"Look, Bruno's very good. He'll get you both there. We have to do it now." She was trying to justify the haste. "Otherwise the fuel won't be enough. And once we lose them off the radar we'll never find them again. Ingmar reckons it's about twenty miles, maybe twenty-two."

"That's a round trip of forty-five miles – maybe more, depending how long we're aboard." I was thinking aloud. Forty-five miles in that sea. Just the two of us.

"Any news on the weather?" I asked as I stepped out of the tent into the windswept dunes.

"It'll get worse before it gets better," she said.

"You know, Cass," I replied, gently touching her arm, "your honesty can be a royal pain in the arse."

She laughed nervously. Laughter seemed a little inappropriate. It was an awkward moment. I pulled a pair of gloves on. "I guess we'd better get going," I strode down the beach towards Bruno with knees of jelly. One of the crew men was carrying a Seahorse engine on his shoulder into the surf, where the craft bounced and bucked in the white surf. He manhandled it onto the transom beside its twin, and then looked seaward. I could read his mind, and his face. He was wondering if this was worth it.

Bruno called to me to bring a bag that was resting further up the beach. He had at least planned far enough ahead to bring a large flask and some containers full of meats and cheeses. That would help, providing we didn't lose them over the side as the boat bounced around.

I tossed them to him and he stowed them under a net stretched over the floor of the boat, then strapped down the net. I stepped out into the boiling surf and pulled myself in as the crew held the craft against the waves that were trying to push us ashore. I sat just astern of the gantry that held the radar. All the electrical equipment, radar and radio, was securely protected by a plastic cover that kept even the heaviest of drenchings out. It would remain so until we found sea smooth enough to operate the unit without fear of it being soaked. Until then were were working on dead reckoning. Somewhere to the northeast was where the rig would be. It traveled at six knots, maybe even less in the heavy weather, so we had a fairly good idea where to look.

Bruno was kneeling in the stern, it being too rough to stand, and lowered the two outboard shafts into the foam. "*Ja,*" he said to the crewmen. "It's good. Let's get going."

Ingmar and his two colleagues thrust the bow out toward the surf as Bruno hit the ignition. The engines spun a moment, and then coughed a white cloud before firing and immediately powering out towards the wall of white water thirty yards offshore.

I turned and waved at Cass standing atop a sand dune watching. She waved back and I saw Bruno too was waving. Then he turned and concentrated on getting us away from the shore.

We actually seemed to be going uphill for a moment as we mounted a huge breaker, which crashed around us, and then we broke through its crest. Water piled into the craft and drained out as quickly through the self-bailers. I was wet outside, but the gear kept all but my face dry. The hood of the jacket was fastened tightly, its drawstrings pulled so that only my nose and eyes were visible. As another dousing followed, I thanked God for the waterproofs, and held tight as the engines began to climb in their song.

Bruno shouted to me, "It's the current, the Channel meets the main flow of the North Sea here." His voice was muffled and only just audible over the engines. "It makes it very rough. You'll have to hold on tight, or you'll be over the side, and I don't have enough fuel to spend hours looking for you."

I thought he was joking. I couldn't tell. I took a closer look at the life vest built in to the wet-weather jacket. It seemed good enough and there was a point for a harness. I took this and fastened it to a rope tied to a cleat on the bow. If I went over, I was at least going to stay with the boat.

We had a tank of fuel — which would last us about two hours. That was long enough to get there, stay aboard a few minutes and then head off. If we were to stay aboard long, we would be unable to reach shore with the remaining fuel. This was Bruno's biggest concern. He knew that if we made good time and located the rig quickly, we would have plenty of fuel. We'd have enough time for me to get on the platform and look around, shooting the condition and proving that these activists were not to blame for any damage.

If, on the other hand, we were unable to find the gigantic structure, we could waste hours looking for it before we located her. By then we'd never have enough fuel to get back ashore. It would be for nothing. As I thought about this Bruno wound up the engines and we began our chase. We quickly accelerated through twenty knots, through thirty, and then quite suddenly things seemed to get a little smoother. We were into deep water, the waves long and slow.

The bow of the inflatable flattened out as it began to settle into long strides, most of the hull proud of the water. Every ten seconds or so we would smack against a new wave, and then sail over it, more like a bird than any sea creature. Soon the regular whack began to jar right through me, and I found myself tensing for it. It was like doing sit-ups for hours on end, tense – and release. Tense – and release. Tense – and whack, the boat would shudder every now and then as we hit a bigger wave and then the cycle would start anew. For the moment we were dry, and we were moving fast towards our goal. And yet even as I watched the boiling surface of the water race by, the wind icy on my unshaven face, I could see heavy black clouds rolling in from the west.

I tried sitting on the floor of the craft, and I tried kneeling. I tried standing and was chilled by the blast of the cold wind, and couldn't keep my footing. I tried sitting on the edge of the hull, as I had been before. After twenty minutes of this I realised I couldn't find respite from the brutal battering of the hull's seemingly never-ending battle with the sea.

How cold and gray that sea seemed. And how hard it felt, too. No softness as we thumped again into the wall of unresisting waves. The light was definitely dropping. We headed into the thickest part of the oncoming storm with increasing speed. I wondered if the storm would make it harder to get results out of the radar. I checked my watch and to my surprise found we'd been on the go for a good half hour.

Bruno turned to me. His eyes were hidden behind goggles and his few days' growth of beard caught the water and held it in droplets. "Steve," he shouted over the sound of the engines, "get the radar turned on, and let it warm up for a few minutes. We need to get a fix on that thing."

I unfastened the rubberized plastic cover and looked

for a switch marked "On." There was an " I O" switch, which when pressed resulted in a few LEDs and a blinking bulb coming to life. I pulled the cover from the viewer, and, peering through the eye pieces at the viewing-scope, I saw a green arm of light begin sweeping around the circular screen.

"Give it a minute or so to warm up," called Bruno.

"How far do you think?" I asked.

"Ten miles, maybe a little less. It'll be well within range." He concentrated on giving us a steady position, our power off a little, but with less spray being poured onto us and the equipment.

I looked again after a moment. "I think I've got them," I shouted, excited now. The image somehow made the whole thing more tangible. Before, the idea of tracking them down had been a vague and desperate plan, even a stupid one. Now, there was an image on the screen, a real indication of the rig's position.

As I looked again I saw that the track of the rig and its four attending vessels was all wrong. They were going due west, they should be moving northwest.

"Bruno, they've changed direction!"

He looked round at me. "Are you sure it's them?"

"I've got one large return and four small, three ahead of the big image, and one about a mile behind. And nothing else, not anywhere on the scope."

"Here, come over here. You take it, just hold the wheel steady," he said. Then he quickly leaned over the radar and took a closer look himself.

"That's her for sure."

"No way it could be anything else?" I asked.

"No, this is the only one that size. No other traffic of

this sort has been mentioned in the shipping hazards report. I'm sure it's the right one." Of course, if we were wrong we might still have enough fuel to find the rig – maybe. But we'd never get back to shore.

"Why change direction?" I pressed. I knew that Bruno wanted to find the rig at any cost. Even if it meant not making the coast with our fuel. Maybe that was why he packed the food. Great. We may live long enough to die of exposure instead of starvation.

"Could be the weather," he said. "I think they know something we don't." He looked to the west, the direction they were now moving. "It has to be the weather. They are trying to put some water between them and the coast. I think they have had a weather update that is scaring them, and they don't want to be caught on a lee shore." He noted the bearing and we switched positions again.

I felt Bruno put in the course correction and we swung off to the left. "Better keep that thing on, but keep the covers on for the moment. We'll be going right into things for a while."

With that we resumed the battering that had gone before, yet this time it was a heavier swell, and the angry clouds in the distance were closing in on us. The wind was right into our faces, and now it carried a light but unmistakable rain. Having fastened the covers on the gear I glanced astern and saw the way the eastern sky seemed almost radiant compared to the darkness we were descending into. It seemed to be an omen.

Chapter 11

A WALL OF WATER SEEMED TO DESCEND on us as we slammed into the side of an enormous gray wave. The weight of the cascading water threw me to the floor of the inflatable, and I then felt myself floating and grabbed the rope handrail, saving myself from being carried out of the swamped boat.

The constant hammering of the hull was hypnotic. Bruno, focused on holding course to our appointment with destiny, and the rig, was less susceptible to the process, whereas I had drifted off into memories long buried in my head. But as we rose to the top of the next wave, a small moving mountain on the surface of the sea, I caught sight of a light in the distance.

"Over there," I called to Bruno, who looked, but already we were descending into the deep again. Moments later we climbed out of the trough and he saw what I was pointing at. There was a running light at the head of a mast, presumably on the rig itself. The light stood out against the gray-black cloud banks in the distance between the mountainous peaks of waves.

Bruno throttled back, and reached into one of the

bags secured beneath the retaining net. He pulled out a pair of Ziess binoculars and bracing his knees on the helm he stood, trying to make out what lay ahead. Somewhere nearby there was a patroling tug, which we had seen on the radar earlier. In this weather it would be easy to miss them, and easy for them to miss us.

Bruno called over the sound of the rising wind, "I can't see that other one. The tug. He's out here somewhere, but I don't see him."

"Let's get closer," I shouted, "I'll try and pick him up on the radar."

"*Ja,* but keep your eyes peeled. If they see us they'll probably try to run us down. I think we really pulled their chain last time."

I eased off the covers and turned the radar on. A few moments later I had the rig on the scope, but as we rose and fell in the deep trough I could see no other vessels.

"I don't have them ...I've got the rig...."

"It's this swell," said Bruno. "It is hiding them. Never mind. Let's go in anyway. We have surprise on our side." He pushed the throttles hard forward and we leaped off towards the huge structure. We saw no signs of another vessel as we closed and, nearing the enormous leg, I moved forward to help us dock onto the moving target.

"Use the strap," said Bruno, "it's stronger than the rope. Wrap it twice round the rung, and then clip it back onto itself."

The waves seemed even larger as we descended under the platform. As they rose and fell, they threatened to dash us against the cold yellow metal of the leg. Bruno nosed the craft in slowly from downwind, but the rise and fall of the sea made our movement erratic and unpredictable.

"I'm going to brush it. Get the strap secured," he urged.

I leaned over the bow and reached out as we approached. Six feet, then three feet, and then we would be pushing metal. We came in too quickly and bounced straight back before I could secure the strap.

"We try again," he shouted.

He came in more slowly this time. We were rising on a wave and then dropped away quickly. The side of the leg seemed to shoot vertically upwards, as though we were falling down a shaft. As the wave bottomed out, I slipped the strap through the rung, and let it play out. As we rose, about eight feet of strap rattled out of the boat as we were lifted on the swell.

"Secure it straight back over itself," called Bruno, "it will be fine." I did as I was told, and the three-inch-wide strap held us firmly. I figured it probably had a breaking strain of two or three tons.

Bruno cut the engines, and a moment later the strap took the strain as we became part of the tow, still moving at a steady five or six knots through the troubled sea. The strap snaked out, till we trailed fifteen feet behind the leg. "You better get your gear. We have to move fast now."

He unclipped his safety harness and moved to the bow, pulling in the strap hand over hand. The pitching of the sea seemed worse now we were secured to the monstrous steel structure. "Okay," he called over his shoulder, "grab the rungs and climb."

I moved forward. About three feet away the rungs led skyward. Looking up, I was shocked at the height we were to climb. It was less than Bruno and François had scaled, but it seemed impossible from where I was standing. I slid my camera bag round my neck on a short strap, so it rested high on my chest. It contained one camera, a couple of lenses and some film. The bare minimum to do the job properly.

Bruno jerked the strap and the inflatable came up against the side of the leg. I grabbed the highest rung I could and scrambled up, suddenly aboard the structure. Its cold metal reality seemed alien in that sea. It could just as easily have been orbiting a planet.

Moments later I was waist deep in freezing water, in danger of being floated off by my own life preserver. I hung on to the tiny rung as the icy water surged around me. Both my hands were crammed into the six-inch-wide rung as I felt the water rise still further, and begin to drag me off. I felt a cut open on my hand as the cold steel bit into my gloved hand. The warm trickle of blood ran to my wrist and up my arm, inside my sleeve.

I could see Bruno watching helplessly. I had mistimed my jump. I should have waited till the wave was at its highest point, but it was too late to think of that now. The freezing water sucked about me and I hung on for my life. If I fell I knew the weight of my gear would pull me down before I even got a breath.

And then, as the wave subsided, I found myself hanging from my hands, my arms burning and trying to pull themselves from their sockets. I could feel blood running down my arm, warm on my skin, yet chilling. Ten feet below me, Bruno stood by, unable to do anything but wait to see if I dropped. I kicked out with my legs and found a foothold on a rung. I scrambled up one, two and then a third rung. I could see the sea returning, racing up. I struggled up a couple more rungs. The wave rose to lap over my rubber boot, but didn't snatch me away. I kept climbing. I was going up to the top, come what may.

The handholds may have been tiny, and the distance great, but I didn't slow till my head was emerging from a hatch out onto the deck, high above the sea. Below, I saw Bruno climbing the way I had. Looking around me on the deck, things seemed strangely tranquil.

Here the deck neither pitched not slammed. I could see our boat far below, trailing at the end of its strap. Far astern, probably a mile or so, I could see a tug. They were clearly unaware of us. I could not see them, but I knew that, were I to move around the rig, I would see the towing tugs. For the moment I just wanted to lie flat on my back and thank God I was on something resembling dry land.

If I stepped over to the leg a moment or so earlier, I would have been lower down, and washed clean off, like a piece of sea junk. For Bruno to recover me single-handed would have been all but impossible.

A light smattering of rain fell on my face, and Bruno's head appeared from the hatch.

"You like to swim, *ja?*"

"*Ja,*" I replied. Bruno could be a real joker.

WHEN I GOT TO THE PLATFORM deck I took a bandage from my camera bag and wrapped it tightly around my hand. It was no longer painful, but gave a steady aching throb. I could see the ropes the Green Rage activists had secured the banner with. They were the white fiber ropes flecked with red, familiar to anyone who has done a little rock climbing. They were fastened with locking shackles, and remained where François and Bruno had placed them. All other evidence of the banner had been cut away.

I shot a frame of the fasteners, and then began shooting other, miscellaneous scenes of the rig. I had Bruno holding the copy of the day's newspaper which Cass had bought. I struggled to think of her as his wife. He held the newspaper, obscuring his face. It looked almost comical, yet it made the point. Green Rage had returned to the rig, and it was undamaged.

The main accommodation area was locked up, but I shot a few frames of Bruno standing at the door with the newspaper. "Did you go anywhere else?" I asked.

"No, we were only up here for a few minutes before we jumped. We didn't have time to get anywhere else."

"They'll make out you were here for days. They think you came aboard in Rotterdam."

"Let's see if we can get in. Maybe we can get photographs of the interior undamaged," said Bruno.

We tried all the doors at deck level. The place was sealed up tight. Climbing the gleaming painted ladders, we reached a control platform for some sort of crane, probably for loading supplies aboard. At the foremost end of it, a hatch gave access to what appeared to be a control room on the side of the structure. I tried the hatch, expecting it to be locked fast. It fell open under my touch.

"Bravo!" said Bruno.

I stepped through the hatch, quickly followed by Bruno. I closed it and followed as he strode across the room to a bank of instruments. "It seems to be a control room," he said, poking around. He looked at a bank of switches. "These are circuits for the electrical system, and look – this is all the lighting arrangements for the platform. What do you think?"

"It's like the bridge of a ship," I said, not feeling as if I was being much help, "but with no wheel."

"It's probably only operational once the rig is sited and anchored in place. I don't see any navigational gear here," said Bruno as he looked about the place. He opened a door to an extensive communications room. I stepped through to investigate. There were seats for three operators, terminals for each user and a rack of radio equipment that filled one wall. A portable Inmarsat terminal was already set up, placed on the main control desk.

It was on, the laptop-like terminal and handset ready for use. Of all the equipment we had seen, it was the only piece turned on. "Bruno," I said. "Look at this."

He stepped in. "Hmmm – Inmarsat. Very nice. Expensive."

"Why do you think it's on?" I asked, a thought forming and alarm bells immediately going off inside my head. "Look," I said. "This is a portable."

"Sure," he replied.

"But it's not plugged in!" I said.

"So, it runs on a battery. . . ."

The same thought formed in his mind. Battery power was good for a while – three or four hours maybe. Five at most. Typically it would be turned on, used to send, and then switched off. The fact that it was here, on, and running on battery meant only one thing. Someone else was aboard and they would be back shortly.

"Quickly, let's get some shots and then get the heck out of here," I said.

I shot Bruno in our pose with the paper again quickly, and then once more, out in the control room. We hastily retreated back onto the supplies deck, closing the hatch behind us.

Our best guess was that there was a small group aboard the rig, possibly in the mess hall, totally unaware of us. We hurried down the ladder, and back towards our entry point. I glanced in a window, and then threw myself to the deck. I was sure I had seen someone moving in there. The reflections in the glass were deceptive, but as I turned to Bruno I saw that he had seen the same thing. Crawling along below the level of the windows, we slowly moved towards the hatch that was our means of retreat.

Our managing to move around so far without detection had been pure fluke. We crouched at the edge of the deck we had to cross. From where we were, no one could see us, but the dash across thirty feet of open space could be our undoing. "Let's get it over with," I said. If word got out, the tug astern would disable our inflatable in a couple of minutes and we'd be stuck.

Bruno said, "I'll go first. Pulling the inflatable up the side of the leg's a tough job. I'd better be first down there, and then once in the boat I'll bring it in close for you. Let's go." He was on his feet and running, and I followed as swiftly as I could. I stashed my camera and sealed the bag before throwing myself down the hatch behind him. As I looked down the descent I would have to make, it seemed an awfully long way. And the sea seemed still more troubled.

Once I was beneath the deck, the full sound of the wind and the waves filled my ears again. I concentrated on rungs below me, feeling the pain return to my hand like a hot iron. The only course was to ignore it and keep moving. Bruno was almost down. I paused to catch my breath and saw him hauling on the red strap. As the boat neared the leg, he threw himself at it and managed to scramble aboard.

I heard the engines start and he looked at me expectantly. I climbed down as rapidly as I could and then, as Bruno danced with the rise and fall of the waves, waited for the right moment.

One minute Bruno was ten feet below, then the next, as a wave lifted him, he was level with me and I was standing in ankle-deep water. He nudged the boat closer, and as he rose up to meet me I stepped aboard, landing lightly on the gunnel and stepping in. My return was considerably better than my exit.

As he eased the throttles ahead, we moved under the rig, then sharply off to the starboard side and began pulling away. I could see no sign of the patroling tugboat astern. Down here in the rough and tumble of the sea, we were practically invisible again.

Bruno checked the compass and set a course southeast, back towards the Ameland coast. The rig was soon left behind us. My gear was stowed and safe, and there just remained an hour of pounding the sea to get us home. The movement of the craft was much more comfortable this time. We had the wind at our backs, and the waves were traveling in the same direction as us. While we still leaped over them with bone-shuddering impacts, they were longer and the motion considerably easier.

At one point I thought I could see a tug far away in the distance following our course, but then I lost sight of it. I must have been mistaken. The rig was quickly lost to view and we made our way homeward.

How Bruno found the right patch of beach and the retreat in the dunes, I will never know. We made our way down a completely featureless, flat Dutch coastline, until he swung the boat hard shoreward and came skidding through the surf onto the shore. For the last forty minutes we had run on a single engine to conserve the dwindling fuel.

Ingmar stepped out of the dunes with François. They greeted us with hot coffee and brandy. Cass tumbled down the beach in a cloud of flying sand to her husband's side.

"We were worried. We figured you ran out of fuel half an hour ago," she said, hugging him. He suddenly seemed about five years younger, the strain having crept onto his face these last couple of hours.

"It was the wind. It gave us a little more range when it was behind us. Damn close, though." said Bruno. We were both chilled to the bone, and stomped up the beach to the tent, where we fell inside and changed out of the sodden clothing into dry gear.

Ingmar said that things had been quiet here ashore. There had been no patrols and they were no longer very concerned about being discovered.

"All the more reason to keep a low profile," said Bruno, ever a voice of caution. "We'll stick to the plan, and make our way north for the next few days. We can worry about what we do beyond that later. In the meantime, Ingmar and François, maybe you would be kind enough to borrow Cass's car and get us some fuel from the village."

Ingmar nodded and arranged moving several jerry cans down to the Toyota. They left quickly, and I knew that after Cass and I left they would be on their way, weather or no weather.

Cass, Bruno and I sat in the tent, while François restored the heat to our bodies with hot vegetable soup and bread rolls.

"You going far in this?" I asked. The weather seemed to be deteriorating further. The side of the tent was being tugged and pushed by the wind.

"I think it will hold off for a while. There are a few islands east of here I haven't been to in a while. I should like to acquaint myself with them again. I used to go there as a kid."

"You grew up round here?" I asked.

"My father and I used to sail down this coast each summer. We camped on many islands on this coast."

"It sounds a great way to spend the summer."

Bruno seemed to soften. "It was. They were good times. It was a good way to grow up. But it seems a long time ago now."

"Childhood always does," said Cass, "but it's with you always. Look at you. This whole coast is part of you. You're a product of it."

"That's pretty profound, Cass," I laughed.

"Yes. Maybe it is, but it's true. And if it wasn't, you'd probably still be floating around out there lost, and out of fuel."

Chapter 12

THE TRAIN PULLED OUT OF GRONINGEN and rattled south. Cass was sleeping, stretched out on the seat opposite me, lost in dreams of Bruno. Their parting had been a little tearful, and I suspected it would not be long before they reconsidered the way they were living.

We flew straight from Amsterdam into Gatwick. I was giving the plastic a good belting, but no one seemed to be complaining. The company must have credited me in advance for my expenses. I wanted to get back to the newsdesk and talk to Marlene about the situation in person. I was also concerned that I had not managed to talk to Guy in the last week. I couldn't duck out of London for the rest of my life, and enough time had gone by for the heat to have died down a little.

I called Guy on the cell, as Cass and I traveled into town on the train. It was late in the day, but when I finally got hold of Guy, he was quite insistent.

"I'm glad you called," he said, understating the situation. "I think we should meet, tonight. How's that sound to you?"

"Sure," I said. "Can you tell me what it's about?"

"Not really, not here. I'd like to chat somewhere away from the office." I visualized him looking over his shoulder as he spoke. It was a picture at once comical and tragic. And yet that really was the reality of the situation. Not knowing who was to be trusted complicated things. I thought about what Cass had said before we left. Strathclyde, the editor, had started this ball rolling.

I felt a growing unease about going in to the *News*. The memory of the beating I received had not faded as quickly as the bruises.

"I have to see Marlene. Is there a problem with me coming into the office?" I asked, hoping he'd be able to give me some kind of indication about what the problem was.

"Yes, I think that would be unwise. I don't really know. I just don't think. . . ." He was clearly uncomfortable with the idea.

"I see. That's pretty clear. I'll get her to meet us away from the office, then. I thought things would have blown over by now," I said.

"Well, they haven't. In fact I should say the opposite. There seems to be a flap on."

"But who, Guy? Who's so interested in us? You said it didn't look like a civil product. You said in that e-mail that you thought it may even be military."

"Yes, or at least government. Someone with some security smarts for sure. Look, I don't know for sure, but there have been strange things going on ever since you appropriated the contents of that hard drive. And they're not cooling down. Not one degree."

"All right," I said. "I'll fix up a place for us to get together and e-mail it over to you."

"No, don't do that," he said. For some reason he didn't trust the e-mail system. That worried me. If he was concerned about the security of his e-mail then we all had problems. "Leave a message on my pager and we'll get together at nine tonight. Right?"

I scribbled down the pager number he gave me and rang off.

"Cass," I said, "I think we'd better be a bit careful about seeing Marlene in the office."

She looked up from reading a newspaper and said, "What?"

"Guy says it's not a good idea." I replied. It sounded a little silly, paranoid even.

She sighed. "What's he saying – Marlene's a problem? Or the office? I can't believe this is still such a big issue. Why does anyone care about it, anyway?"

"Search me," I replied, just as exasperated as she was.

"No," she said. "I'll drop your film with Marlene and see her. If you don't want to go in, then that's fine, but I've had enough of this.

"Where are you staying tonight?" I asked. This was a subject we had both avoided thinking about. Were we going to be returning to a London fit for work-weary journalists and photographers dying to go home, or a London full of people wanting to restructure my face? Or hers, for that matter. I felt very nervous about leaving Cass on her own.

"I don't know," she said. "Maybe we'd better stay over my parents' apartment again. Just till we know there's no one hanging around waiting for us. That's smart."

"Yeah," I said. "You're probably right."

"Look, Guy didn't say you'd have a problem in the

office. It might be fine for you. I'm the one they seem to want." I said it without conviction. At least sleeping over with her, I could be sure she'd be fine. It would have helped if I'd known what I was supposed to be so worried about, but that would have to wait until I'd seen Guy.

"You go on up to the apartment," she said, digging around in her pocket for a key, then handing it to me.

She went back to her paper, reading the home news intently. "Boy, did we miss some fun!" she muttered.

THE APARTMENT WAS as we'd left it. That was a relief. I had been worried they would track us down and trash the place, but that wasn't the case. I picked up the phone and dialed Guy's pager and told him to meet me outside the recording studio on Abbey Road, and we'd go on from there.

I had a little time to kill, so I dialed my apartment, to see if Sykes was back from his sister's on the south coast. The phone rang and rang, but there was no answer. Knowing Sykes, he was either down at the Prince Of Wales, or still on the coast.

I remembered I had Shandra's number in my wallet. I pulled it out and dialed her apartment, not really knowing what I was going to say. The phone rang twice before she picked up. My heart was in my mouth, for no good reason, and then I realized the voice on the other end of the phone was an answering machine.

"Hi, Shandra, it's Steve. Just wondered how you are, thought I'd give you a call. You can get me on my cell, you've got the number. See you around. Bye."

Not too committed, not too hungry. I figured it was about right. Maybe she would call me. Maybe pigs would start flying in and out of the Docklands Heliport.

Cass had not shown up when I left the apartment an hour later, to meet Guy. I left a note for her saying I should be back within about an hour, and that there seemed to be something wrong, and that we could work it out when I got back. I left the note on the door, and slid the key beneath the doormat.

I stood around the crossing for ten minutes before Guy's battered old Saab pulled up. The door swung open with a resounding creak, and I slid inside. The fastidious blond engineers who created the car would have been appalled. He pulled away, back into the slow moving stream of evening commuters.

"Where to?" he said.

"Let's park on the edge of the Heath," I said.

He pulled away and headed towards Hampstead.

The neon glow of the yellow street lights reflected off the clouds, lending a ghostly atmosphere to the Heath as we walked the tree-lined path. A cool breeze lifted the first autumn leaves. They danced away at knee height down the path.

"Well?" I asked, impatient now. I wanted solid answers and I was tired of vague suspicions.

"Very strange," he said. He looked like an extras in an old war film, the sort who represent the "back room boys" with thick glasses and an ungainly appearance. It was an image that suited him perfectly. I suspected he cultivated it intentionally.

"It's their encryption. It's very good. Really, I've not seen anything quite like it, which is why I think it may be military or at least government. I was in that data yesterday and tried an old trick. You find documents that start with similar formatting, and look for sequences. You don't even need to know what the numbers are. If you have a short line, followed by another – say around thirty-five characters long, and then another with only ten characters and then one with less than eight, well obviously it's an address...."

"Right," I said sarcastically. "Obviously."

"And then there's usually some sort of date somewhere nearby, and then you get a line that starts XXXX and then XXXX or XXXXXXXXX or something. Anyway, those first four Xs spell out the word "dear." You see what I'm trying to do?" he asked.

"Not exactly," I replied.

"I'm trying to find the start of a letter. From there I trace through the address, down to the words 'Dear Whatever-his-name-is.' Once I can find the word 'dear' I have the first two vowels and a couple of consonants. And that gives you four out of twenty-six characters. Two of them are vowels, see! Fill in those, and you start to get partially complete words, and then you guess other letters, until you have something that matches, and you start to get more letters. Anyway," he said warming to his subject, "I've modified the dictionary in Microsoft Word, and I think I can have it broken sometime tomorrow. The spell checker will actually end up cracking this thing for us."

"Blimey," I replied, "I knew that thing was good for something!"

"But look," he went on, "I think you should know, there's someone inside the company who's very interested in you. I wondered if maybe it has to do with this story."

"Who?" I asked. The list of people taking a professional interest in my welfare was growing. There was Hanson's partner, whoever he was, and the police because of the Green Rage incident, just for starters. Allied Resources might want to have a word, too. Chances were they probably had some heavies trying to find us.

"I don't know," said Guy. "I just stumbled across it a couple of days back."

"What do you mean?"

"I sent you an e-mail by mistake the other day, and so I figured I'd go into your mail and lift it out."

"You can get into my mail?" I said, wondering what private material I might have that would embarrass me.

"Of course, anyone's in the company, actually." He was quite matter-of-fact about it. Interesting.

"So what did you find?" I said.

"Well. That's the funny thing, you see," he said, as if only a complete fool would fail to understand. "I didn't find anything."

"So?"

"I mean I couldn't get in. I got this error message saying the files were already being accessed. So of course I figured you were in there checking the messages – that would be normal. Only thing was we had some phone troubles yesterday, and the main switchboard was down."

"Yeah, so what?"

"So you couldn't have been dialing in. Could you? Nobody from outside the office could dial in. Did you try?"

"No. I don't think I did dial in yesterday, now I think about it."

"Well, someone was in your mailbox. You see, there's a file-locking mechanism. If someone's in one of those files, another user can't get in."

"You're losing me, Guy."

"Okay, think of it like this. Only one person can check your mail at a time. When I tried — the system wouldn't let me in. That can only mean someone else was in there. And checked out your e-mail and for all I know your other files too. After all, if they were in your e-mail, and they were inside the building, they would have access to the network, and probably had a good look through your machine. Anything in there to worry about?"

"No," I said, "nothing that I can think of."

"I've got something else for you." He handed me a sheaf of papers, stapled and folded. "This is a list of all the phone numbers I have already got from his machine. They seem to be just a set of contact lists, but they were scattered about a bit. Not all in the Exchange files. Maybe they'll help you. Maybe you'll recognize something."

"Thanks, we need something to work on. It's about time we brought this thing home once and for all." I shoved the sheets into my jacket. We turned and headed back towards the car.

"Guy," I said, as I climbed back into the Saab. "Would you do me a favor? I know you've already done so much. And this is a bit tricky, but maybe it's important."

"Go ahead."

"See if you can get any information on Jeremy

Carfax; he's a shareholder and some sort of super-suit with the company."

"Carfax, okay. He has e-mail with the company. I've seen his name on a few network lists."

"Any idea what he does?"

"Not a clue. I'll check him out."

"Thanks, Guy," I said, as he pulled away and headed back the way we had come.

SITTING AT THE KITCHEN TABLE, I worked my way through the sheets of contacts Guy had pulled. As he had said, this was a convoluted collection of names and numbers. Some made a little sense, while others made none whatsoever.

As I flicked through the list I began segmenting them by the first three digits, to get a rough idea of location. I started with Kelly Watson. Her number started with 289, so I looked for others with that prefix. There were several, but it wasn't long before I stumbled over an unexpected break. Another name had that same number. Patricia West, not only sharing the number, but also mentioned with another number further down the list. I wondered what it meant. Something, that's for sure.

When Cass arrived a while later I showed her the lists Guy had pulled, and she scanned down the names, looking blank. "Look at this," I said, showing her the name with the same number as Kelly Watson. "What d'you think it means?"

"Well, it looks to me like she used to share the girl's apartment, and then moved. I can tell because in my own address book I often have someone listed more than once. When they move I put their new details in, usually before deleting the old ones. It looks like he forgot to delete the old details. I've done that myself. Which means we have someone – complete with phone number – who used to live with the girl, and is also connected to Hanson."

"Not a particularly nice club to be in," she said, then added, "And she lives quite close. This is a West Hampstead number. That's going to be very close to here. I think we need to find out everything we can about this Patricia West person. She may be just the break we've been waiting for."

Chapter 13

THE FOLLOWING MORNING WE TRACKED DOWN Patricia West. It only took one phone call to the number listed in the documents Guy had supplied.

The phone rang twice before being answered. "Marble Arch Hotel, can I help you?"

Cass hung up the phone and twenty minutes later we were outside the imposing Edwardian structure. The hotel was typical of its time: too small to be particularly profitable, but too big to be converted to a luxury residence. It combined the functionality of the age with the poor design of purpose-built hotels of the thirties. And yet it did merit four stars, which glowed on a highly polished plaque by the doorman, who eyed us suspiciously as we walked straight in. We were clearly not tourists, and probably not affluent enough to afford the luxuries of this joint.

Once inside I flicked my exhausted cigarette through the revolving door, not quite making it out, which earned a withering look from the red-coated doorman. I winked at him and carried on to the reception desk. I didn't know what I could attribute my mood to, but I was feeling pretty gung-ho. After all, I had been knocked from pillar to post in the last month, and now we were getting a real break.

"I'm here for Patricia West," said Cass to the receptionist. Nice line, I thought. It carried authority with the right mix of interrogation.

"She's expecting you?" said the receptionist.

"Of course," said Cass. How could Patricia West not be expecting us? "Is she still on the third floor?" she asked, after an awkward silence.

"She's in 407," said the receptionist.

We turned and walked to the elevator. A moment later we were walking along the corridor looking for Room 407. It was the last door, right at the end of the corridor.

I knocked, and as the door opened a crack, I slid my foot inside. I could see a young woman of twenty-one or twenty-two, dressed in a bathrobe, and looking as though she had only just woken after a heavy night. She squinted at us and tried to adjust her vision.

"Miss West, we'd like a word." Cass sounded quite firm. It crossed my mind that she could be here with a burly friend who would delight in knocking my remaining teeth out. Best let Cass go first. "You don't mind if we come in, do you?" said Cass, and then barged her way inside. I followed and closed the door behind me.

"Who are you?" the woman asked, fear mixing with outrage at the intrusion. "Are you cops?"

"No," said Cass, "there's nothing to be afraid of."

"Well?" she said, trying to gain composure and seeing we weren't to be put off. "Who are you? What you doing coming in here at this hour?"

"We're reporters," said Cass.

"Oh my God!"

"It's all right!" I said. "There's no trouble. We just need your help with something."

"We know you used to share an apartment with Kelly Watson," Cass went on. "We're investigating her murder."

"Her murder?" Ms West looked shocked. It was clearly news to her, or she was an accomplished actress.

"You hadn't heard? It was in the papers," I said. "Was she a close friend?"

"No," she said, clearly shaken by the news. "Not really a close friend. Just someone, you know, I used to hang out with. Shared a place with." She sat down on a sumptuous chaise longue, and folded her legs beneath her. "So, what happened to her?"

"She was stabbed. Several times, I think. It was pretty messy."

She let out a gasp and clutched her shoulders in a study of sudden insecurity. Then she said firmly, "I'm not telling you anything, you know."

"It's okay," I said. "We don't need to quote you, we just need to straighten some stuff, that's all."

Then Cass chimed in, "We know about her work, Ms West. We're just tying up a few loose ends. Like, when you moved out. . . ."

Ms West was remaining tight-lipped.

Cass continued, "Of course, since you're so close to Kelly the police would probably be very interested in chatting to you, wouldn't they?" That got her attention. Cass went on, "But we wouldn't think of telling them about you. Not with you being so helpful. . . ."

"I moved out about a month ago. It was getting difficult. A really bad atmosphere." She shifted uneasily.

"You used to take clients back there?" asked Cass, cutting to the jugular.

"Yeah, it was a good pad," she replied, as if it was the most normal thing in the world. "We shared all the costs, so it worked pretty well for both of us."

I figured I'd better leave Cass to this. I was way out of my depth.

"What happened with Hanson?" she asked.

"You know. He was getting greedy. More greedy than ever, actually. You know, she was so bloody thin because she could hardly afford to eat!"

"Come on," I said, unable to resist the opportunity, "she must have been coining it in there!"

"Not after Hanson took his piece of it!"

"How much was that?" asked Cass.

"He was taking about eighty percent. That way she'd pay him off in two years, if she worked hard. That's what she kept saying. That was about all that kept her going. That bastard!"

"That's a hell of a lot to pay back," I said. She must have been into the guy for a lot of money.

Ms West continued, "She's been working almost solidly since she got here."

Cass was nodding, "Uh-huh. How long was that?"

"She said she got in about a year ago, but I didn't like to pry. She liked some privacy."

"I'm not surprised," said Cass. She looked at Ms West expectantly.

"He fixed her up with the name, after getting it from some fella in Belfast. 'Kelly Watson' – and her hardly able to speak a word of English!"

"Yeah," said Cass, thinking way ahead of me. "I could

see how that would cost! And the others?" She was shooting wildly in the dark now. I felt sure she'd come unstuck any moment. Still, what was the harm?

"We never got to meet them, but he would come on Tuesday and Sunday mornings to pick up the money. He usually had a lot of it. He was going round most of the girls and picking it up all at the same time. He must have had at least four or five, maybe more."

"Same arrangement?"

"Yeah. He fixed them up and made sure they had documents, and they paid him from what they earned."

"He must have been making a packet!" I said.

"Oh, he was doing all right," she said, "but it wasn't just him! It was that other fella, the toff. He was the one doing really well. He used to come with Johnny, picking up the cash − I don't doubt he kept a good wedge of it. And he always wanted something extra."

"I see," said Cass.

Cass and I looked at each other. So far we'd winged it completely. Now we were at a loss. Hanson had to be working with someone, and they had been the ones who had abandoned him. They were probably the ones behind most of his rackets.

Cass stood, and said, "Thank you, Miss West. You have been very helpful." She was obviously ready to leave.

I followed suit, wondering why we were leaving.

"Do you think they'll find out who killed her?" asked Ms West.

"I don't know," said Cass. "Probably not."

"If they do, we'll let you know," I muttered.

"You do that," she said, as she closed the door behind us.

We left the hotel quickly. Outside, we walked to a nearby coffee shop and sat for a moment to regroup.

"So he was smuggling people in and buying their papers. Is that what this thing is about?" I said as I carried two weak coffees from the counter to a table by the window.

"That seems to be it," said Cass. "Then they go on the game and Hanson gets paid back." She paused, and looked into the distance for a moment. "Some poor parents probably thought they were doing their daughter a favor to get her out of wherever it was she came from," she shrugged. "Romania or Bosnia, maybe. They hear he can help, and all she has to do is pay him off when she gets a job. Only he sets her up with another kind of work, where the pay is cash and he can manage her affairs."

"So all the girls end up doing this?"

"It fits – unless you have a better idea."

"No – I think you're there. I just don't understand who the other person is."

"Other person?" said Cass quizzically.

"The one she said was a toff. Remember, she said there was another guy that came round and collected the money with him sometimes. What's going on there? It sounds like he had a partner."

We walked back towards the tube and headed for Fleet Street. Beneath the News Consolidated building we retrieved Cass's Escort from the company parking garage. It coughed and spluttered up the ramps until emerging out onto Norfolk Street. Cass swung south and headed for Tower Bridge. We then drove south over the river. It was time to go and chat with Mrs. Hanson.

A REMOVAL VAN was parked outside the house as we walked up the drive. Two enormous men carried an even more enormous sofa out of the front door. They were followed by two more, each carrying crates carefully packaged by moving professionals.

"Hello Mrs. Hanson," Cass called through the open door. "Can I come in?"

A voice came back from the kitchen, "If you're selling anything you can fuck off."

Cass glanced at me, then called back, "No, not selling anything, not today anyway."

"Come on in, but keep out of the way of the gorillas. They'll flatten you as soon as look at you."

We both stepped inside, and found the source of the voice in the kitchen. I recognized the bleached blond hair the moment I saw her. This was the woman who had come to the house while I'd been raiding Hanson's hard drive, hiding in the flowerbed. To the best of my knowledge she hadn't seen me. Strange, the secret pleasure of knowing more about someone than she knew about me. I liked that feeling.

Mrs. Hanson was sitting on a stool. Her gold handbag was on the kitchen counter. I could picture her in a bar like that. She wore skintight trousers with a leopard-skin print and a tight black top with a neckline that plunged towards her navel, revealing a full cleavage. She had a sunbed tan, nicely setting off a gaudy gold necklace about her slim neck, which was rivaled in bad taste only by the rings on her slim and uncharacteristically elegant hands. She was dressed to shock, but quite probably always dressed this way. It had the desired effect on me, but I sensed Cass wasn't very impressed.

"Well?" she said looking up from a gin and tonic, her gaze level and not in the least bit intimidated by the two strangers before her. She leaned forward slightly, in mock anticipation. Her cleavage adopted new proportions and depth. I glanced out the kitchen window and watched the birdbath in the garden. A late summer swallow was shaking itself after a bath. An animated ball of blue feathers

"We wanted to have a chat about your husband," said Cass.

"Ex-husband," she replied. "Or at least he will be shortly. The papers should be served later today, if the lawyer is as good as he's always saying he is. No more Mrs. John Hanson. I think I'll find a better name than that. What d'you think'd go nicely with Julie?"

"That's a tough one. Jetson, maybe?" said Cass. "I'm sorry about the divorce."

"Don't be. Ending five years of fun and ten of misery's nothing to be sorry about. Now, what do you want?"

"We're...."

She cut Cass off, "I know what you are – 'reporters.'" She sneered the word out. It seemed to lie on the carpet between us, quivering.

"This is Steve and I'm Cass...."

"You were the one at the window, weren't you?" she said, looking at me. I immediately felt the blood course to my face in an embarrassed blush. The secret voyeuristic pleasure I had enjoyed vanished like a burst bubble.

"You knew?" I stammered. She watched me squirm, and a smile came to her lips. She was enjoying herself.

"'Course I did! Not at the time, but within a day or so!" she laughed, quite matter-of-fact about it. "You think you're so damned clever, and you never saw the remote camera, did you? No, they've been looking for you for a while. Asked me to look at the tape, see. Wanted to see if I knew who you was. You looked a sight cowering down behind the roses, right below the camera. Ha! Don't ask me about it, though, I don't know anything worth telling. Johnny was mixed up with some right nutcases, and they went apeshit when you came in and lifted that information off of their computer. Absolutely apeshit. Believe me, they gave me a grilling about it. Not that I knew anything, except that you'd been sniffing about."

She drank slowly, watching us and enjoying my discomfort.

"So, how are you involved in this?" asked Cass, clearly as puzzled as I was.

"One thing I will say for Johnny, he was smart enough never to tell me nothing. He knows that when I get on that plane he doesn't have to worry about anything. I won't tell anybody anything, because he never told me nothing. That was his best gift to me. You know what I'm like! Can't keep a secret for toffees."

"What plane?" asked Cass.

"Lovey, in two hours I'll be drinking Gordon's and tonic in Spain, and there's nothing anyone can do to stop me. I'll be on a British Airways flight from Gatwick in about forty minutes, and then I doubt I'll ever see this dump again. I'm thinking of doing a degree at the Open University, you know. Sociology, I thought. Luckily enough the villa is in my name, so I'll be happily out of it while Johnny spends the next ten years repenting his sins in the Scrubs." She drained her drink. "A divorce won't be difficult under the circumstances. Between you and me, there are probably five other Mrs. Hansons in the equation – and that's just the ones I know of."

"He was a busy boy, wasn't he?" said Cass.

"He wasn't all bad. Just got in with some bad company recently. He got into some stuff he should never have touched. But like I said, I don't know nothing about it." Then she added confidentially, almost under her gin-laden breath, "I suspect he'll find relief in the Book. You know, the parole boards love a born-again Christian. And let's face it – he needs a bloody miracle about now! Ha!"

"We know about the girls," Cass said, fishing. "The one who was killed was on his payroll. The police'll be hearing about it soon enough." Julie showed no reaction at all to this news. She was totally in control of the situation.

"That's all fine, and I don't know anything about it, my dear! Like I said, he kept it to himself. Him and his partner would go off on a Saturday morning and I wouldn't see him all day. Silly bugger should have been home with me. I guess he probably thinks that too, now. A bit bloody late though, isn't it! Typical Johnny – always just a bit bloody late! "

"Can't have been much fun for you," I volunteered. I lit up a cigarette and offered one to her. She took it and lit it with a large and clumsy gold lighter, in a rolling motion. It was strangely sensual, the way she did that. Then she held out the lighter and lit my smoke for me, looking straight in my eyes. She was playing me like a fiddle, but I liked the tune.

"We had our fun," she said confidentially. "That was a long time ago, though. Times change. Time for something new now. A lady has her needs, you know. And he hasn't been much use to me for a while." Cass might not have been in the room.

" I see," I said, weakly. "Yes," I repeated, drawing my eyes from hers. "I see." I repeated idiotically. I noticed Cass looking at me with distaste.

The sound of glass breaking in the distance interrupted the moment. The movers were finishing the place off. A voice called out, "Sorry."

"Well, you want anything else you better go and talk to Johnny. He's on remand in the Scrubs. I have a plane to catch." She said it with a note of finality.

"Help us with one thing," I said. "Who was his partner?"

"You'd love to know that, I'll bet," she chuckled. "But I won't be the one to tell you."

We followed her as she walked out and picked up a small case in the hallway, then out into the drive. She took a remote control from her handbag, open the garage door with it, and tossed it into the road. Inside the garage was the red Porsche.

She slung the case in the back of the car and stepped inside. As she pulled out of the garage she stopped and lowered the electric window. "You must be careful, Steve. These boys will rip your tackle clean off if they find you. Oh, and by the way," she smiled, "give Johnny a big hug from me and say 'bye-bye.'"

There was a squeal of tires as she roared out into the road, running over the remote and smashing it to a hundred pieces. The red Porsche disappeared, and Julie

Hanson was gone, leaving nothing but the smell of burnt rubber.

I slumped into an armchair on the lawn by the removal van. It was quite comfortable, and Cass came over and sat too. She was still looking in the direction of the recently departed Julie Hanson.

"Well!" she exclaimed.

"Well, well!" I said.

"Isn't she something!"

"She certainly is," I concurred. "But she had a very good point. Maybe it is time we went to see Hanson."

"What makes you think he'll have anything to say to us?" asked Cass, perfectly reasonably.

"If I were going down for years – I know we don't know how many, but it will be for a good while – and my wife had just left me, I'd want to talk to someone. Wouldn't you? Besides, what's he got to lose?"

"That's true," she said thoughtfully.

"You'll have a problem with reporting restrictions, but it's worth seeing what he has to say, don't you think?"

Cass was on her feet and walking towards the car. "Come on," she said over her shoulder, "I might be able to get on the afternoon visiting schedule. I used to do prison visits for one of the prisoners' rights groups. I still know the schedule sergeant at the Scrubs. With a bit of luck he'll let me in."

I got to my feet and two removal men whisked the lounge away. I supposed she was probably having it shipped to Spain. That or a relative. On a whim I walked up to the foreman, who was drinking tea from a flask in the cab and reading the racing page of *The Sun*.

I knocked on his window and he wound it down. "Can you help me with something?" I said. "She said she wants some stuff delivered, but I don't think I got her address down right." I fished in my pocket and pulled out a notepad. I squinted at the page before me and pulled a face. " Blimey," I said, "Casa de what?"

The foreman pulled a clipboard from the dashboard and handed it to me. It was a destination in the south of Spain, in Marbella, complete with phone number. I scribbled the details into my note book.

"That better, mate?" he asked.

"Much better," I replied. "Much better!"

Chapter 14

CASS WORKED HER WAY BACK ACROSS THE RIVER and west through the busy London traffic, heading towards Wormwood Scrubs. As we crawled through the midday traffic, I read the morning paper.

Something was troubling me. I said to Cass, "You know, I'm sure there's more coverage of race issues recently."

"Of course," she said.

"Like Hanson," I went on, "that should be a human interest story, right? I mean, he's married more than once, his court appearances, the charges, they all scream tabloid to me. 'Bigamy' is tabloid fare. And yet it's handled as a political story, even carried on the political pages.

"I mean, I can see there's that angle too, but why not go with the good old-fashioned moral outrage stuff? And actually, why hasn't someone got to Julie before? She's great for a tabloid story – 'My awful life with bigamy beast!' I'm sure she'd go for it. See what I mean?"

"Well, yes. But then, why not make it more serious? Besides, it's all connected with the political mood of the moment, isn't it?"

"What exactly is the political mood of the moment?" I asked.

"This amendment the Immigration and Nationality Review Board wants to the Immigration Act is a big deal. It's going to make it much harder for people to get citizenship. I've got friends in one of the immigrant rights pressure groups who say it will close the doors to all but the wealthiest immigrants. They also think that there's a lot of cases pending that will just be thrown out if the amendment goes through. People who already have family here, and just want to stay with them."

"That's pretty serious stuff, isn't it? There are a lot of second-generation immigrants who are going to be caught out by that, I should imagine. They come over and later their relatives might want to join them. I don't know much about it, but I hear it happens that way."

"Well, under the new rules, the new immigrant'll not get any credit for the existing family already in the country. In other words, they'll have to satisfy the conditions independently," she explained. "That may not sound so unfair, but you have to think how some of these people grew up."

"What do you mean?" I asked.

"Well, the eldest male in the family, say from Nigeria, is going to be the one who gets the best education and possibly gets the university degree. A female child won't get much of a chance to go to university, in most cases. It's just not their cultural practice. If they are lucky the younger siblings may get into college, but if the family has limited resources it's unlikely.

"So later the boy comes to England, and decides to immigrate. He has to prove substantial assets for a start, and then he has to satisfy other conditions, including educational ones. In his interviews with the immigration staff in the embassy in Nigeria he sails through with no trouble. The sister is another story. Her level of education will usually be lower, and her resources much less. She will apply and may not even get an interview at the embassy, as she fails to reach the educational criteria. At present the fact that she has a relative in the United Kingdom would help her. If the recommendations of the Immigration and Nationality Review Board are accepted then she won't get in – she'll almost certainly lack the educational qualifications. I believe she'd need a degree. There's almost no chance of that, in most countries."

"Isn't there some other category she could get in under?"

"If she was an investor with seven hundred and fifty thousand pounds in government bonds, or invested in an approved British company, and had at least one million pounds to transfer into a British account then she would find she benefited from recent changes to the law."

"That seems a little unlikely for your average Nigerian villager," I replied.

"Our immigration law is generally acknowledged as the most complex in the world. However, if you are a wealthy investor, ironically, it is easier to get into than most other countries. The way things are set up, all our current system does is encourage immigrants to try to get in outside the law. If they change the law the way they hope, it will just make that situation a lot worse."

Cass dived through an opening in the traffic, cutting off a taxi. Her driving was breathtaking at times. I wondered if the tube went anywhere near the Scrubs.

"I read a story not so long ago about a Nigerian woman being deported," I said. "The police had to be called in to carry her on to an aircraft bound for Lagos. They stuck her in a straightjacket and had to sit on her chest to get her to stay aboard the aircraft, and she had a heart attack and died. The plane was still on the ground at Heathrow."

"And?"

"I don't know," I said. "It just seems a shitty way to end a life.

"The police can be pretty brutal in these things. No one sticks up for an immigrant being deported. There's not many votes in that sort of thing. Who the hell cares?"

"You think that's all it comes down to?" I asked, wondering if she was really that cynical.

"What else?"

"And that's what all these riots have been about?"

"Of course! These people don't want to lose the right to bring in their families."

"Well, ripping the place up doesn't do much for their cause," I said.

"You can be sure there'll be some real headcases around to make sure there's trouble. Most demonstrators are probably peaceful, even if it doesn't quite get reported that way."

"I haven't really been following it, but the press coverage has been fairly damning, from what I've seen," I said.

"Yes, it's weird, that. It's almost like that's part of some – plan. Though who might be behind it, I couldn't begin to guess." She was just speculating, but a shiver still ran through me. That would be too farfetched, surely?

I stared through the windshield and thought back to

Hanson, to how this whole thing had started. There was something badly wrong with it all. Why was Hanson getting all this attention, why was he getting so much play, and why was the slant always the "unstoppable flood of immigrants"? I was developing some very uneasy feelings.

THE WOODEN GATES of Wormwood Scrubs loomed high as we drove past, and Cass began looking for a place to park. The frontage of Wormwood Scrubs is unusual for British government buildings. The Victorian gatehouse has some of the brickwork picked out quite gaily in white paint. It is very distinctive and probably goes back to the time when the Scrubs was a military prison. It now houses upwards of eight hundred male prisoners, some awaiting trail while on remand.

Unlike some maximum-security prisons, the Scrubs has an unfortunate history of escapes. Some put this down to the fact that the prospect of staying inside is so awful, escape is more readily considered. The fact that serious offenders can mix with others remanded before their trial, and in some instances underage offenders, has been a point the media has returned to periodically, and will until the prison authorities move themselves out of the Victorian era some of their prisons were created in.

In spite of its origins, the Scrubs has a few quite advanced features, several of which were evident as we drove by. These included cameras mounted high above us and viewing from several directions, as well as a series of powerful lights that would doubtless flood the night-time gate. So good to know that visitors were being watched and their visit preserved on film. For whose safety? I wondered what happened to those videotapes.

"I don't think I'll be able to get you in, Steve," said Cass as we walked towards the gates. "One person maybe, but two is going to be stretching my luck. Heck, he may not even see me. Hanson's probably been warned off, and won't see anyone."

"You'll have to say you are someone he knows. Try saying you're Julie," I suggested.

"I'll think of something."

I glanced up as someone stepped out of the gate and walked in our direction. It was a woman with her head down, obviously in hurry, and looking quite agitated. There were a few of those who had walked out of those gates, I guessed. I caught a glimpse of the side of her face. In a moment I recognized the profile, and her ears. In fact, not the ears, exactly. The earrings.

I kept walking, glancing over my shoulder. She hadn't recognized me.

"Cass," I said quietly, "that woman, the one who just walked past."

"What about her?" said Cass as she looked back at the woman.

"She was at the trial. At Hanson's trial! I know I saw her there."

"Reporter?"

"No, I don't think so." Then I realized I'd seen her somewhere else, too. It was at the party with Shandra. She had been with Carfax. "She was also at a party I went to. I think she's important."

"Then follow her," Cass said urgently. "Go!"

"I'll see you at the flat," I turned and ran after the

receding figure. She stepped out into the road and crossed the street in the distance. I darted out into the traffic and dodged cars as I crossed the busy road.

She was wearing black, and wore a hat making her easier to spot, but as I ran, trying not to lose sight of her, she swept down a subway, and disappeared from view. My heart was in my mouth as I sprinted along the road to where she had disappeared. As I ducked down, taking the steps two at a time, I realized I didn't have a chance in the Underground.

I've lost more people on the tube than anywhere else. Most photographers acknowledge that if they were being photographed they would duck into the nearest tube station and lose the person after them. Now this woman, whoever she might be, and whether she was aware of me or not, was doing the same.

I pulled out my season ticket and pushed through the ticket gate, scanning the crowd. She was nowhere to be seen. The way ahead split into westbound and eastbound routes, the eastbound heading back into town. I took a chance and ran down the white-tiled tunnel heading east. As I emerged onto the platform I saw a black coat flash into a carriage as the doors began to hiss shut. I hurled myself through into the carriage next to hers. The train rattled out of the station and I made my way down to the end of the carriage, my breath coming in gasps. I would have to kick those damned cancer sticks before I became entirely useless.

Through the window at the end of the carriage I could make her out. I had got lucky. She was oblivious to me and I had a clear view of her. It was definitely the same woman. It proved nothing at all, but if I stuck to her, maybe something would show up. Or maybe she'd lose me at the next stop.

But she didn't. By now I was sure she hadn't seen me, and I wanted to keep it that way. I ducked behind a small group of tourists as she changed trains and managed to stay on her. After four more stops she left the train at Westminster. I hung back, keeping about thirty yards and a good crowd between us. She was an easier target as she reached the escalator and walked up the moving stairway. She walked quickly and very purposefully. I wouldn't want to do this for long.

Outside she crossed Parliament Square and walked a couple of blocks north. I was far enough away to keep her well in sight, and see what she was up to, and then suddenly she walked into the foyer of an office building. I approached the glass frontage of the building and, looking inside, watched as she waited for an elevator. There were two other people waiting with her. As they stepped inside the elevator I slid through the glass doors and watched the numbers light up as the elevator moved up the floors.

It paused on floor seven, and then again on floor twelve before returning to the foyer. I went to the listing of offices, laid out neatly in plastic letters placed on a board on the wall.

Floor seven was BMP Metals (Accounts and Administration), which I noted in my notebook, and floor twelve was simply not listed. Just following her up was too much of a risk. As an elevator full of people arrived in the foyer I slipped my notebook back in my pocket and retreated to the front door. I had no idea what was going on, but felt I was getting warm.

I decided to go back to Parliament Square and consider my next move. I walked to the Saint Steven, a pub popular with members of Parliament. This was on account of the fact that there was a bell running directly from the House to the bar room to tell them when a vote was imminent. The bell would ring and they would return to their seats in time for the vote. Very civilized. As I sipped half a lager, I wondered what was on the twelfth floor. There was no choice but to go up and eyeball it. Doing so immediately after the woman had led me there would have been unwise. I would have to get in there before lunch, when people would be coming and going. A quick look would be enough to give me some idea.

I was about to leave when I felt a tug at my sleeve. Then a voice said, "That was quite a pee you went for. After two hours I figured you weren't coming back." It was Stella, the radio journo I'd last seen in Amsterdam.

"Well, don't I get some kind of explanation?" Of course! I had left her in the café in Amsterdam.

"Sure, I was kidnapped," I laughed.

"Yeah, right," she sneered.

"Sorry! I really didn't mean it to happen like that. I enjoyed myself. It was very rude, but I swear I didn't have much choice."

"Pity you had to go. I lost you at the summit too. Couldn't find you anywhere." It was a question in statement form. Some journos don't just come right out with it and say, "What the heck were you working on?" because they think you're hiding some secret story. I put her out of her misery.

"You saw the oil rig pics?" I said.

"That was you?" she said, astonished.

"Don't spread it around. The cops think we fucked the place up. There'll be trouble over it."

"I won't tell a soul. Hey, that was a nice one! How the heck did you catch that one?"

"Like I said, I was kidnapped. The story just sort of came to me. You see, I told you – it does happen."

"I don't believe a word of it. Look, I'm just wrapping something up over here, let me finish this one off and then you can tell me the truth. Give me ten minutes."

"I gotta run."

"Steve," she said, "don't be such a bastard, you're always running out on me. Don't you like me?" she pouted.

"You know I do," I said, not wanting to hurt her feelings. Then I realized she was teasing me.

"Well, call me in the next couple of days; I've got big news for you. I'd better get back or my interview'll walk right out of here."

She pressed a card into my hand, and slipped away into the crowded bar. I would call her, too.

I hurried through the square and back to the office building. In the elevator I pressed the button for the twelfth floor and waited. As the doors opened I stepped out to find myself in a corridor smartly paneled in some impressive dark red wood. There was one door directly in front of me. A small brass plaque beside it said in simple brass lettering "Immigration and Nationality Review Board." Below, someone had stuck a handwritten notice: "No Soliciting."

I had all I needed and turned to find the elevator door closing. It left before I could hit the button. I pressed the call button several times and waited. It seemed to be taking an age, and as I waited I could hear voices just beyond the door. It seemed absurd that I should be so worried about seeing someone from the office, but I had a very bad feeling about the prospect. At last a lift arrived and I stepped inside. As I did so the door of the office opened and I looked out of the closing door of the lift, right into the unmistakably cold eyes of Jeremy Carfax.

THE FIRST THING I did was get back to the Saint Steven. I needed a good shot of courage. I made it vodka. Straight and without ice. Like I drank when I was on assignments in Africa. Mix water in it and get sick, that was always the way. Few germs can survive the blue-labeled Smirnoff. Come to that, few livers can, either.

The liquid calmed me. What the heck was Carfax doing there? He had been in that news report too, I remembered. So this girl, who had been with him at the party, and had been at the trial, had visited Hanson, for Carfax? But why? What could Carfax have to do with some hood like Hanson? Could he be Hanson's partner?

I WALKED FOR A WHILE until I found myself in Saint James's Park on a bench, looking at civil servants walking up the avenues to pass their lunch hours. I considered what it might be like to work in one of those offices. I'd rather make a living digging roads.

A duck with something wrong with its webbed foot was badgering a couple nearby, wanting some of the sandwiches they were sharing. They tried to ignore the creature for a while, until the young man threw a handful of crumbs in the direction of the duck, in the hopes of satisfying it. From nowhere a half dozen more appeared and crowded the couple. The traffic seemed far away for a moment, and here in the center of London there seemed an uncanny peacefulness, much like the center of a hurricane must be.

My cellphone bleeped and I pulled it from my jacket.

"Steve, it's Guy. I have some good news and some bad news."

"Go on," I replied.

"Well, I've at least partially broken the encryption. I have a series of files that seem to be some kind of database, contact files. I can't make much sense of them; they seem to have been erased at some point, but have left some trace on the disk. I can read some of them. That's the good news."

"And the bad news?"

"Well, there's a couple of people in that database that shouldn't be there. At least, it's very strange that they're there."

"Who would they be?"

"Our very own editor, for one. Malcolm Strathclyde – office, private line, cell phone and home number. What do you make of that?"

"I don't know. Maybe he is in a lot of contact lists. Maybe he's just on some press list?" I speculated.

"No, this is a contact list which doesn't seem to include any other media staff, at least not on editorial. There's another cell phone here which is listed to *News Consolidated*, with lots of notations which I can't decipher. Seems to be important, judging by the number of notes in the database – only I can't read the damned things."

"You've tried phoning it?"

"It just rings."

"What's the number?" I asked.

"It's 499-8181. It just rings. No idea whose it might be, but it's certainly ours. We've been paying the bills for it since the account was opened. I know a lot of those "499 8" numbers are ours, so I checked it out on the off-chance."

"Smart move," I said. "Anyone else?"

"I'm only partway into it, and that's all I have so far. But there's something else I wanted you to know."

"What's that?"

"Check your e-mails. I think Marlene wants you and Cass back in the newsroom."

I thought about this for a second. "What makes you think that?"

"I was snooping around this morning. She's been getting flack from the suits over you."

"What do you mean?"

"She seems to be under pressure to get Cass on the desk and you back in the office. There's all kinds of shit happening about you getting on to that rig, and it seems that the Allied Resources is hosting a news conference tomorrow night and is suing people left, right and center. The paper is likely to be sued for being party to an act of piracy."

"That's not good," I said.

"It's not. Apparently no one's aware that you were out there, but the pictures are known to have come out of *News Consolidated*, which puts them in a rather awkward position. On top of that, this Hanson trial has been moved forward to be heard next week. They want you on that. Someone feels you've been wasting time on an investigative effort that has come to nothing, and that your place is closer to the office."

"Who's thinking that?" I asked, ready to be defensive.

"Strathclyde. I read his e-mails and he sent something down to Marlene about it this morning."

"That's very strange," I muttered. "I don't think he knows who I am, so why is he taking an interest in me suddenly?"

"No idea. But he does know who you are, and will probably know more about you after the meeting this afternoon. Marlene, Bonnie and Strathclyde are meeting with the lawyers to discuss the paper's involvement on that rig. Your name may come up."

Suddenly I was wanted back in the real world. The last few weeks had been an adventure, and now, just when things looked as though they might be going somewhere, it was falling to pieces. I was silent on the phone, thinking it had been a while since I actually took a photograph. Maybe it was all for the best.

"Okay, Guy, thanks for the news. Do me a favor, keep trying to crack that hard drive. I know it's important. I just don't know why."

"You know what, a funny thought occurred to me."

"If it's as funny as all the other things you've said, I'm not sure I want to hear it," I replied.

"It's like this was a machine that was lent to someone. Some of the stuff I'm finding has actually been erased from the hard drive, but because no one has overwritten the files, I can still read them using a tool I have. In other words, it's like someone wiped out a load of data, and the machine then got lent to Hanson. Those first files we found were easy. They were Hanson's. This other stuff, with the encryption and stuff, this isn't consistent with someone with limited computer skills. This has to be for someone else entirely."

I thought about it for a moment. "It could be his partner's," I said.

"Did he have a partner?" retorted Guy.

"Yes, according to his wife. We just don't know who. But I'm beginning to get an idea," I said.

"Well, when you know, let me know 'cause he'll be really pissed that we've got this stuff, whatever it is."

"I will," I said, and rang off.

The ducks came to try their luck with me, but I snarled and they scattered.

CASS ARRIVED IN THE APARTMENT about ten minutes after I did.

"Well?" I asked.

"There's something very sinister about this whole thing, Steve," she said, as I poured some tea.

I was glad that she too was coming to that conclusion. Without being too much of a conspiracy theorist, I found it hard to avoid the conclusion that there was an undeniable link from Hanson the thug, to the Immigration and Nationality Review Board. It went via the nameless girl, a.k.a. Kelly Watson, through Jeremy Carfax, part-owner of *News Consolidated* papers, to that office in Westminster. I wanted to hear Cass's suggestions before I elaborated further, at risk of sounding like the most crashing buffoon.

"When you say 'sinister,' " I said, "do you mean, 'Hanson's a sinister thug'? Or something broader?"

"Definitely broader," she replied. "More like, 'Hanson's a small cog in the gearbox of a particularly nasty machine.'"

"What did you learn at the prison?"

"Hanson is out on his

own for sure. He's going down in a big way, and wonders why we took so long to get onto the angle about Kelly Watson being a hooker, and an illegal immigrant. He says that the police don't know anything about his connection there, but that he's going to tell the whole story at his trial. That's fair enough; we should have worked harder on Kelly Watson from the start. I'm kicking myself for that now. But he keeps saying he's the fall guy, he's been set up."

"Which is predictable, but I think also think probably true. I just don't quite see why. It's what everyone will expect him to say, and so no one will believe it."

"He's going down regardless, and will be implicating his partner, who he says he won't identify until his trial, in the hope of a plea bargain. He's feeling pretty sure of himself now, because he's convinced he can show that his partner was involved in Kelly's death."

"He told you this?"

"He was happy to talk to someone interested in doing something other than nailing him. He says he's not the bad guy in this whole thing. He's done some bad stuff, but he's a petty thug compared to his partner."

"Hmmm. What else did he say about the partner?" I asked.

"You'll love this. It will appeal to your tabloid

instincts. Sit down and I'll tell all."

I settled down in the living room and Cass pulled her notebook out and started flipping through the pages of notes she'd made.

"He says his partner got him into the whole business of illegal immigrants, and setting up marriages. Later, it turned to forging identities or buying identities of existing or dead citizens. He said he couldn't believe how easy it was, and then went on to talk about the prostitution side of the story.

"There are twelve girls working for them at present, but no one's managing them. They all work in the same way Kelly did, and pay him a percentage each week. They're all young eastern European or Indian girls. He says they ran into trouble when his partner started using some of the girls to entertain at parties. He'd have a couple of them come along to liven things up."

"What a mess," I said.

"Yes, it was a mess. He started to see them as his own private toys and started to do things they didn't want any part of. He wouldn't leave them alone, and didn't mind laying down a little muscle to get what he wanted. Apparently they dreaded him coming over to collect the weekly take, because if it was a little low he'd expect what Hanson called 'a little bonus.' Hanson had about had enough of it when he finds himself up on a charge.

"At first he figures it's just a bad luck rap, and a good lawyer will get him off. Then he figures someone tipped the police up at Southwark off, and that he was set up. Then the charge is upgraded and he finds himself hauled off to the nick. Then his charge is upgraded still further to something he'll probably end up doing time for."

I cut in at this point, "And that's when he decided to blow the whistle on his partner?"

"No," said Cass. "At first he figures he'll just weather the storm. If he has to do a year, then he can do it. Might even get out early with luck. By the time he gets out, his girls will have earned him a small fortune, if his partner can be trusted. Then he hears about Kelly Watson. A little after the fact, as it happens, but when he hears about it, he panics. He contacts his partner and asks what the hell's going on.

"What he hears isn't good. His partner doesn't care what he thinks, and says he doesn't need a partner who's locked up in the Scrubs anyway. He tells him in no uncertain words that their partnership is dissolved. He also says that if he has any problems with this, Julia will be sent the way of Kelly."

"No honor among thieves these days!" I said.

Cass went on, "This sends Hanson off the deep end, and he's been pulling his hair out ever since. This morning he finds Julia's done a bunk, and good for her, she might be safer that way. Before I saw him he gets a message from his partner to say that if he keeps his mouth shut and plays ball he might get some help at the trial, but he figures he's been turned over so many times already he's not interested. Then I come along, and he's about ready to tell me anything. Except," and here she sounded despairing, "who the partner is."

"Yeah," I said. "I can see his point. If he tells you who his partner is, and you leak it out, then the cops won't trade for it. Right?"

"That's what I figure," she said, her story finally over. "And what did you find out?"

"I think I know who the other half is." I watched as she took this in. "I think it's a guy called Jeremy Carfax. He's …"

"He's a major shareholder in *News Consolidated*," she burst in.

"You know of him?" I said, surprised.

"Sure. He's a right-wing twit who plays amateur politics in his spare time. What makes you think he's involved?"

"I followed that girl back into town. She led me to an office. You'll never guess whose." I waited but she shook her head.

"Immigration and Nationality Review Board."

The phrase hung in the air.

"But why?" said Cass.

"No idea." I replied. "They operate out of a discreet office near Parliament, and as I was checking it out, who should emerge but Carfax."

"And how is he connected to Hanson?"

"It's tenuous, I know, but there is a link. I saw that girl, the one at Hanson's trial, one other time. I saw her at a party in Dolphin Square. She was with Carfax."

She looked at me wonderingly, no doubt speculating what I was doing at such a party, and then said, "Maybe she's just his secretary or something incidental. Maybe she's just a colleague."

"These two have more than a passing acquaintance, I assure you."

"Well, what's Hanson doing involving himself with them?"

"Beats me," I said.

We discussed the subject back and forth until it made

less sense than before, and we were sick of the entire issue. Then I remembered Guy's warning.

"There's something else I should mention," I said. "Guy tipped me off that we are being called back into the office as soon as they can find us. There's quite a fuss being made about our involvement on that rig. The lawyers have been called in, and they may have to do something to placate Allied Resources."

"What's their problem?"

"Well, we may have been party to an act of piracy – or so Allied Resources will claim."

"That's completely ridiculous. Besides, we've got pictures to show there was no vandalism."

"Allied Resources is holding a press conference tomorrow night, and *News Consolidated* wants its position clear, in case it has to answer any serious charges."

"There are no grounds for worrying about that. You've done nothing wrong, and nor have I. If it comes out that I'm involved as more than a journalist then I'll be hung, drawn and quartered, but we trust each other, don't we? You won't drop me in it – will you?"

"Of course I won't," I said. I was a little offended that after all this time she was still not entirely ready to trust me. "Anyway, we'd better get things sorted out and get into the office tomorrow. Maybe if we lay all we know in front of Marlene she can make some sense of it. Hell, there's something there – though God knows what!"

I needed air. It was getting claustrophobic in the apartment and I needed a smoke. I walked down the stairs and along Abbey Road, smoking a cigarette. I wasn't really headed anywhere, just drifting along wondering where my feet might lead me.

I was depressed at the thought of going back to the office. I wondered if I would have other visitors at home. I felt I knew less than when the whole Hanson deal had started.

My cellphone interrupted my depression, and I spoke above the early evening traffic.

"Yeah, this is Sinclair."

"Steven," the caller said.

For a moment I wondered if it was my mother, the only person left on the planet who still called me "Steven".

"Yeah...."

"It's Shandra. I'm so glad you called me, I was so worried about you."

"How are you, Shandra?" I said, my voice softening. Her Oxford accent was quite disconcerting at times. It sounded more exaggerated than usual.

"To be quite honest, I'm exhausted. It's been a big day. I'd love to talk to you about it. Can you come over?"

"I'm on foot," I said. "Notting Hill is a bit of a walk...." I didn't want to mention Cass at this stage, she might get the wrong impression. "You could pick me up, if you want...."

"Love to," she replied. "Where would suit you?"

"Let's meet at Swiss Cottage." I gave her directions and walked on, forgetting my woes in an instant.

I SAT ON THE BALCONY of the Notting Hill penthouse apartment. Far below, the evening traffic was oblivious to those of us so high above.

Shandra wandered through, moving like the lower reaches of a river. She brought a Scotch for me and a martini for herself, then she stood next to me looking out at the busy city beneath us. She didn't say a word.

She wore a flowing, deep purple shift, simple and delightful. Her shoulders were bare, and the night breeze must have chilled her. Some Clapton blues were playing in the living room, the sound swelling and joining us through the sliding doors. What excellent taste she had. Some people can just be relied upon.

I stared across the city, a little sad that this evening marked the end of a special time for Cass and me. Tomorrow would be back to business – and a time to account for the recent past. But I couldn't have cared less about that at this point.

I was here with a Scotch warming my stomach and a beautiful woman by my side. What could possibly be more promising? And I had a feeling deep within my trousers that said things were only going to get better.

"You were mentioned at a meeting I was at today." Shandra eased into conversation and brought me back to earth.

I waited for her to elaborate.

"You've been busy, it would seem," she continued. This was interesting. I wondered how widely it was known I'd been involved with Green Rage.

"Go on," I said, sending my cigarette butt sailing to the ground far below. One day someone would be walking by when I did that and it would disappear down their collar. My closest shave to date had been hitting that cyclist in Amsterdam. Smoking really is a dangerous thing. I made up my mind to quit soon.

"I know all about Holland. Very naughty goings-on," she said, and sipped from her towering martini. She had a look of mischief on her face.

"Well, there was no harm done," I said.

"That's a matter open to debate. The owners of the rig are looking for a hundred thousand pounds in costs for damages to it."

I smiled inwardly. They obviously had no knowledge of the fact that we had got aboard a second time, and that I'd photographed an undamaged rig. This would prove interesting. I would keep the existence of the photographs of the second visit secret for the time being. They were safely stashed at the office; Cass had seen to that.

"I doubt they have much of a case, do they?" I asked, trying not to look too smug. My security lay in the second set of pictures. They were more valuable than any lawyer's argument.

"We'll see tomorrow. They've asked to meet us. Maybe they'll put their cards on the table. Who was the journo with you?" She asked the question in passing and I hardly noticed it till I began my answer.

"I ... I don't know. I never actually met the journo," I said. "I traveled up with one group and someone else wrote the story. I don't actually think she was English."

"You don't?" she said.

"No. Did you read it? Very sloppy, I thought. But what do I know! I just take the pictures." She was watching me closely. For a moment I felt like I was being hunted. Maybe lawyer types do that. I don't know. I guessed she was just naturally curious. That would be normal enough. Why shouldn't she be curious about the one part of working on the *News* that we had in common?

"Nice pictures," she said, and slid away inside for a moment.

Some women have a way with kitchens. They don't actually cook, but just go in, lift a tray of food and return with it. They are mostly on soaps on the TV or in unlikely fiction. They never burn food, set dishcloths alight by accident, or drop bowls of trifle. Nor do they have to wash up, peel potatoes or gut fish. Whatever their secret, Shandra was privy to it. She wafted into the kitchen and a moment later returned laden with a tray of Indian delicacies. I couldn't even begin to describe them, but the aroma and the colors of the various sauces and chutneys made me want to rush back to St. John's Wood and get my camera gear. Photography can afflict one like that.

We shared the meal sitting around a low table in the living room. Clapton gave way to the Floyd and I wondered where Shandra had found such music. It was all "me," and no "her."

The cool of the evening washed over me as I lit another smoke out on the balcony. London at night. Romantic.

The Scotch in my hand felt good, and in my head too. I leaned on the balcony railing and watched the traffic below. A Porsche pulled up at a café across the road. Nice car. Not that I want one. Tube does me fine.

Someone climbed from the Porsche. He was a long way off, and, funnily enough, it must have been a trick of the night, it looked almost like Carfax. I had the guy on the brain! I shook my head, trying to rid myself of the impression, then turned and went inside.

"That really was a nice meal," I said to Shandra.

"I'm so glad you enjoyed it. I suspected you would, though. I think you like to try things that are out of the ordinary."

"Yeah," I said. Now, this is the point at which were this a pornographic story the narrator would say something like, "And naturally the conversation turned to sex." Actually that's not what happened. I followed Shandra into the kitchen to get a glass of water. The curry was still working its magic on me, and I needed a little coolant.

"I really liked it," I said filling a glass from the tap.

"Let me stick some ice in that for you," she said, turning to the fridge and getting a tray of ice. She banged it on the counter and took a handful of the cubes and dropped them into my glass.

"Do you have to be somewhere?" she asked.

I thought of several replies. Saying "No, let's get straight in the sack, love," seemed a little gauche. Shandra wasn't that kind of lady, I could tell. I like to think I am a good judge of character, and Shandra seemed quite reserved. I said softly, "No, not really. I'm very happy right here, Shandra."

"Good," she replied. "Why don't you come through here and enjoy your drink."

So much for being reserved. She walked into her bedroom, leaving the door open for me to follow. As I stepped in I sensed the closing of a trap. Had there been a metallic "Kerlunk!" it could have been no more obvious. But there wasn't. Instead I was sitting on her enormous black silk-covered bed, looking at her, much as a thirteen-year-old schoolboy looks at a teacher he has an incurable crush on.

"Yes." I said meekly and took a sip of my drink. " I could do that," I mouthed quietly.

Standing before me, Shandra kissed me. She bent down, her hands around my face, pulling me irresistibly to her. Then I felt her pushing me back on the bed. She pushed my shoulders hard and straddled my unresisting body.

She was laughing, astride my chest. I rolled and pinned her down, holding her arms by her side, and she lay unresisting. I kissed her neck, then traced a line along her shoulders, gently massaging the strong muscles there. She gyrated beneath my touch, at once yielding and wanting.

She reversed positions with me, then slowly, very deliberately. She unbuttoned the first two buttons of my shirt. Then she reached across to the bedside table and I heard her rummaging around for something.

The glint of the blade caught my eye, and I felt the cold gray steel on my chest. "Snick," it said – cutting away a button, and then "snick," again. In a moment I had no buttons.

I laughed nervously. Looking at her, it struck me this may not be the first time she had used a commando dagger to undress a lover. I wondered if the spiders in India ate their mates after sex. I suspect they do. My laughter became slightly more nervous.

She pushed me down flat on the bed, then seemed to shrug her shift away to reveal a black bodice, suspenders and stockings beneath. She was immaculate, her body the strong form of a woman in peak physical condition. Sidling up to me, she stroked my head, and I moved to place my arms around her, but she pushed me down.

She ran a hand over my chest, then down over my navel, sliding her long index finger over me as if tracing the path a scalpel might take. Then again I felt the cold steel. This was a little frightening. It was fantastic, but horrifying. I took a mental snapshot of myself. What the hell was I doing?

I felt the blade running softly over my belly, then lower, to my waist. It was inside the band of my trousers, and then in a slick motion she pulled it away, parting my trousers and boxers in a single slice.

"My ...," she said. "What a proud fellow you are!"

"Shandra," I said.

"Quiet. You like it. I know you do. Don't fight it. ..." She was compelling. Part of me was screaming, "She's playing knife games, now get the fuck out of here now, you raving loony." And yet, another part of me just said – "Oh, wow!"

I couldn't fight it.

As she leaned over me I ran my fingers through her hair, massaging her scalp. I felt the cold blade rest against my groin. This time when I pulled her to me she kissed me deeply, her lips parting and drinking me into her like a glass of Campari. I could still hear Clapton playing blues in the background.

Her body was firm under my touch. As I stroked her breasts she thrust herself against me and for a moment I thought I was going to be sliced open by her damned knife, before I realized she'd dropped it and I was feeling her hand on me.

"Just wait a moment, Steven," she said getting up and walking to a closet. She still called me Steven, just as my mother did. That was sure as heck where the similarities ended. I thought for a moment she was going to sort out some "precaution," but instead I found her returned with some objects at once exciting and also sinister.

I looked as she picked up a black silk blindfold. Shandra said, "I think you should put this on, don't you?" She held out the blindfold.

"I don't know ...," I replied.

"Oh, I think you should," she said, very reasonably, but leaving no room for argument. I felt her hand on my nipple grasp it firmly between thumb and forefinger and twist, slowly at fist, then harder, sending a bolt of pain through me.

"Yes, yes," I said, and the pain stopped. "I should wear it. Of course, you're right."

She placed the blindfold over my eyes, then tied the silken straps behind, holding it firmly. Next I felt the cold steel of some cuffs being placed on my chest, clink clunk. They rested there a moment, cold and heavy. Nervously, I laughed again. This really was getting more than a little beyond my realm of experience. "Er. Shandra."

I felt a sharp slap across my face. The stinging pain of it shocked me. It was more surprise than pain, but it had the desired effect.

"You want the cuffs, don't you!" she said.

"Well, actually Shandra. . . ." She cut off my protest with another slap. This time it was harder. My head rolled in rebound. I felt her roll me on my side with surprising strength.

I was ready to quit and about to say so, when I felt her hand take first one wrist firmly and close the steel jaws of a pair of handcuffs, and then the other, leaving me with both hands firmly cuffed behind my back.

Shandra said forcefully, "On your feet!"

I maneuvered myself off the bed and felt her strip what remained of my trousers and boxers from me with the knife. She grabbed my hair and pulled me to my feet. I felt her pull my head down to her chest, the warmth of her breasts intoxicating.

She held me like that a moment and then I felt something securing the cuffs. Then the sound of a rope being pulled. I felt my arms rise behind me, then further, forcing my head down. This was beginning to hurt.

"Shandra," I said. "That's enough." The rope was pulled tighter and I felt my arms begin to burn in their sockets. This was no longer fun.

I heard the door close. Shandra had left the room. What the hell was this about? I could hear a voice. It sounded like it was a phone conversation. She was calling someone.

The door opened again after a couple of minutes and she returned.

"Shandra," I said pitifully, "this isn't my idea of fun. Can you undo this...."

She was standing before me; I could sense her rather than see her. She touched my hair, tenderly. She pulled me towards her, and I guess my face must have been against her warm tummy. She caressed my face a moment.

"Pity.... you could have been such fun!" She sounded disappointed, letting out a little sigh.

"What?" I said. "I don't understand.

"No, you don't, do you? That's been your trouble all along. You just have no idea...."

I had no idea what she was babbling about. Only my

growing unease prevented me from saying, "Show me what I don't understand." It seemed unwise.

She stroked me a moment more, and for a brief instant I thought I might actually enjoy this. Then I heard the door across the room open. What now?

She moved away.

I heard a heavier footfall.

It was followed by the unmistakable sensation of feeling an iron bar crash against both my shins at once, sending me falling and spinning against my bound arms. The flames in my arms and legs raged as I swung like meat on a hook. I screamed once, and then a gag was thrust into my mouth. My next scream burst forth from the pit of my stomach but got nowhere further than the back of my throat.

The night took a definite turn for the worse.

Chapter 15

IN THE ROAR OF MY AGONY I could hear someone moving around the room. No wait, two people. I hung, swinging from the rope attached to the cuffs, my hands held fast behind my back.

Suddenly a hand grasped my hair, jerking my head back roughly.

"In trouble again, aren't we, Mr. Sinclair!" It was the voice of Jeremy Carfax. What the hell was he doing here? He wasn't a part of my evening plans at all.

I struggled to my feet, relieving the pain in my arms. I tried to remove the blindfold, but I couldn't reach it, no matter what I did. My shins throbbed in pain.

Then in a burst of light it was ripped from my eyes, revealing the besuited and sneering Carfax before me. With him was the thug Sykes had slugged in my apartment. In a very few moments I would be paying for the time he had spent locked in the trunk of the car outside my apartment. Carfax also would want a settling of debts.

I nodded recognition to the heavy-set form, and Carfax noted it. "You two have met, of course," he said.

"But I'm forgetting my manners, you haven't been properly introduced! Steven – may I call you Steven? – this is Claude. He's been hoping to have a chat with you for a little while. Tracking you down was not a simple matter."

"Hi, Claude," I said wincing in pain and unable to think of anything more appropriate. He replied by moving forward, the iron bar in his hand raised, but was halted by Carfax placing his effeminate slim hand onto Claude's football pitch-like chest.

"And, of course, I have an outstanding matter with you too, don't I?" continued Carfax. Turning, he said "Claude, darling, just wait. You'll have your turn."

I didn't like the way he said that. Sinister beyond belief.

Carfax returned his attention to me and went on. "Yes, very difficult to track down. It wasn't until I put two and two together about that silliness in Holland that I realized we'd been looking in all the wrong places."

"Well, I …"

"Shut up and listen," said Carfax sharply. Claude was swinging the iron bar with a look that said he'd like to have another go at my shins, so I kept quiet.

"Yes, that business was most amusing, it even provides me with the means to get rid of you once and for all. But first let's sort out the matter of that data you stole."

"Data?" I said. Perhaps acting innocent would help me out of this mess.

Carfax looked almost disappointed. Then with a look that said, "We'll do it his way," he turned to Claude and said, "You have five minutes."

I had no desire whatsoever to be left alone with

Claude for a moment, and said "Okay, I. . . ." But he was already leaving, not interested.

He turned and walked from the room. For a moment my eyes met Shandra's as she was framed in the doorway, before the door closed, leaving me alone with Claude. She wore a pink dressing gown, and a frown. She had obviously been listening at the door. Hanging there naked but for a pair of socks with the image of Homer Simpson saying "Doh!" on them, I must have looked pathetic. I tried to project a message across the space that said, "This isn't my idea of a good time, babe," but my thoughts ceased abruptly as Claude slammed the iron bar into my legs again. The blow sent my body tumbling away, held up only by the restraining rope behind me.

The next five minutes seemed like five years. A very bad five years. Whatever else Claude may have been, where his work was concerned he was a craftsman. He knew precisely how to inflict enough pain to leave me writhing, but still leave me conscious to experience the sensation.

He concentrated on my legs, beating them mercilessly with the bar, before turning his attention to my back and pummeling my kidneys.

By the time Carfax returned, this time with a clear drink in his hand, gin and tonic probably, I was ready to welcome unconsciousness and death. Out of breath, I tried to focus my attention on him.

"Are you ready to talk now?" he said.

"Yes," I gasped. "What do you want to know?" I am not a hero. I am the first to admit I handle mindless, brutal torture rather badly. I was ready to tell him anything he felt like hearing.

"I think you know what I want," he said, pulling the chair from before the dressing table. With a chuckle he added, "And if you don't tell me I'll have to ask Claude to continue."

"What do you want?" I muttered again, trying to ease my breathing.

"You removed some data from John Hanson's computer. I'd like to know what you did with it. That's all."

"That's it?" I stammered. "That's all you want?"

"Well, it will do for a start."

"It's at *News Consolidated*. In the IT department. One of the computer staff tried to help me with it. The material is sitting in a file. No one can read the stuff."

He sneered. "And what exactly were you trying to do with it?"

"Just to look at it, see if there was anything interesting there."

"And did you find anything?" he asked, almost nonchalantly.

"No. It was encrypted somehow. Nothing we could make any sense of. Just some files that no one can open. You're welcome to them."

"Well, that's very helpful. Not so difficult, was it?"

He looked at Claude and smiled. I thought he was about to tell Claude to release me, the ordeal being over. Instead he said, "Very well. I'm done." I let out a sigh of relief. Then he added, "Claude, he's all yours."

A blow behind my knees sent me sprawling before I could even turn and see Claude. Carfax left the room as I felt another kick into my kidney and the room spin above me. Pain exploded through my body and my back seemed to crack as he slammed a punch into my lumbar vertebrae.

"Carfax, you bastard," I shouted. "I'll fucking get you," I screamed.

The door open and he leaned back in for a moment. I could see Shandra looking worried in the background.

"I think not," he mewed. "Look at yourself, Sinclair! You're pathetic! You've been pathetic all along! You have absolutely no concept at all what's happened, have you? You stumbled over something, a very small thing as it happened, and completely missed the importance of it. No, you not going to 'get me.' You're not going to 'get' anyone or anything – except perhaps for 'getting' yourself arrested in the morning. I think you're going to find Allied Resources want to hold you personally responsible for the damage to their rig. Quite amusing that, really!"

"What the hell are you on about?" I groaned.

"Oh, you don't know, do you. Let me explain. You see, the pictures you got on the rig – with the man with the newspaper over his face – showing that there was no damage on the rig the day after those anarchists got aboard …clever, that! Quite a smart move. Well, you see, the problem is that without those pictures it looks very much like you were part of that whole incident. You're the only person who can be found who has any connection with the affair at all. That looks rather bad for you, don't you think?"

"The cops don't know I was there," I said rather weakly, knowing what was to follow.

"Well, one of your fellow photographers will be tipping them off in the morning. A freelancer who wants your job. You see, you'd be arrested immediately for your involvement. And I expect they'll hold you for a good long while. What with your history of violence."

"History of violence?"

"Oh, we'll be sure to let you have one from the Personnel department at *News Consolidated*. We like to give our staffers helpful references."

"Bollocks," I said. "The News'll print those pictures, and then you can't do anything. They'll print them and I'll come out of this thing looking like a bloody hero." As I dangled there, naked and bleeding, the image seemed a little optimistic.

"No, Sinclair," he said slowly, "they won't print them." He drew a roll of negatives from his jacket pocket. "And you won't look like a hero." Holding the negs to the light, he looked at them, then held them in front of me. Sure enough, they were my shots, my only way out. "They can't print something they don't have. In fact, the newsdesk'll look pretty silly trying to wriggle out of this whole foul-up. If your news editor knows what's good for her, she'll bite the bullet and let you sink."

"You bastard," I said. A moment later Claude clubbed me and I staggered under the blow. I could feel the warmth of the blood running over my face. The heat of it was comforting, and trickled down my naked body.

I was unable to see and kept falling over at that point. I could feel Claude slamming into me now and then, and then far away I heard Shandra's voice. I think I was unconscious, just hearing the voice in the distance. She was saying, "No! Stop it! You've done enough!"

Then more clearly I heard Carfax, "What's the matter with you, you jumped-up little whore? No stomach for it now?"

"Just stop it!" she was screaming. "Look at him! Do you want him to end up like Kelly?"

"Shut up, Shandra – that was an accident." For a moment there was silence in the room.

Shandra ended the silence with the words, "Well, just leave him now. For Christ's sake – look at him, he's half dead anyway."

"Maybe you're right. Claude, leave him," he called. "Besides, I want to get down to Fleet Street and get that data back. He's not going anywhere for a while."

I WOKE TO FIND SHANDRA wiping the blood from my face. My wrists were free and I touched my head where a pulsating throb spread across my forehead. It was painful to the touch.

"What the hell happened?" I said.

"Claude laid you out with that iron bar. I don't think you even saw it coming." She was cradling my head where I lay on the bedroom floor. "This is going to hurt a little," she said.

"Oh God!" I replied, thinking that some new horror lay in store. Instead, she was washed the cut with a diluted antiseptic, the pungent smell replacing her perfume of half an hour earlier.

I rolled over on my side, and tried to get to my feet. "Just stay away from me," I said, recoiling from her as I gained some sense.

"No," she said. "Come here."

"So you can do something else to me? You must be mad."

"I'm helping you, Steven, now come and sit down before you do yourself an injury."

"No. Why should I trust you? You just turned me over

to Carfax, didn't you? You expect me to think you're some kind of healing angel now?" I caught my breath, it was still painful breathing. "No way, lady. You sold me out once, but I'm not so stupid as to let you do it twice."

"You don't have to worry," she said. "I'm not going to do anything to hurt you. Besides," she added bitterly, "he's got you sewn up so well there's nothing new I could do to you, even if I wanted. I wouldn't want to anyway. I am sorry about all this. ..."

"Yeah, right."

"I am. I didn't want any of this. I just did what I was instructed to."

Again I tried to get to my feet, but the pain in my legs overcame me. I slumped to the floor and she swabbed the newly-flowing blood from my face. I looked at her, and for a moment she seemed genuinely concerned. Funny, that. I thought I could almost believe her.

"I got rid of him. When you were unconscious I told him to get that animal Claude off of you. He was ready to beat you to a pulp just for practice." Something registered about that in my head. I had half-heard a conversation in my semi-conscious state.

"Is that what happened with Kelly Watson?" I threw the comment out.

"Shut up. Don't even think about that. You dodged that once, he won't be sloppy like that again. If he really wants you to carry the can for that, he'll make damned sure you do. You were lucky to have been called at the right time on your cell phone. He was sloppy. I know how he works. You were very lucky. It was a stupid idea from the start – just something they did to scare you off." She went on, clearly appalled at the monumental arrogance of Carfax. "They found themselves with a body on their hands and you started nosing around at the same time. They just made sure you and the body landed up at the same place at the same time. I don't think they even meant it to stick. It was just a scare tactic."

"So why are you telling me about it?"

"Because I've had enough of it. I hate what he does. I will never do what he wants again."

"What makes you so virtuous all of a sudden? Remember you tied me up for him, set me up beautifully."

"Yes, but I didn't know he was going to do this. I didn't know he was going to get so ... carried away. That's what happened with the Watson girl."

"What did he do to her?"

"I don't know the details. He told me they were playing some game and she ended up getting stabbed. I keep my face out of that stuff!"

"I can see how that could happen," I muttered. I watched her, unable to trust her for a moment, but relieved that I was unchained. She could say what she liked, as soon as I could I'd make break for the door.

"He's mad, you know. Completely mad. He has no conscience whatsoever. He really believes he can get away with things like that."

She rose to her feet and walked to the wardrobe. As I watched her, I wondered what instrument of torture she was going to come back with. She pulled out a heavy towel dressing gown. It was a deep blue color, soon to be spotted with red. She helped me into it and pulled me firmly to my feet. Then she eased me onto the bed.

She left the room then, and I tried to pull my thoughts together. There was just a shadow of a chance that she really was telling the truth. Claude could have puréed me without restraint. Her explanation of the fate of Kelly Watson sounded vaguely plausible. Some sort of rough session that got out of control, though no one would ever be able to prove that.

There was a way to find out if she really was telling the truth. I waited for a moment, and then heard her footsteps returning.

She moved to the bed, still wearing her pink dressing gown, carrying a tray with two mugs of hot chocolate.

"If you're serious about being sick of Carfax, then you'll do something for me. You'll tell me what the hell this is all about!"

"You never really knew, did you?"

"Knew what?" I asked, frustration mounting.

"You and that journalist, you've been bumbling around not really knowing what it was all about. Incredible really. So many people were so worried."

I sat up in the bed and turned to her, "What the hell are you babbling about?"

"The hard drive you copied. That's what it's all about," she said.

"Well, I know that. I figured there was something that linked Carfax and the Watson girl. Or something that tied him to Hanson's racket."

"Yes. Well, that's not what he was worried about. He has plenty of ways to distance himself from Hanson, don't you worry."

"If not that, then what was so threatening?" My head was beginning to throb again. I drank some hot chocolate.

"It was the computer. It was supplied to Hanson from Jeremy's office. It had been Jeremy's private machine. There were security features built in that made it quite useful."

"No kidding. No one can do anything with the data."

"Well, when he got a new machine that one became spare. Hanson needed a machine, and in a moment of thoughtless and uncharacteristic generosity, Jeremy offered him the spare – with all the protection features. He thought this was a great idea, to stop anyone learning of his involvement with the girls Hanson was running. He's like that with people. Incredibly generous at first, and when they fall out he's ready to have them hung out to dry."

"So he gives him an old computer. So what?"

"There was a cock-up. No one cleaned off the old data. Someone was meant to do it, but it got overlooked. There's stuff on there that would put Jeremy Carfax and a lot of other people behind bars for years."

"Like what?"

"Stuff you will find hard to believe."

I lay flat out, my eyes closed, as Shandra sat there spelling out the full extent of my stupidity. "Try me," I replied.

"Plans for the manipulation of the media, of public opinion, to help factions of the government get legislation through Parliament. That's one of the things he does, along with some other cronies, all of whom are listed in those files. Bribery, blackmail...."

"But surely," I said half groaning as the aches coursed through me, "Hanson would have seen that and asked him about it."

"Hanson never opened those files. He never had the codes to. He was too dumb to figure out what he had anyway. It was so far beyond him he was not a concern. They retrieved the computer the day after you scanned it. That was when they realized they had a problem. When you hooked up to it, the camera started monitoring you. So they knew exactly who was busting into the unit. Jeremy recognized you from the party, and put the word out to get you under control."

"What's to stop me going to the police with this information now?" I asked.

"If you go anywhere near a policeman you're likely to find you're arrested on the spot."

"For what?" I said, confused again. My head hurt and my legs were in agony.

"You are going to be marked as little short of a terrorist because of that rig business. And don't think the *News* will help you. There's no evidence to suggest you are anything but a confederate of whoever got on that rig. You're finished there, he's seen to that."

I thought about that for a moment. Ironic that I should be branded the enviroterrorist, when Cass had infiltrated the paper and was precisely that. But Shandra was right. The *News* would keep its head down if there was no story there. And without my pictures, there was nothing. A rogue photographer's word against Allied Resources'. If I was laying money on the outcome, I'd be backing Carfax and Allied Resources. In fact anyone but Steve Sinclair.

Shandra went on. "This afternoon, they found that the pictures you had taken to clear yourself were missing, I was told to draw up a letter firing you from the paper, to be presented to you when you arrive for work tomorrow. He's got you nailed down tight."

"Someone would believe me."

"Maybe. But how will you prove anything? No one'll help you. It's not their fight. You're on the edge of something much bigger than you. The people involved in Jeremy's other activities aren't going to let you spoil their game. Not after they're about to pull off their biggest victory."

"And what is that?"

"I'm amazed you didn't guess. I don't know how you can have got so close without knowing." She shook her head in exasperation.

"For God's sake, stop telling me how dumb I am and spit it out!"

"Hanson was a small element in a campaign to create a short, sharp reaction against immigrant populations. He was a tiny part of something much bigger. Maybe you heard about the race riots in North London?" She was being sarcastic. "Or Birmingham, or Bristol?"

"Yes, of course," I replied.

"They weren't just spontaneous outbursts. They were orchestrated like the evening television schedule. The timing set to coincide nicely with the introduction of new immigration legislation. You have no idea ... the polls back it up, they'll get this piece of legislation through without a hitch. Then everything'll settle down."

"That's monstrous." I sounded a little old-fashioned, but it got the message over.

"It's politics. It's power."

"But you, of all people. Why did you get involved?" Surely she could see the irony in it.

"I'm his personal lawyer as well as a staff lawyer at *News Consolidated*. I've been working for him for years. This was just the last in a series of recent projects."

"But, Shandra, you're from an Indian background. Your roots are with those cultures. How did you let something like this happen? Didn't he ever question your loyalty?"

"It's funny, isn't it? I've been working with him long enough I don't think he even thinks of that − that I'm different to him. Which of course is a rather intriguing angle on racists. Even they can have their eyes closed to color after a while. I don't know, he's certainly never mentioned any concerns to me. But then he is a weird person. Maybe he gets a thrill from the idea that I'd go along with him in this, because I'm paid to."

"There has to be more to it than that!" I said.

"There is. Carfax bought me, and paid for me long ago. He paid my university costs and he's putting my sister through as well. He reminds me from time to time. Turning the screws, you see?"

"But why?"

"Because that's how you buy loyalty. Steven, you really are very naïve at times." Her exasperation showed in the lines around her eyes. I noticed again how slim she was, yet this time it looked more like frailty. A leaf to be blown in the wind.

"He paid to put you through your training as a lawyer?"

"No one else was going to," she shot back sharply. "And don't talk to me about the principles of the thing. Principles don't sit well on an empty stomach."

"And now?"

"I figure I've paid him back in full. I'm not certain, but I'm thinking of talking to the police. Not yet though."

"Well, when? Now strikes me as a bloody good time!" I stammered.

"No. I have to do it right. I have to be sure to make it work. If it backfires I'll be finished. You've seen what he's capable of. This has to be handled just right. Which brings me back to you."

"Me?"

"Yes. As it is no one will believe me, without a witness. Or at least some kind of corroboration. And that's where you come in."

"What do I have to do?" I said.

"You have to write down exactly what happened. Everything. Which hospital you were in after Claude beat the crap out of you, anything you can about the rig, anything to show that you were doing the things you claim to have been doing."

"I don't want to implicate the Green Rage people. They've done nothing wrong."

"Just write it as best you can."

"That's not going to be easy if I'm going to be arrested in the morning."

"No. It isn't. But then, this isn't going to be easy for anyone."

"Do you have any suggestions? After all, if Carfax finds out about you, then you'll be history before I am."

"I can keep him in the dark a little longer. It won't take long. Four days or so. Four days you have to be kept out of trouble."

"It sounds so easy."

"Not really. Can you walk? We have to hurry," she said, getting to her feet.

I tried to stand. It was painful, but I could manage it.

"In two hours you're leaving to fly out of here. We have to get you somewhere. Anywhere away from here. We'll take things from there."

"There's another reason we should hurry," I said, wincing in pain as I tried to walk.

"What's that?"

"In a few minutes Carfax is going to find out that the laptop isn't at the office at all. I don't think he's going to be too happy about that."

HEATHROW AIRPORT at 1 a.m. is a hive of activity. If there are places that never sleep, major international airports are their centers. I checked in at the Swiss Air counter and bought a ticket to Geneva, paying cash supplied by Shandra.

We stopped near the apartment before leaving for the airport. I hobbled along the quiet street, and into the apartment building. Cass was talking into the phone as she came to the door, and hurriedly hung up.

"What happened to you?" she said, seeing the bruises on my head.

"I finally found out what happened."

"Was it worth it?" she asked.

"I don't know. Probably not." I gathered together my gear, then said to Cass, "There's going to be trouble tomorrow. They'll try to have me arrested for my involvement on the rig. I think you might be safe, though. Only Marlene knows you were on there, right?"

"I think so. I don't think I mentioned it to anyone else – but what do you mean, 'they'?" asked Cass, as I gathered my stuff.

"Jeremy Carfax. It's all been to do with that computer. He's got the data by now. He headed off for the office about three hours ago. It's too late to change that now."

"So what was so special about that data? We never really got anywhere with it."

"We figured out the connection from Hanson to Carfax and Kelly Watson, but that was nothing compared to what else is in there. Apparently Carfax has been running some kind of media operation of his own. It all ties in to the race riots and the way Hanson's been reported. Loads more things too. Stuff that can be used to sway public opinion before Parliament votes on the changes to the immigration legislation. He's a spin doctor of incredible proportions. He has the whole country fooled. That's about as much as I know. They beat the daylights out of me to get the stuff back, so they sure as hell figured it was important."

"So what will you do now?" asked Cass.

"I have to get out of England, before I get arrested. Then I'll write it up and get it back to someone here. She'll try and do something with it. You might think about lying low for a while, but I think you're fairly safe. No one knows about your involvement. And tell Guy to watch his back. Best tell him just to drop the whole thing." I noticed a few suitcases stacked in the hall. "Looks like you're doing some traveling of your own."

"I'm off," she said. "I think the gaff's blown for me here. A taxi's already on its way."

"Looks like I got here just in time, then. You'll be all right?"

"Sure, I will," she said as I hobbled out the door. "I'll be with my husband in a few hours."

What a joyous reunion that would be. I left carrying my camera bag, the laptop and a change of clothes in my rucksack and hurried painfully back to Shandra's car. I made sure she had no idea who I'd visited, and she was smart enough not to ask any questions.

A hurriedly prepared ice pack on my head and bandages on my legs allowed me some comfort on the journey through west London and onto the M4. Shandra drew cash, which she handed over, on the basis that my successful getaway was an important component of her plan. I also drew out a thousand pounds sterling from my company credit card, before cutting it in half. It would doubtless be canceled first thing in the morning.

"I'll get something back to you in a few days," I said.

"I'll need it within four days." She scribbled a fax number on the back of her card and handed it to me. "This fax number will find me, but make sure it gets there on time. The timing's important, so that when I blow the whistle I have all the information I need."

"Okay, I'll see you get it. I don't know where I'll be, but I hope you nail him. God knows, someone has to."

I left Shandra at the gate, partly pleased to see her go and partly saddened by it. I wished we'd met some other way.

FROM GENEVA I FLEW ON to Nairobi, where the three thousand pounds I had in my pocket would go a little further. On the verandah of the Fairview Hotel I sat working at the laptop. For four days I typed relentlessly. Breaking only for a Tusker and a smoke now and then, I managed to commit most of the events to paper. After several tries I managed to fax the completed document out to the number Shandra had given me back in England.

Beneath the overcast Nairobi afternoon skies, I sat watching the rain as it washed the foliage of the tropical trees spotless and shiny. Long, lazy days running into each other. I hadn't taken a photograph in weeks.

I'd had no word from London. Shandra seemed to have evaporated. There was no trace of Cass, and Guy, who I could still reach by e-mail, was my lone contact with a former life. At least that one friend remained. When I was handed a telegram in the foyer of the Fairview Hotel, informing me that he was shortly going to arrive at Jomo Kenyatta airport, I couldn't have been more pleased or surprised.

"Good trip?" I asked as he strode out of customs.

"Bloody awful," he replied.

As the taxi lumbered along, struggling to get back from the international airport without falling to pieces completely, Guy brought me up to date on the events of the last month.

"It seems to me that half of London wants to find you and jail you, and the other half wants to find you and hire you as a witness for the prosecution!"

"What do you mean?" I asked.

"Well, the police are convinced you're the mastermind behind Green Rage. Flattering, eh? You're credited with the entire rig business, and they're trying to piece together your movements over the last few years, to see if there's any way they can link you to the organization's previous activities."

"Bloody great!" I cussed.

"Cass's vanished off the face of the earth and Shandra – now there's an interesting lady – she's been trying to find you. You wouldn't know where she is, I suppose?"

"No idea," I replied. "Does the news get any better?"

"Yes, I believe it possibly does. It depends, though. Do you still have the laptop from the office?"

"Well, I was going to return it. . . ."

"Yes, I'm sure you were. Eventually. They were a little upset about that." Guy played down the oversight. "You see, it's just possible," he went on, " – if you haven't interfered with that laptop – that there's still a copy of Hanson's data on it."

I thought about this for a moment, then said, "So what? You couldn't get into it last time. What makes you think you can this time?"

"Well, Steve, you never mentioned to me that you had the password." •

IN THE HOTEL Guy unpacked his computer, and attached a telephone cable from his modem outlet to the one on the laptop I had held on to from *News Consolidated*.

"You see, Cass told me some time ago that you'd got this tape form an answering machine. She gave me copies of everything she had, you see, when you started asking all these questions about Hanson, in the hopes that I might be able to help."

"The files can't have been very interesting. We didn't get much really."

"Well, you see, that's where you're wrong. Do you remember the answering machine tape?"

"Of course, Cass lifted it from the house. Nothing on it, though."

"Wrong again! I had a listen to it. There's a transmission, but it's not a fax transmission. It's a log-in to the computer. If I'm right, I'll be able to play that sound into your modem port and log in – even though I have no idea what the code is."

"That sounds quite clever." I must admit I had only the slightest idea what he was talking about. "You mean the answering machine recorded the sound of a computer being logged into?"

"Yes. Exactly. It's too back and forth to be a fax transmission. I've loaded it and cleaned up the sound a little, and it appears to be a log-in script." He fiddled with the connection and rattled something off on the keyboard.

"Of course," he added, "I could be completely wrong." He started an application on his machine and I heard the high-pitched whine of a transmission. The laptop began to respond and a moment later a totally unfamiliar screen appeared on Guy's machine. "There we are. Quite simple really."

"And now?" I asked expectantly.

"And now we disarm the passwords, and look at what the heck we have here."

I watched over his shoulder as he skimmed through the directories. There were accounts files, details even I could understand. Payments to organizations, publishers, and the name of more than one judge appeared on the books.

For two hours we looked at the material, seeing a

catalogue of Carfax's activities – from diary entries to e-mails. A complete financial record testified to his involvement with activities as diverse as Hanson and his immigration scam, to suppression of evidence before the courts.

"Do you think any of this would stand up in court?" I asked.

"Almost certainly not," replied Guy, "but it will give Scotland Yard somewhere to start. And maybe someone in here who is willing to talk. And then they have him."

"And Shandra?"

"She's keeping a low profile at the moment. Love to get in touch with her, you know. You wouldn't know where she is, would you?"

"No," I said again. "Not a clue."

"She stirred up the police, and they've already opened a file, but this will give them something to chew on," he muttered, as he copied the data from the laptop to his own machine. I watched as he finally deleted the data off the laptop, and felt a great sense of relief. It was gone now. Maybe some good would come of everything I'd been through after all.

"As long as it's not me they're chewing on."

"This will make an enormous difference," he said, tapping his machine as he put it away. "I'll take this back to London, if that's all right with you. I think it's a problem for the cops now. And besides, your co-operation will probably get you off the hook, I shouldn't wonder."

"Lucky me," I replied sarcastically. "I won't be hurrying back for a while. Besides, I like it here."

"Probably a good idea," he said. "All things considered."

The feeling of finally knowing there was a good chance Carfax would be nailed filled me with an over-whelming warmth. It lifted me, held me up, and added a spring to my step for weeks.

AND THERE THE ENTIRE MATTER would have rested. That I didn't hear from Guy for a while was of no concern, communications in Nairobi never being very reliable. In time, I moved out of the Fairview, into a nearby apartment, making my trail still more difficult to follow.

I picked up work stringing for this paper or that, and occasionally went on assignment for AP. As luck would have it, I knew several of their staff from time they had worked in London. I was in and out of Somalia, and Ethiopia quite regularly, sometimes being away from Nairobi weeks at a time.

When a letter postmarked London found me through the AP office, I was hardly surprised. My name went out on pictures from the Nairobi bureau regularly. At the time I was dropping into the office to pick up supplies before hurrying out to the airport on a new assignment. I stuffed the letter in my bag and promptly forgot it until aboard the British Airways flight for Monrovia, where I was being positioned by AP as the situation deteriorated in strife-torn Liberia.

I read it, drinking a cold lager served by an attractive young stewardess from Romford. The letter was from Shandra.

Dear Steve,

I want to thank you for your help with Carfax. I'm sorry, but I don't think there will be any charges laid against him, in spite of my efforts. It has been a terrible experience for me, and my sister, and I have brought the most incredible shame on my family. I feel awful about it.

I saw your byline on a photograph out of Nairobi and am hoping this might find you. I want to warn you about something. The network administrator you mentioned – Guy Mctavish – stopped working at *News Consolidated* shortly after you left. I happened to learn he helped Carfax out towards the end. I believe there must have been a payoff, as he apparently erased all the data quite willingly from the system at *News Consolidated*. The police found no traces whatsoever of any data that might have a bearing on the Hanson/Carfax business.

Before Carfax realized I was turning information over to the police, I heard talk of Guy being commissioned to find you and ensure that no copies of the data existed anywhere on another machine you had retained. Word was, you still had a laptop from the company with a copy of the data on it.

When I saw your byline I immediately tried to reach you. I can only hope I have found you before they do. When you get this message, please, whatever you do, protect that data – don't let Guy get his hands on it. He'll destroy it, and that will be the end of any hopes of bringing Carfax down.

You can reach me through my parents' address at the head of this letter,

Best of luck,
Shandra